D1738394

TUNNEL
OUT OF
DEATH

TUNNEL
OUT OF
DEATH

Jamil Nasir

TOR®

A TOM DOHERTY ASSOCIATES BOOK
NEW YORK

TUNNEL OUT OF DEATH

Copyright © 2013 by Jamil Nasir

A Tor Book
Published by Tom Doherty Associates, LLC
175 Fifth Avenue
New York, NY 10010

www.tor-forge.com

Tor® is a registered trademark of Tom Doherty Associates, LLC.

Library of Congress Cataloging-in-Publication Data

Nasir, Jamil.
    Tunnel out of death / Jamil Nasir.—First edition.
      p. cm.
    "A Tom Doherty Associates book."
    ISBN 978-0-7653-0611-1 (hardcover)
    ISBN 978-1-4668-1361-8 (e-book)
    1. Private investigators—Fiction.   I. Title.
PS3614.A754T86 2013
813'.6—dc23

                 2012043361

Tor books may be purchased for educational, business, or promotional use. For information on bulk purchases, please contact Macmillan Corporate and Premium Sales Department at 1-800-221-7945 extension 5442 or write specialmarkets @macmillan.com.

First Edition: May 2013

Printed in the United States of America

0 9 8 7 6 5 4 3 2 1

TUNNEL
OUT OF
DEATH

1

Ransom International's conference room was upstairs in the 1930s mansion that Heath Ransom used as both home and office. It had an antique cherry-wood table, an ambience system that was currently pumping out the invigorating air of a mountain pine forest, and remote conferencing lenses in the ceiling. Unfortunately today the lenses were dark: instead of a hologram, the actual physical body of a young man continued down past the surface of the table and pressed heavily into one of the conference chairs, which made slight sounds when he moved. Particularly unfortunate because the young man—a large, handsome, impatient person whose business card said "Dr. Eugene Denmark, President and CEO of GeneMark LLC"—had an unusually disturbing neural-field leakage, full of apprehension and grim determination, as if whatever business deal he wanted to propose to Ransom International was a matter of life and death.

Field leakage was a muted background murmur that Ransom heard around people, like a low-voiced discussion going on in the next room. He had bought this house to minimize such distractions: the spacious grounds that separated it from the street and neighbors kept it quiet enough for him to conduct his endovoyant investigations business, and relax when he wasn't working. His neurological bug/feature also made it tricky to choose employees: like Charles Tobin, the small, elegant man sitting next to him, they had to be both competent and benign—a less common combination than you might hope.

Tobin, well aware of his boss's sensitivities, was taking the brunt of the meeting, and Ransom had gratefully allowed his attention to wander. Just now he was discreetly watching out the window as a retro-style hippie minibus passed down Anglia Street in the distance beyond his lawn and autumn-colored trees, meter-high letters on its side scrolling out the message REAP WHAT YOU SOW. The current mania for religions had brought out amateur preachers all over the country. Not only that; more and more of his clients nowadays wanted religion-related services, like proving doctrinal fraud or locating the resting places of saints. An unpleasant feeling came over Ransom; he disliked that sort of work, which presumed he was some kind of witch doctor—

The unpleasant feeling grew stronger, and with a start Ransom realized that it had not come from the thought of his religious clients at all. Rather, his guest's field leakage had suddenly taken on a grating tone, and in some confusion Ransom realized that the man was staring at him.

He tried to take in what Denmark was saying. "—isolating Class One humans for long periods in a specific nerve-growth medium stimulates unusual development of the medulla, and consequently of the telepathic and clairvoyant faculties. We theorize that the enforced sensory and social deprivation stimulates activation of the telepathic areas to overcome the isolation. Then, once the subject emerges from the tank, you have a ready-made telepath or clairvoyant."

"Wait a minute," Ransom said, now roused completely. "Is this some kind of government research? The NGF tanks you're talking about are USAdministration military, aren't they?"

Denmark's eyes went vacant for a second, as they had every time Ransom had talked during the meeting. Of course, one of the few reasons anyone would ask for a physical meeting nowadays was to sneak snoop gadgets into the venue, and RI observed the usual business protocol of ignoring such things if they weren't too intrusive. On the other hand, business protocol also prescribed that the wired party keep his surveillance subtle. Did this Denmark really think he was going to close a deal by making a bug-eyed display of peeping all over Ransom's somatic indicators during their talk?

Denmark's attention came back. "Mr. Ransom, I can assure you that there are no legal or national security strictures barring GeneMark from selling this technology, or you from buying it."

The sentence came out smoothly, but Denmark's background murmur had changed. The man wasn't exactly lying, but he was holding something back. This made Ransom uneasy. NGF tanks turning out ready-made telepaths would have been huge news in the endovid detective community, but he had heard nothing about it. Could Denmark be a federal agent? USAdmin made an enormous income from industrial espionage, using spy technology that was illegal for nongovernment entities to possess; but it was rumored to still be light on endovid talent. Catching a prominent investigator breaking federal law—by trying to buy top-secret government technology, for example—might be a good way of blackmailing him into working for them.

Tobin's field also expressed unease. He used his own smooth voice: "Frankly, Dr. Denmark, we would normally consider such a radically new technology only if it came from one of the established firms in the field. I for one have not had the pleasure of dealing with GeneMark previously."

"GeneMark is a start-up formed specifically to market this technology."

"I would think that most start-ups couldn't afford the FDA licensing costs. Has FDA cleared you to do Phase Two studies?"

"Ah, right, let me explain," said Denmark, smiling. There was a slight stiffness about his face, Ransom thought, as if he had recently had some cheap plastic surgery, like a mobster. Or maybe the man's bad vibes were making him imagine it. "Your concern is understandable, but this technology is actually perfect for a start-up like GeneMark. Under FDA's regulations, gene-expression modifications taking place strictly in response to environmental factors are presumptively Class One. That means that the burden of any testing would be on a party trying to prove that our medulla enhancements are *not* Class One."

"And *are* they Class One?" Tobin asked.

"We believe so, yes."

Again the murmur from Denmark's etheric "other room" underwent a change. There was an iceberg somewhere under the tip the man was showing. But even if there hadn't been, as far as Ransom was concerned the meeting was over. Nowadays even some Class Two mutations were legal, but he had grown up in the late twentieth century, and such things disturbed him. He had been a successful endovid for almost three decades without any engineering; if his competitors started packing on gene enhancements that left him in the dust, he would simply close up shop. He had more than enough money to retire on, even if they kept up the advances in life extension.

Providentially, at that moment his assistant Clarice buzzed. With a murmured "excuse me," he took her out of his pocket and looked into her attractive Japanese face. "Sorry to disturb you, Heath, but a prospective client is requesting an urgent meeting. They're here in person. Anna is with them in your office. They say it's an emergency."

"In person?" The knot in his stomach tightened; two physical visits in one morning.

But he wasn't about to look a gift horse in the mouth. He

said: "Dr. Denmark, I'm terribly sorry, but I've just been summoned to an emergency meeting downstairs. I want to thank you very much for coming in to talk to us. Obviously, we'll have to discuss your proposal internally before getting back to you."

Denmark looked taken aback. "Well, actually, Mr. Ransom, I was hoping very much to have a few minutes alone with you. To discuss a somewhat delicate—"

"I'm really awfully sorry," said Ransom, rising. "I hope you'll send us any additional materials you think we need in order to evaluate your product."

"But it's very important." Denmark stood up, too. A flare of panic suddenly expanded from him like a flame, catching Ransom off guard. He steadied himself against the edge of the table.

"Perhaps I could continue with Dr. Denmark while you run to your meeting," said Tobin, reading Ransom's body language.

"Good idea," said Ransom dizzily, now desperate to get away. "Dr. Denmark, my assistant Mr. Tobin has my complete confidence. I will rely on his recommendation in any event."

For the first time during their meeting, Ransom felt that Denmark looked into his eyes without the split second of glassy distractedness. "This is something you need to hear, Heath," he said, too loudly, as if trying to get his attention in a crowd. Ransom had not invited him to use his first name. "Reality is more malleable than you can imagine. This fact is being exploited. I need to talk to you—to you personally. Someone very dangerous—" He stopped talking abruptly, as if he had said too much.

With difficulty, Ransom maintained his professional demeanor. "I really am very sorry, Mr. Denmark, but I have to rush."

Denmark's field was hopeless now, as if he had lost a fatal

gamble. Wordlessly, he leaned across the table and held out his hand. Long practice at being polite overcoming his reluctance to touch another person, Ransom extended his own. Denmark's hand was cold. And at the touch, the unfocused murmur of the man's psychic leakage suddenly sharpened.

A still summer morning rose up around Ransom, nearly erasing the conference room. Birdsong and the gentle wash of surf were the only sounds. He stood at the top of a high bluff, a sandy path leading down among trees to a beach. But a feeling of menace and danger hung about the peaceful scene, like ominous music at the beginning of a horror movie.

Quickly disengaging his hand, Ransom nodded politely and found his way unsteadily from the room.

2

Shaken, Ransom took the stairs to the first floor. If only Viewing could be confined to when you were actually working—but of course the brain didn't operate that way. Years ago he had tried low doses of neuroleptics, first in the evenings and then only on weekends, but they had occluded his trances. He was going to retire one of these days, he promised himself for the thousandth time, and then he would take whatever drugs made him feel better and subtle perception be damned. He especially hated getting impressions from people who, like Eugene Denmark, seemed to have some serious misfortune in the offing: natural scenes where a path or road led to a geographic boundary—like a shore or cliff—were usually auguries of death. But without an investigation using his full array of techniques and analytic systems there was no way to tell for sure, and so the information he had picked from Denmark was cryptic and garbled—a source of distress rather than enlightenment.

And what the devil could the man have meant by "reality is more malleable than you think?"

He had a moment of swelling anger at Denmark, at everyone who pressed upon him with their uncontrolled leakages and incomprehensible fates. He quickly calmed himself. It was his own "talent" that made him vulnerable, not anyone's intentional intrusion. Besides, he had a meeting—with a prospective client this time, not a salesman—and it wouldn't do to go in full of angry self-pity.

Anna Heatherstone was waiting in the hall outside his

office, tall, slim and dark-haired, wearing a fashionable 1940s-style suit, her freckled Irish face lighting up when she saw him. Ransom felt himself relax. Anna's emanation was like barely suppressed giggling, and being with her always made him feel that nothing was so terribly serious. She murmured a five-second summary: Boston society people, family issue, research shows they have plenty of money but also plenty of debts, refuse to talk to anyone but the boss. Ransom nodded, and Anna briskly opened the door to the large, paneled office.

"Mr. and Mrs. Merrivale, Dr. Heathcliff Ransom, President and Principle Endovoyant Investigator of Ransom International," she said to the two people sitting in the visitors' chairs.

The male Merrivale stood up and gave Ransom a firm, manly handshake accompanied by a firm, manly look in the eye. "John Merrivale," he said. He was over six feet—which made him half a head taller than Ransom—looked about ninety, wore 1940s-style yachting clothes, and his silvery hair was cut short enough to suggest both late-middle age and virility. Ransom glanced at the hair enviously; he had to keep his own head shaved for the View tank induction leads. The female Merrivale stayed seated and gave Ransom a long, slender aristocrat's hand, smiling and murmuring politely. She was a handsome, slim woman, also silver-haired, with bright blue eyes, perhaps a few years older than her husband. In the murmur of their psychic tone Ransom could feel confusion and anxiety.

Everyone sat down, Ransom behind his desk. He looked at the Merrivales benignly.

There was an uncomfortable pause.

"We've come to see you on a matter of some delicacy," began John Merrivale. "Great delicacy, actually." He glanced at Anna.

"Ms. Heatherstone is my trusted employee," said Ransom. "She assists me in my investigations, so I will have to apprise her of the facts in any case."

The Merrivales exchanged a look.

"Our aunt— Ardice's aunt, actually," said Mr. Merrivale finally, "fell ill several days ago, and went into a coma."

"I'm sorry."

"There was no sign of any health problems. It came out of a blue sky."

Ransom nodded sympathetically.

"We—well, to be very blunt about it, Mr. Ransom, we suspect foul play."

The Merrivales looked at him plaintively, as if there was no more to say, until Ransom felt obliged to continue. "And you want me to try to identify the malefactor?" He sometimes got cases like this based on his years as a Metropolitan Police Force forensic endovid, but he usually didn't take them; they were often ugly, and the police resented private operators mucking up the waves for their own people.

"Well—not exactly," said John Merrivale. "We want our aunt back."

Anna Heatherstone shifted uncomfortably in her chair.

"I can certainly understand that," said Ransom sympathetically, waiting for more.

Mrs. Merrivale spoke up for the first time. "Mr. Ransom, we hoped you might be able to help us." Her hushed, mon-eyed voice had a warmth Ransom felt in the middle of his chest. "Aunt Margaret isn't dead. Her consciousness is still somewhere on or near this plane. We are told that you find lost things, and that you are the best in your field. Will you find Aunt Margaret and bring her back to us, Mr. Ransom?" She said it as if she were willing to seduce him if necessary, her wide, appealing eyes on his face.

Ransom exchanged a glance with Anna. "I'm terribly

sorry, Mrs. Merrivale; I find corporeal objects, not people—
or rather, the people I find are still alive. Or if they're not, I
find their bodies, not their . . . spirits."

"But John's friends in the police department told us that
you have solved crimes by contacting the spirits of the recently departed."

"Well, it's more complicated than that." Long practice
had given Ransom an instinct for which version of his intro-
ductory spiel to give which clients, though the current religious upheavals and schisms made it a constantly moving
target. "It's true that in trance you often speak to people, but
the working assumption is that this is just anthropomorphized information. The theory—though it's not accepted
by everyone—is that the endovid's brain acts like a radio,
somehow tuning in to fluctuations in the vacuum field left
there by specific thoughts or other mental events. But because the mind has no model for this kind of cognition, it
dresses it up in familiar forms: so you may experience it as
someone talking to you, the spirit of a murdered man nam-
ing his killer, for example."

"Or it *could* be that you are actually talking to a person's
spirit, couldn't it?" asked Mrs. Merrivale. "Isn't that what
souls are—semi-stable torsion waves in the Hamiltonian?
And bodies, too, for that matter? Aren't we—both body and
soul—just anthropomorphized information?"

"I take it you are a religious woman, Mrs. Merrivale?"

"Ardice and I belong to the CUEC," said her husband
quietly.

"Well then, I'm not telling you anything you don't already
know," Ransom said, shifting gears smoothly. The Cosmic
Universal Evolutionist Catechism was a little far out for wealthy
people of European stock, but anything was possible these
days. "Holographic torsion wave interference patterns in the
vacuum field constitute the forms of this world, including

the forms of what we call matter and consciousness. The matter patterns of the body dissipate after death. Do the consciousness patterns also dissipate? I leave that to the theologians. But if they *do* persist, I know of nothing to suggest that they do so in any part of the field accessible to living humans. And even if they do, I have no experience or training for finding them, much less reconnecting them with their bodies. In the couple of cases you heard about I was looking strictly for information—time of death, location of the body, and so on— and I didn't care where it came from. I have no idea whether the people I seemed to talk to were spirits or completely nonpersonal etheric field fluctuations that my mind invested with human shapes and voices. A lot of luck was involved, too." Not to mention neurological and psychological wear and tear, he thought. And a great deal of the client's money.

"But you might apply the same methods to finding Aunt Margaret, mightn't you?" asked Mrs. Merrivale. "That's how flux doctors work, they say—they find the person's consciousness field and communicate with it, coax it back into the body."

"So they say. But I have no training as a flux doctor. I would have no idea how to—"

Mrs. Merrivale's eyes, which had been brimming, overflowed. She bowed her face into a lacy handkerchief she had taken from a tiny, precious-looking handbag.

John Merrivale put a large hand on his wife's shoulder. The gesture gave Ransom the sudden, odd feeling that he was watching a play, though the Merrivales' field leakage indicated that their distress was real enough. "We understand that you can't guarantee results," said John Merrivale. "We just want to turn every stone, make every effort we can to pull Aunt Margaret through."

"It's not just that I can't guarantee results. I wouldn't know where to start. I can refer you to a couple of excellent—"

"We can't afford to waste time on uncredentialed operators," said Merrivale. "Aunt Margaret's coma is what they call labile. She could deteriorate on short notice. Our only choice is to go straight to the top, get the best help available. That's why we're here." He glanced at Ransom almost bashfully. "I'm sure it doesn't make any difference to a man like you, but we're willing to pay a premium, if only you'll take a stab at it. We'll stipulate a minimum fee payable whether or not you succeed, plus a bonus if you do. You'll have a free hand to try whatever measures you think necessary."

He named a sum of money.

As it happened, Merrivale had been wrong. Money on the scale mentioned *did* make a difference to a man like Ransom. After a decent pause, in which he pretended to hesitate, he took Clarice out of his pocket.

"Clarice, will you get Mr. Lewin into my office? Anthony Lewin is my lawyer," he explained to the Merrivales. "It will have to be understood that I'm taking the case making no representations as to results."

Mrs. Merrivale looked up from her handkerchief, joy showing through her tears, and her husband stood up to fold Ransom's hand in another manly handshake.

Ransom had met Lewin in person just once, and the man's fussy, hostile emanation had driven him to distraction. But Lewin was smart, and he could work fast when he had to. He did so now, his holographic bust floating an inch above Ransom's desk like a hectoring ghost. Within twenty minutes a heavily customized version of Ransom International's standard retainer contract appeared on the electronic paper Anna Heatherstone handed out, and were duly thumbprinted. In return for a handsome guaranteed fee, to be secured by a priority lien on one of the Merrivales' homes, Ransom would initiate his investigation immediately, preempting all other matters whatsoever, and exercise his best efforts to reunite the body and consciousness of Mrs. Margaret Biel, relict of the late Raymond Fenton Biel. At the mention of Raymond Fenton Biel an uncharitable suspicion formed in Ransom's mind, but he kept it silent.

After Lewin had evaporated, Ransom and Anna, joined by Bobby Mandelson, their intern, listened to the Merrivales' story. Mrs. Biel, widowed, age 132, had been in good health and socially active, with everything to live for. She hadn't been depressed or shown any symptoms of stroke or organ trouble. In fact, the only cause for complaint she had given her doting relatives had been her sudden preoccupation with an upstart religion, the Church of Mind and Beauty of Greater Boston, Inc., which appeared to worship fashion models.

"I couldn't understand it at all," Ardice Merrivale said in her hushed, exciting voice. "Aunt Margaret asked me to go with her when she first joined, and they have their services in a lovely half-size replica of St. Peter's Basilica in a sub-basement of the Bank of China building. They said the models were symbols of the eternal self-renewal of the natural world, and of the beauty of the spirit that infuses all things, but to me it seemed—well, they seemed to put a lot of emphasis on the 'erotic power of youth,' and the altar girls were naked!

"And they did tricks—magic tricks. I don't know how, but they were—they seemed impossible. The priest said they were demonstrations of the mutability of reality, and that anyone with the determination and resources could use that same mutability to turn back time and regain youth. Aunt Margaret seemed simply hypnotized by it all. And then when I learned that she had changed her will to leave this church a large sum of money, I was naturally concerned that they had taken advantage of her."

"Touching, isn't it?" said Anna Heatherstone subvocally in Ransom's earpiece, her face still turned toward the Merrivales. "Because before the Mind and Beauty Church came along, the Merrivales were in line to inherit the Biel fortune." Ransom had noticed Anna's eyes going in and out of focus as she concentrated alternately on the meeting and her online research.

"Are we talking *the* Raymond Fenton Biel?" asked Ransom via the private channel that he, Anna, and Bobby Mandelson shared, willing his speech muscles to work without actually moving them so that his nerve mike could pick up the impulses.

"None other."

"How much money is involved?"

"A lot. Unless she wakes up and changes her mind, the Merrivales only get a few million."

"—then three days ago," Mrs. Merrivale was saying in a voice that quavered with emotion, "the morning coffee maid couldn't wake Aunt Margaret up. They rushed her to the hospital and took all possible measures, but they say her condition is deteriorating." At this point, Mrs. Merrivale dissolved into tears again. "If those horrible Mind and Beauty people have hurt her, I'll never forgive myself," she sobbed. "I tried to get her to stop going, but she wouldn't listen."

"Steady, old girl," said John Merrivale gallantly. "It wasn't your fault. There's nothing you could have done."

"Oh, gag me," said Anna in Ransom's ear.

"Do you have a police agency on retainer?" Ransom asked out loud.

"We have Pinkerton," said John Merrivale. "But they say there isn't any evidence of foul play." He sounded indignant at their disloyalty.

"All right," said Ransom. "It takes me a couple of hours to prep for a Viewing. In the meantime, Mr. Mandelson will accompany you to Mrs. Biel's home to pick out a few objects intimate to her that I can use to get a spoor. I can't spend more than about twenty-four hours continuous in the tank, so we'll know soon whether I've had any success, say within thirty-six hours. Oh, and would you please provide me with a picture of Mrs. Biel?"

He helped Mrs. Merrivale on with her coat, glad-handed her husband out of the office, and closed the door softly behind them and Bobby Mandelson.

"Raymond Fenton Biel," said Anna Heatherstone, wide-eyed.

She and Ransom took a side door out of the office and walked quickly down a back hallway into what had been the servants' quarters a hundred years ago, Ransom shedding jacket and tie and talking in rapid-fire to Clarice, rescheduling appointments and the Viewings he had just displaced by taking on this astonishingly profitable job.

"Heath," said Clarice, "Mr. Denmark is still in the upstairs conference room waiting for you. He insists he has to see you before he leaves, says it's a matter of life and death."

"Tell him I'm very sorry, but I have an emergency Viewing, and I won't be available for at least forty-eight hours. Ask him to make an appointment for next week, and then make sure someone else meets with him."

"You're supposed to get your blood exchanged and your lymphocyte firmware upgraded this afternoon. You've already rescheduled twice, and your tissue readings are down."

"I know, but this really is an emergency. Tell them to come at the same time tomorrow. The day after tomorrow."

"Okay," said Clarice with resignation.

"Did you find out anything else?" he asked Anna, as they reached the prep room door.

"It appears the Merrivales are in debt up to their eyebrows. So maybe being left with only a few million euros really does mean abject poverty for them."

"Figures. Anything else?"

"Well, there's one interesting thing. Margaret Biel isn't the only super-rich old person to go into a coma recently."

"Meaning what?"

"Meaning that in the last eighteen months at least three other fabulously wealthy people over a hundred and ten have had sudden comas that sound a lot like Mrs. Biel's: one other in North America, one in EU, and one in Japan. All of them have died within a week or two. A few conspiracy data-miners have commented, but no one mainstream has paid any attention."

"Huh. Weird. Not members of the Beauty Church or whatever, were they?"

"No, the Church of Mind and Beauty is strictly Boston. On the other hand, at least two of them seem to have gotten involved in some kind of cult right before they went under. I tried checking whether those are tied to Mind and Beauty, but I have to do more research. From what I've dug up about Margaret Biel, she would just love a church dedicated to youth and beauty. She's had an interesting life, if you're interested in parties, weird sex, divorces, lawsuits, and rehab. And spending money like a geyser. She was very good-looking at one time, too."

3

Ransom, with his endovid bug/feature, had not been a good family man. His children, alienated almost from birth, were strangers to him, having moved away with their mother after only a few difficult years. Taking down his Christmas tree a few years after that, it had hit him that the days when having a Christmas tree made sense were gone, never to return. A sadness took his breath then, and he had to sit down for awhile to let it pass. But it had never passed altogether.

The memory came as he followed Interstate 85 through the pine woods of North Carolina on his way back from a weekend at the beach, where he and his latest girlfriend had split up. As the hovercar autopilot rushed him along the deserted, potholed asphalt somewhere between the Coastal North Carolina and Richmond, Virginia, infrastructure islands, endless ranks of trees flashing past on both sides, he realized that the breakup hadn't really made him feel sad. Instead of being an emotional event, it was as if the breakup had been a metaphysical one, erasing all traces of his former life; or rather, as if his life had left so few traces that even the ending of a desultory romance had brushed them away like cobwebs. Loneliness contended with exhilaration inside him as he sat suspended in an amber of speed and yellow afternoon, like a man who has faked his own death but not yet decided on his next move.

The Irony of Modern Life, they called it: now that people lived longer, relationships were getting shorter. Or maybe relationships had always been short; maybe the only difference was that now you had time to depart them voluntarily rather than being swept away by disease, accident, or age. Maybe longevity had simply allowed humankind to see through the romantic illusions that accompanied short lives, to realize that people, like cars or clothes, could suit you for a while and then no longer suit you. Maybe loneliness and disorientation were simply how freedom felt: the discomforts of an organism that had not yet adapted to having enough time to think.

His car slowed and took an exit off I-85, followed a county highway, and then a narrow, crumbling asphalt road with an occasional tiny house backed up to the woods, ramshackle cars in sandy driveways, and a short while later he stood at the top of a wooded bluff, a breeze cooling the diamond heat of the sun, and before him a sandy path led down among trees to a beach, beyond which the ocean sparkled blue-green, and on the horizon he could just see a vague green line of distant land—

Cold fear shot through him as he recognized the vision he had seen shaking hands with Dr. Eugene Denmark.

And suddenly he knew where he was.

The drive along I-85 was a frequent transitional episode, a sensorium his mind projected at the beginning of Viewings before the initial trance confusion subsided and he remembered what he was doing. As his mind cleared he remembered the Merrivales, their Aunt Margaret, his emergency Viewing—

But why had he come *here,* to this scene, which was connected with some unknown calamity involving a man he had met only today?

But no, he had been mistaken. With relief he realized that what he had thought was a dirt path was actually a wooden walkway; the thick woods on either side were really just beach grass and a few young palms growing in the twenty meters of sandy soil between two big beach houses. The walkway did lead to a beach, but down only a couple of steps, not a bluff, and this beach was wider than the one from his vision, a hundred meters of white sand almost too bright to look at in the noon light. Between gusts of breeze the sun on his bare head felt heavy, like hot lead. Seagulls wheeled, mewling high in the air. There was no land at the limit of the horizon; instead, clouds towered offshore as if piled there by the stiff ocean breeze. Two distant figures up to their knees in the choppy surf seemed to be fishing; other than that, the beach was deserted.

Looking around, Ransom saw that he was near one end of a narrow coastal island. Big beach houses sat atop the massive stilts that kept them above the hurricane-season surge-tides and, a hundred meters to his right, beyond the last house, the island ended; across a kilometer of choppy water Ransom could see the near end of another island, lying, like this one, a few hundred meters off the coast, with its own tiny palm trees and beach houses. To his left, the island on which he stood stretched away into the distance, the houses along it built atop a shallow rise where the beach ended and the palm trees, beach grass, and aloe started. The whole place had the luxurious near-desertion of an upscale summer resort.

Then, on one of the warm gusts came a smell. A smell he recognized.

Margaret Biel. The sensory analogue his mind had made of the aura fields lingering on her watch and hand mirror, which he had held before getting into the trance tank. His physical body was still suspended there, but his concentration on the aura fields had drawn his consciousness to a stratum in the astral world where Biel, or some trace of her, lingered. He need only follow the "smell" to find her. Or at least that was how it would work if she were a lost dog or child or an absconded husband with the normal collocation of body and consciousness. Where the spoor would lead in the case of a coma patient was anyone's guess.

He sniffed, turning his head back and forth, trying to get a sense of where it was coming from. Down the beach to his left was his best guess. His feet made a hollow sound on the wooden walkway, and then a faint squeaking in the sand beyond. He was wearing Dockers, he noticed, but even through their soles his sockless feet could feel the sand's heat. He also had on a light seersucker suit over a T-shirt; the stiff breeze flapped the skirts of his jacket as he reached the firmer sand along the water's edge, where the smell of the ocean was stronger. He turned left, squinting in the sunlight, fumbled absently in his pockets and put on the floppy fisherman's hat and wraparound sunglasses he found there.

He had walked perhaps half a kilometer, passing only a few beachgoers in all that distance, when the smell suddenly grew stronger. He was approaching a beach umbrella, this one set up only a few meters from the gentle surf. A young woman sat under it watching a toddler. The toddler had fat red cheeks and dimpled legs, and wore a comically large sun hat; she was digging ineffectually at the wet sand with a plastic shovel. Ransom was about to walk toward the umbrella when he realized that the spoor was coming not from the woman, but from the tiny girl.

In a few steps he was standing over her. She looked up, squinting in the sunlight, then held up a shiny wet rock, showing him the spoils of her prospecting. There was no doubt about it; the aura traces he had sensed on Margaret Biel's possessions and the spoor pouring off this child were identical. He was being offered a rock by the astral analogue of Margaret Biel.

A movement in the corner of his eye made him look around. The woman had come out from under her umbrella. A tall and strikingly good-looking woman, but doing the worried mother.

Ransom gave her a friendly nod. "Cute kid," he said, and resumed walking. No use causing a ruckus and possibly disrupting his View until he figured out what to do next. There had been no time to make plans for getting Margaret Biel's spirit, soul, or consciousness—or whatever it was the child symbolized—"back into" her body; in fact, he hadn't even expected to find her in the first place, he now realized. He wondered whether the toddler manifestation was the etheric world's metaphor for brain damage associated with the coma. If so, what was the mother? Ransom glanced over his shoulder at the woman, now back under her umbrella, the child engrossed again in trying to dig in the sand, a spent wave washing an inch deep around her chubby legs.

Then another unexpected thing happened. Walking away from the little girl, he had expected the Biel spoor to diminish; instead it seemed to grow stronger again. And now it seemed to be coming from somewhere ahead of him, and to the left.

That was unusual but then again, bobbing for comatose dowagers was new to him. The source of the spoor now seemed to be somewhere inland of the beach houses. Ransom trudged back across the hot sand and between palm trees, through a sandy yard, up a driveway bordering a sharp square of manicured lawn, and out to the road that ran level and straight down the middle of the island until it was lost in a bright haze. If this was a typical resort, the road would eventually pass through a small "downtown" of shops and restaurants, their high prices part of the force-field of luxury and private security that kept the common masses away.

He started along the sidewalk in that direction, following the spoor. The big houses slumbered on their stilts in the heavy sunlight, cars and SUVs parked in the shade underneath. A sunburned kid rode by on a bike, and a couple of cars passed, but Ransom met no one else walking at this broiling time of day.

A couple of blocks down, palms overhung the sidewalk. When he reached them he stopped for a minute in their shade—and was surprised by a sudden cool gust. For a moment he thought the clouds piled up over the ocean had come onshore, bringing a rainstorm, but when he looked up he realized that far more than that had changed.

He was no longer in an upscale beach town at midsummer. The trees arching above him now weren't palms, but oaks and maples, a few of their leaves yellow with the very beginnings of autumn. He was on a suburban street somewhere far from any coast; the air here was cool, dry, and still, and the houses had big yards with flower beds and mature trees. The street was deserted except for a skinny preteen with a school backpack walking slowly toward him. She seemed lost in thought or fantasy, looking down at the sidewalk in front of her, lips moving occasionally as if talking to herself. As soon as she became aware of Ransom, though, she crossed the street. It wasn't only the spoor that told him she was Margaret Biel: he could see the resemblance to the old woman in the photograph. He crossed the street after her.

"Excuse me, miss?"

She stopped walking and turned toward him suspiciously. Her face was defiant, stubborn, frowning. Already at ten or eleven she looked formidable.

"I'm sorry to bother you," he said. "Are you Margaret Biel?"

"Fuck off, pervert."

"What a charming little girl." He stopped two meters away from her. "Are you Margaret?"

"If you try to kidnap me, I'll kick you in the dick."

"Don't worry. I only kidnap nice kids."

"What do you want?"

"I want you to—well, I guess I do want you to come somewhere with me."

"If I scream," she said, dropping her backpack and backing up, "everyone around here'll call the police."

"Will you listen to me? I want to ask you something."

She backed up some more, watching him balefully. Her hands were curled into fists.

"You don't have to go with me if you don't want to. But—"

"I don't want to," she said. Then: "Where?"

"I—it'll take some explaining. Is there somewhere we can talk?"

"We can talk here." Then she added: "Do you have a cigarette?"

"I'll buy you some cigarettes if you want," said Ransom. "I just want to ask you something."

"I thought you wanted to take me somewhere," she said mockingly. She was flirting now, Ransom realized. She had gotten over her fear and was practicing being a grown-up, looking at him coolly through narrowed eyes, as she had probably seen the actresses do on TV. A foolhardy kid, with balls.

"I will, if you want," he said. "But I want to ask you—"

And then he was somewhere else again, as if the whole world had decided to answer his question.

4

There were still trees around and above him, but they were bigger—big country oaks, elms, and beeches, their leaves fluttering in a breeze that carried the faint, sweet smell of summer. The sky was vivid blue with a few puffy clouds, and the afternoon sunlight was August yellow. The sidewalk was gone; he stood on the gravel shoulder of a road that wound through a beautiful, hilly countryside, the peak of a house or curve of a long driveway visible here and there among the trees. Margaret Biel's spoor came distinctly down the road, from over the next hill.

And now he understood what was happening. It should have been obvious from the start, but he hadn't investigated a fatality in a long time, and maybe he had unconsciously absorbed the Merrivales' confidence that their aunt was alive somewhere. It was known that at death consciousness—the soul if you were religious—passed through a series of images or scenes, places and events from the life that was ending. No one knew how these "terminal dream" scenes were selected; they seemed usually to be mundane moments, solitary and quiet, as if before its departure the spirit returned to those few times when the mind had become still and transparent amid the rush and worry of life, allowing it to look out; as if the soul in departing returned to say good-bye to the only moments in this world that it remembered clearly.

It seemed obvious that Margaret Biel was undergoing this process now, and that Ransom was following her through her terminal dream. She might already be gone for all he

knew, departed to the place where no one living can follow—
if it *was* a place, rather than just nothing. But the scenes she
had raised for herself in the astral world still had some resid-
ual life force animating them, allowing a pursuer to inhabit
each of them briefly, following her spoor like someone
tracking a woman through the halls of a picture gallery by
the smell of her perfume.

Could he catch her before she stepped across the brook or
over the stile or through the gate symbolizing the irrevocable
end of her life? And even if he could, what then? Reflecting
that he was being paid a huge sum of money to figure that
out, he draped his jacket over his shoulder and started up the
road, his Dockers crunching on the gravel shoulder.

At the top of the hill the breeze was stronger, cooling his
sweat. Halfway down the slope ahead of him a driveway ran
off to the right between ornamental stone gateposts. The
spoor came from there. Ransom trudged down to the gates
and made the hot, quarter-mile hike up the drive, which
curved through well-kept grounds to a graceful stone mansion surrounded by flower beds. The clip of shears came
from somewhere out of sight, and sprinklers sparkled and
hissed over lawns. The big double front doors of the house
stood open to take advantage of the breeze, screen doors
dimly revealing a big, airy hall within.

They were unlocked. Ransom slipped inside. As his eyes
adjusted he saw that a wide staircase rose from the left side of
the hall, reflected in a huge antique mirror framed with
mother of pearl on the opposite wall. Tropical plants grew in
enormous glazed jars. The sound of a vacuum cleaner came
distantly from somewhere.

Margaret Biel's spoor poured down the staircase.

Ransom climbed it quickly and quietly. If the person
whose mind had reified this etheric sensorium was dead or
had passed her attention elsewhere, an argument or fight

would quickly drain its energy. It was important to be quick and calm, to get the information he needed before the sensorium started to curl up and fade—unless Margaret Biel was still alive and maintaining it with her attention, in which case the analogue of her he met here would be the woman herself—and then he would have to figure out what to do next.

In the upstairs hall a heavy wooden door was ajar; the spoor came from the room within.

He went in and closed the door quietly behind him. It was a corner bedroom, breeze stirring the curtains in big windows. A girl wearing jeans and a black Ramones T-shirt was lolling on a massive oak bed, listening to earbuds. She craned her head backward to see him.

"I told you—" she started angrily, but broke off when she realized it wasn't who she had thought. She pulled the earbuds out, squirmed around, and sat up. "Who are you?"

She was fifteen or sixteen, very pretty, her short hair dyed black and half a dozen studs in one of her ears, but unmistakably the same female whose photo Ransom had seen before getting into the View tank.

"My name is Heath."

"Are you the doctor?"

"Come again?"

"The psychiatrist."

"No. Do you need a psychiatrist?"

"My mother thinks I do. Who *are* you then, sport?"

"I'm an endovid investigator." When she just stared, he went on, "I go into trances and track down things for people. Lost things."

"Cool. Have I lost something? My mind, maybe?"

He smiled. "You seem okay to me."

"No, I'm dysfunctional," the girl said bitterly. "I have poor impulse control. I'm socially maladapted. I'm not interested in school. You can cure all those things with drugs and sympathetic understanding, you see. But I don't see why she wants me to see you."

"She doesn't know I'm here."

"Are you a rapist?"

"No. I have a purely professional interest in you."

"Do you have a car?"

"Sorry." He didn't have any of the things that the Margaret Biels wanted, he reflected.

She leaned forward and looked out one of her windows at the driveway in front of the house. "Then how did you get here, sport?"

"I appeared out of thin air."

"Uh-huh."

"I have to ask you some questions, okay?"

She had been looking him over as they talked, and now she seemed to make up her mind about something. "Lock that door, okay?"

He locked it, and when he turned back she was pulling off her T-shirt over her head. "You want to fuck? We have to be quiet, or my whore mother'll hear." She stood up and unzipped her pants, stepped out of them, and sat back on the bed in her underpants and lithe, new-made body. She grinned as she watched Ransom look at it. But sex would dissipate the sensorium's energy—unless this was the real Margaret Biel.

"Honey, I'd like to, but—"

She pulled off her underpants, and tossed them away dramatically, then lay on her side, head resting on her hand, grinning at him. He came and sat on the edge of the bed.

"Okay, you're very persuasive," he prevaricated. "But can you answer a question first?"

She took his hand and put it on her hip. It was smooth and warm and a little bit sweaty. "What?"

"If you were almost dead and there was some way I could bring you back to life, what would that be?"

"Fuck me," she whispered, and he didn't have time to find out whether that was an answer or a demand, because a hard knocking started at the door.

A woman's angry voice came through. "Meg? Meg, I told you not to lock this door! What are you doing in there?"

"Go away, bitch!" the girl screamed, sitting up, her face contorted with rage.

"Margaret, open this door at once! Do you hear me?"

With a snarled curse, the future relict of the late Raymond Fenton Biel sprang from the bed and went to the door, slender muscles rippling in her young flanks and buttocks. Ransom stood up behind her as she threw it open. The woman Ransom had seen under the umbrella on the resort beach stood there, fifteen years older, eyes blazing. The eyes took in her naked daughter and Ransom almost at once, and horror came into them. She slapped Margaret, hard. Then she turned to Ransom.

"Get out of here," she hissed. "You get out or I'll call the police."

"It's not what you think, Mrs. Biel—" Ransom started soothingly, but the woman's attention was diverted to Margaret, who, knocked off balance for a second by the slap, now punched her in the face.

Suddenly, the walls, floor, and ceiling of the room seemed to pop outward and multiply into smaller copies of themselves. As the sensorium ran out of energy, the dimensions it occupied collapsing like a balloon with the air coming out, its internal light was circling inside a smaller and smaller four-dimensional sphere, so that the reflections of the furniture, the two women, Ransom, and the view out the windows multiplied and narrowed, closing in around them, getting smaller and smaller until they imploded altogether, silently, taking the sensorium with them.

Margaret Biel's smell, however, remained.

5

It was this smell that brought Ransom, with only a moment of disorientation, to the next scene in the picture show—the last, he guessed.

He stood in an orchard on a beautiful summer day. In every direction rows of trees receded in diminishing perspective—peach trees, he thought, their low, broad-spreading branches canopied with dark green leaves and immature fruit. The air smelled of sun-warmed vegetation, and it was very quiet. Far ahead of him, the orchard sloped upward, and raising his eyes he saw the towering slopes of a mountain, its almost vertical summit disappearing into mists and clouds.

You didn't have to be a poet to see the metaphor: the walk through the beautiful orchard, then the climb up to the mist-shrouded realms from which no one returns.

Margaret Biel's spoor came clearly among the trees from the direction of the mountain.

So he had failed; as predicted, he wouldn't be bringing back the aunt who laid the golden egg. Biel had been here, and had headed toward the mountain, and was probably already gone into the mist.

With a sigh he started walking anyway, his professional reflexes taking over. But he was already thinking about his next job, a missing-documents case he had put off to take the Merrivale matter, and which he now had to reschedule. The spoor headed straight for the mountain, never straying right or left. His feet swished softly in the crabgrass as he followed it. He was halfway to the mountain's foot before he sensed that something was wrong.

At first it was just a vague discomfort, almost like a sudden bad mood or upset stomach. Then he began to hear a buzzing. It got louder as he walked, as if he were approaching a beehive, until he realized that it wasn't a buzzing at all; it wasn't even a sound; it was more like *static* that he could feel in his viscera and fingers, and as a nausea in the pit of his stomach. He wrung his hands and shook his head, trying to get rid of it, but it got stronger as he walked; and now the orchard began to look grainy, like a hologram full of white noise. In all his years Viewing ether he couldn't remember anything like it—bone-deep, stomach-turning static, which seemed to smear and scramble the sensorium and his own guts.

When its source finally came into view, his curiosity turned to apprehension.

It was a hole. It hung in the air a meter above the ground, strangely artificial-looking, like a picture of a black cave entrance pasted crudely onto the orchard. Pan-sensory static poured off it like smoke from a tear gas canister. As he drew cautiously closer, he saw that it was *moving,* rotating with a pixelated glitter, like a low-quality digital rendering of a rotating black pit, and that the static spraying out of it seemed to break off green, gray, and gold shards of the orchard sensorium along its circumference like pieces of shattered stained glass, which then swirled down into its onyx darkness. It pulled at Ransom, too, in an indefinable way, like some kind of metaphysical whirlpool; but after a second of panic he realized that its pull was weak and seemed to be getting weaker, winding down.

Then his relief turned to dismay.

Margaret Biel hadn't gone to the mountain after all. Her spoor was coming unmistakably from the sintering onyx whirlpool.

For a sickening moment he wondered if she had somehow gone badly haywire and turned into this thing, but he quickly rejected the idea. He could see that the thing was a *passage,* a tunnel bored somehow into the sensorium; Margaret Biel's spoor was coming from it not because she had turned into it, but because she had *gone* into it.

Ransom's professionalism, though strong, did not extend to jumping into sinister and possibly dangerous mystery holes. He had been conducting endovoyant investigations for nearly thirty years, and few appearances frightened him anymore: he faced them with the equanimity of a man who knew that he was actually lying safe in a tank of smart liquid in the basement of his mansion, and that if things got too bad he could invoke his extraction protocol or, at worst, his vital signs would register distress and his assistants would pull him back to his comfortable life as one of the most sought-after endovid investigators in the country. But this black tunnel chilled him. Even in a world where the uncanny was routine it felt strange; something alien in a place to which he had thought nothing could be alien.

He moved cautiously toward it, trying to see into it. It already looked a little smaller than when he had first seen it, its pull still weakening. It was hard to guess the distance to something that didn't seem part of the sensorium in the first place, but he thought he was about two meters away from it.

Cautiously, he put out a hand.

The hole gaped and roared like the maw of an enormous animal, and the orchard stood on end. Ransom fell. He didn't even have time to be scared before the light of the orchard receded, and blackness closed around him.

At first he struggled, trying to right himself, but then the speck of light that had been the orchard disappeared and gravity, time, and motion were gone. There was only a silent, bellowing roar of static, vaporizing him at the center of a black sun. Chaos, said his last shred of thought, the terrible, boiling dissolution even of atoms, even of their fundamental particles—

Then even thought was gone.

But after an immeasurable interval a speck of light appeared, and with it his erasure seemed to reverse: a speck of sensation, feeling, thought grew larger and larger, and just as suddenly as he had entered the tunnel he was out again, resurrected into pearly gray light and sweet air. The joy of it, the gratitude at simply existing, at being able to see and feel, mind and body reconstituted, were so strong that for a minute he didn't notice or care where he was; he sobbed, and tears streamed down his face.

Then he gave a yell of fright and flailed his arms and legs wildly.

He was a thousand meters up in the air, falling toward a rocky coast and an immense blue water.

6

Not falling but floating, he realized after a second. Drifting downward through alternating currents of thick, cold ocean air and warm, earthy air from the land. Simple levitation, commonplace in the astral/etheric world.

He took some deep breaths and tried to relax. He realized that he felt sick and was trembling violently. With sudden fear he looked around for the black tunnel, and caught a glimpse of it very high above him, small and receding. He scanned for any others that might be lurking nearby, but everything else looked ordinary; there was nothing to suggest that he wasn't back in the everyday astral world, where appearances such as floating a thousand feet above a coastline of rock cliffs were routine. He was back on his old stomping ground now, where he had nothing to fear.

He focused once again on the sensorium around him; he had been drifting toward the land, and he saw now that there was a town perched atop the coastal cliffs. He fixed his eyes on it, which made him move toward it faster. It looked like a small town, streets and stone houses hugging rocky slopes, villas along the edge of the ocean cliff with bright green gardens inside their walls, bridges crossing two deep gorges that ran down to the water. As he came closer he picked a street to focus on, and at last landed gently in the middle of it like a man stepping off a bus, a steep, deserted back street narrowed to one lane by cars parked along both curbs, faint smells of motor oil and dust replacing the primal smells of the upper air. The gray sky and the mild, gusty breeze made it seem calm and somnolent. Ransom adjusted his jacket and hiked up his pants. There was nothing like flying to disarrange your clothes, as he knew from long experience.

Then it struck him. Something wasn't right.

He couldn't tell what it was at first, but then he knew. The spoor that had led him in each of the previous Biel sensoria was missing. He turned all the way around in the street, sniffing, but he smelled only the scents of the town. It might as well have been a real street in a real town, where such things as etheric spoors didn't exist.

After a minute's hesitation and more clothes adjusting, he began to walk. One rule in the astral was, when in doubt, wander around. If you did that long enough, you usually ran across something that told you why you were wherever you were.

A few blocks down the street, people sat at sidewalk tables outside a café. None of them wore anonymizing gear, which meant that he was somewhere with either low per-capita income or laws against info-push marketing. As he approached, he realized that the people were speaking Italian.

No one looked up as he entered the tiny café, where a man resembling a sleepy walrus leaned on a counter, an espresso machine hissing behind him.

Ransom approached him with his shaky Italian. *"Buongiorno."*

The man just looked at him sleepily, a cigarette stub between his fat fingers leaking smoke.

"Sto cercando una donna americana," Ransom said after a pause to work out the syntax. *"Una signora con capelli marroni, occhi blu. Ha visto chiunque come quello?"*

The man continued impassive.

"Do you speak English? *Comprenez-vous Francais? Parlez-vous*—uh, no—*parla Italiano?*"

The man took a drag on his cigarette, but was otherwise unmoved. Ransom had sometimes encountered such rudeness in Paris, but never in Italy, where people invariably at least paid attention to you. He turned away. "*Buongiorno, signore.*"

Emerging onto the sidewalk, he addressed the people at the tables. "*Signore e signori, ho una domanda di importanza.*"

They went on drinking and talking imperturbably, ignoring him.

Ransom had never heard of Italians so ungenerous, even etheric Italians. By creating them, the sensorium was doubtless trying to tell him something. In the astral world the sensorium itself often had to be considered a character in whatever drama was unfolding; constructed as it always was (consciously or unconsciously) by some sentient mind, it often had points to make and meanings to reveal. You just had to poke around until you discovered them.

He followed the sidewalk downhill, scrutinizing the small shops and elderly one- and two-story stone buildings for hints as to why he had landed here. Though maybe there were none, he told himself. Maybe Margaret Biel had died in her Boston hospital, and that was why there was no sign of her anymore. Maybe she had ceased to emit the spoor that gave direction to his search, and that had thrown him more or less haphazardly into a random sensorium. Maybe that could explain even the terrible chaos hole.

Anyway, he would look around for a while longer, and if the trail stayed cold he would extract. He felt he had already gone far beyond the call of duty on the Merrivale matter. He had other cases to work and fees to earn.

Following the path of least gravitational resistance soon brought him to a street that ran along the top of the ocean cliff, at the very bottom of the town. A row of big holiday villas with high garden walls mostly hid the view of the Mediterranean, but he found himself enjoying the mild breeze, the smell of flowers from the gardens, and the picturesque houses perched on the hills above. The street was empty and very quiet, and not even one security drone buzzed out of a garden to check on him. He walked all the way to the end of the village, where the street became a narrow highway hugging the hills. There were no villas here, and he could see the water; he stood admiring it for a few minutes. Then he turned back and retraced his steps.

Back in the village again, he sat down on the narrow sidewalk, against a garden wall overhung by the fronds of a palm tree, closed his eyes, and began the extraction protocol, visualizing the silver astral cord stretching from his navel to his physical body lying in the dive tank, the cord pulling him, rushing him through the sky so that he could feel the alternating warm sunlight and clammy cold of clouds. Soon he had the sense of being inside the tank again; he visualized the feel of it, the neutral nontouch of the thick polymer liquid on his skin as he began to move, anticipating the momentary sense of suffocation before it withdrew from his lungs, the red light above his head, and the calm female voice repeating his name, giving him another focus by which to pull himself back from the View trance, his body weak and trembling. When the sense of being back in his body was strong enough, he opened his eyes.

He was still sitting against the villa wall in the pleasant Italian afternoon. Sunlight filtering through palm fronds dappled a small amphibious Fiat stained with bird droppings parked at the curb; there was a scent of jasmine in the soft, humid air.

He closed his eyes again, for longer this time, concentrated more intensely, until the inside of the tank felt crystal clear. But when he opened his eyes again he was still in the village.

That was unusual, but not unheard of. It probably meant

that the sensorium, in its role as actor, was not going to let him go until it showed him its secret, the information for which he had come. Which meant there *was* information, and thus some reason for him to be here after all. He sighed, got to his feet, and started walking again.

He had gone only a few hundred meters when he picked up the spoor.

It was weak, much weaker than before, but still unmistakable. It came from one of the narrow three-story houses on the less expensive inland side of the street, each surrounded by a low wall around a tiny garden. As he had thought, the sensorium had something for him. Margaret Biel, or what was left of her, was here.

The front door of the house was narrow, high, and arched, with metal grillwork over opaque white glass. He could see from the green light on the keypad that the sensor was operating, but no one answered even after he had stood there for a couple of minutes. After a moment's hesitation, he went in anyway. No alarm sounded and no security drones stung him, so he guessed someone was home and would be out shortly in response to the front door's announcement. He stood and waited in a high-ceilinged foyer floored with stone, which opened onto a large room with floor-to-ceiling windows that made it as much glassed-in porch as sitting room. The windows on the left and right showed woods growing almost up to the sides of the house, a few birds flitting among the branches; the back windows showed a narrow strip of grass and a rocky verge that fell three hundred meters to the gray-blue ocean. The smell scheme matched the holograms: a fresh, outdoor tang of leaf mould in clean ocean air. The house was very quiet except for the distant sound of simulated waves on a simulated shore.

The Biel spoor came down a narrow flight of stairs to his left.

He climbed them silently. The spoor leaked out around a closed door at the top. He went through it into a dim room stuffy with the warm, musky smells of sex and sleep. A boy and a girl, perhaps in their mid-twenties, lay on a futon bed. The room looked like a temporary living space: a couple of suitcases stood in an open closet, two chairs were draped with clothes, and some expensive multimedia hardware was set up on the floor against one wall.

Margaret Biel's oddly muted spoor came from the sleeping girl. Ransom went to stand over her.

She was fair, blond, and delicate, with high cheekbones and pale freckles. As Ransom stood puzzled, searching for any hint of resemblance to Margaret Biel, the girl opened her eyes and looked straight at him.

He jumped backward, almost falling over a chair. "I'm very sorry," he said, recovering. "I didn't mean to scare you. I'm looking for someone I think lives here, and no one came to the door, so—"

The girl sat up slowly, and slid from under her side of the bedcovers as if taking care not to wake her companion. She was naked.

Ransom looked away gallantly. He hadn't scared the girl into hysterics, at least, so hopefully the sensorium would hold up long enough for him to figure out what was going on. "Do you know someone by the name of Margaret Biel?"

When she made no answer, he shot her an oblique glance. She wasn't looking at him. She was sitting on the floor rapidly putting on clothes.

"Excuse me, miss," said Ransom, confused. He moved forward and stood in front of her. Her eyes moved between her clothes and the sleeping boy as if Ransom were invisible.

Invisible—suddenly at least something made sense. The people at the café who hadn't seen or heard him; the absence of security drones even in as lax a country as Italy;

and now this girl completely unaware that he was standing
in front of her. And then it struck him that he had walked
right through the closed doors of this house and this room
without opening them, his mind eliding the incongruity.

In this sensorium, he was a ghost.

What did it mean? What was he supposed to understand
from it? And why did this girl, who looked nothing like
Margaret Biel, seem to emit Margaret Biel's spoor?

Done dressing, she crouched by a backpack and unzipped
it with silent slowness, her eyes fixed on the boy. He lay fast
asleep on his stomach, arms and legs stretched out. The girl
took a small, white packet from the backpack and tore it
open silently, the disposable plastic shriveling and smoking,
sublimating as she dropped it. There were two objects inside, one red and one blue; Ransom saw with surprise that
they were disposable hypodermics of the kind the military
used, color-coded as narcotic and stimulant. She dropped
the blue syringe next to the futon and armed the red one
with trembling hands. Then she slowly and carefully pulled
the blanket covering the boy aside until his tanned, muscular legs were exposed.

With a sudden movement, she pushed the red syringe
against the inside of his thigh. It made a slight spitting
sound.

The boy rolled over and sat bolt upright, stared at her in
confusion for a full second, and then jerked his leg away as if
he had been stung, the movement throwing the exhausted
syringe onto the rug. He looked confused.

"Barbara, what—" he began in English. But then he
stopped. His eyes crossed. He seemed to have trouble holding up his head. He reclined slowly onto his elbows and then
onto his back with a deep sigh. The girl, wiping the syringe
on a dirty T-shirt she had grabbed from a chair, fumblingly
put it in the boy's hand, then stood up and backed away

against the wall. She and Ransom stood frozen, spectators to an awful scene.

The boy didn't notice the thing in his hand. He had settled peacefully onto the futon, looking straight up at the ceiling, but now his breath was shallow, his eyes glassy. A set look of concentration came into his face, and his breathing trailed off to nothing. His eyes stayed open, but he began to turn gray, like a boy poured from cement.

Then two things happened.

The first was that the room stretched out and curled as if it were made of water being sucked down a drain, the vortex pulling at Ransom with sudden, terrifying power. He grabbed wildly at the furniture, the wall, but it didn't help: everything seemed to have turned liquid and was twisting down into the whirlpool. He clawed and scrambled with terror to try to keep away from it, flailing against the undertow of the liquid room.

The second thing was that the boy stood up out of his gray body and drifted unconcernedly with the current, not looking back.

What happened next was a blur. Ransom knew he was being sucked into the death hole that had opened for the boy. Scrambling and clawing in panic, he suddenly felt something solid. He gripped it, held on as he had never held on to anything. He had a confused glimpse of the boy far inside the vortex, but now he seemed to be walking through a beautiful meadow toward the edge of a forest.

Ransom refused to follow. Hand over hand he pulled himself painfully against the overpowering whirlpool, slowly into the safety of the solid thing he had found, which was like a narrow tube, just big enough to squeeze into. The effort was titanic, tearing; his whole world shrank to an agony of holding, pulling, squeezing himself into the narrow safe place—

And suddenly the pull of the vortex ceased. A wet, heavy solidity enveloped him. He was lying on his back, looking up at the blurred ceiling, but now everything was throbbing with waves of darkness. He couldn't breath. His body was wet concrete, a corpse glued to the floor by its own weight. He was suffocating—dying.

Somewhere above him a blond blur moved and was gone.

An exhausted numbness filled him, and he could feel something opening, feel the beginnings of the ravenous vortex current starting to swirl around him again. Supreme panic roused him, and he forced his now nearly blind eyes to see. Taking a breath was the hardest thing he had ever done, a thousand years of torture in which every moment soft voices told him to let go, relax, rest in the soft darkness just for a moment—

With a last agony of effort he willed himself to shout. He didn't know if he succeeded, but he couldn't hold out any longer.

He fell into rushing darkness.

7

Ransom heard sounds; he tried to open his eyes. After a long struggle, he succeeded. He squinted and blinked against bright light, tried to dispel double vision. There was a smell like antiseptic. He was lying in a narrow place, and for a moment he thought he was in the dive tank, finally coming out of trance. But it didn't feel like extraction; there was no headache or receding red lights like car taillights in a tunnel. Instead he felt exhausted, dizzy, nauseated. He tried to move his hands. They were sensitive and clumsy, as if he had never used them before. As his eyes slowly cleared he realized that he was lying on a plastic alloy table that had shaped itself to his body so that its hard surface felt soft and comfortable. Half a dozen delicate, jointed robot arms protruding from a console were poised above him, holding neural induction electrodes, acupuncture needles, and syringes. Wires and tubes ran to various places on his head, neck, and arms, and screens showed his vital signs. He tried to sit up, but he couldn't.

He was in a medical bay. Two other people were crowded in there, too, standing over him, their eyes intent and anxious. The woman was young, no more than forty, he guessed, with brown hair and dark brown eyes. The man looked about his own age, with graying hair. They both wore fashionable, flattering 1940s-style clothes. Instinctively Ransom listened for the tone of their psychic leakage, but he was too dizzy and weak to pick up anything recognizable.

"*No, non muoverti.* Don't move, Michael. I will call the doctor," the woman said in what, after a moment of puzzlement, he realized was English spoken with a strong Italian accent. She left the bay.

He had been in the Italian town, he remembered. In the house, in the room with the blond girl and the boy. The girl had given the boy a shot—

The man was leaning forward, looking into his face. "How do you feel?" he asked, also with an accent. There were fine smile wrinkles around his eyes.

Ransom had to swallow a couple of times before he could croak: "Okay."

The woman came back in with a small, round man in blue scrubs and a rakishly professional expression.

"Ah!" the small man said in English, throwing up his hands in celebration. "You are awake! Welcome back to the lands of life!"

The medical bay was by this time uncomfortably close quarters, but the three people standing over him now had what sounded like a heated argument. Ransom, with his limited Italian, was able to discern that it was actually the man and woman asking the paramedic if they could take him home, and the paramedic saying yes.

The paramedic looked at some of the instruments. "How do you feel?" he asked, lifting his splayed hands palm-upward from hip- to head-level, as if depicting the disgorgement of the entire soul.

"Okay," said Ransom. "Good, I guess. Where am I?"

"*Ospedale di Santa Maria*, St. Mary Hospital, Sorrento. The local branch. And you are a very lucky young man. You could easily have died, and you would have died, if these people had not given you the epinephrine, eh, and brought you to me at once. They say you are not a habitual drug user?"

"No, not at all."

"But on your thigh we found the mark of the syringe, and your blood was full of narcopine to kill three men. It is still illegal in Italy. Lucky you left the epinephrine by the bed. You are American, eh? You must know that it is still illegal in Italy, and that I would have to call the police but for, eh, the words of these friends of yours, who say that you are not a habitual drug user."

"I'm certainly not. Thank you. I don't know— I don't know what happened." It was the young man the girl had given the shot to, not him. Had she given him one, too, after he passed out?

"Perhaps you were trying to perform suicide?"

"No, certainly not. Not at all. I was afraid, very afraid I was going to die."

"We heard you cry out from the bedroom," said the woman, eyes wide, voice trembling. "Your voice was"—she gestured richly and looked at her husband—"*come si dice, 'il corvo'*?"

"The crow," he said.

"Your voice was like the crow."

"If they had not brought you here in that moment—" the paramedic gestured and shrugged. "But if it was not suicide, and if you are not a habitual drug user, then I will tell you. A casual user must always take less than a habitual user. The habitual user builds up a resistance, so that the same amount he uses will kill the casual user. You understand?"

"Yes, but I didn't take any narcopine. I— I lost consciousness, but I didn't take anything."

The paramedic studied him keenly. "Do you remember what happened to you?"

"Um—"

"Do you know what day is today?"

Ransom tried to think back to before he had gotten into the View tank.

"Do you know the month?"

"October," he said before he realized that it couldn't be that late in the year in this sensorium.

The three Italians looked at one another.

"Do you remember the names of your friends?" asked the paramedic, tipping his head toward them.

"No. I don't know these people."

The man and woman looked at him anxiously, the doctor gravely.

"But Michael," said the woman gently, putting her hands on his arm, "you don't remember us, Lucia and Tomas?"

"You must have me mixed up with someone," said Ransom. "My name isn't Michael, and I'm sorry but I don't know you."

"But you and Barbara have been staying with us for two months. You don't remember?"

The boy had called the blond girl Barbara. "The blond girl?"

"Yes, yes, the blond girl. You remember Barbara, no?"

"I think I saw her," said Ransom cautiously. "I saw her give a shot to someone, a boy who was sleeping. Don't you have the domestic-violence monitors turned on at your house?"

The woman—Lucia—put her hand to her throat. "Michael, did you beat Barbara?"

"What? No! What— I told you, my name isn't Michael. You have me mixed up with someone. But do you know the boy I mean? Brown, curly hair, about twenty-five, muscular? Is he okay?"

The three Italians exchanged a look, and the paramedic gestured with elegant nonchalance at the other two to follow him, and all three went outside the bay and had what was probably supposed to be a low-voiced conference. Ransom caught the words "memory," "house," "very, very carefully," "a few days." Then the three of them came back to cluster around him again.

"Come on, Michael," the woman, Lucia, said to him gently.

"Let's go home. The doctor says you will be well. Come on, *caro.*"

The paramedic flicked his fingers through some holographic icons, and straps that had been holding Ransom to the table loosened. The man and the woman, Lucia and Tomas, helped him up, the paramedic giving advice and encouragement in Italian and English. They took off his hospital gown and helped him on with a pair of jeans and a T-shirt. No one seemed to realize that it would be a lot easier if there weren't four people in the narrow space. He was still dizzy, and his vision kept going blurry. They unfolded a wheelchair and pushed him out into a small area with a nurse's station in the center and two other medical bays opening off it, then through a sanitary lock into a small front office. The paramedic shook hands all round, and Ransom, Lucia, and Tomas emerged into a ripe late afternoon, the sky a deep blue, the warm, humid air saturated with the smell of the sea. Tomas went off somewhere, and Lucia stood on the sidewalk in front of Ransom in his wheelchair, studying him with her large, emotional brown eyes. Returning her look, Ransom noticed something peculiar. He tried to pin it down. Everything around him—the yellow sunlight, the clinic driveway, the rocky hills, even the smell of the ocean air—seemed perfectly authentic, but it had a strange *feel* to it, a flat, insubstantial texture, as if he were looking at it on a video screen.

"This is all very kind of you."

"Shh, *caro,* don't say that. We are your friends, of course we will do anything for you. You really don't remember? Tomas and Lucia Pagano?"

"That boy—is he all right? The girl gave him a shot—" He poked his leg to show where, and was surprised to feel a pain, as if he too had been given a shot in the same place.

"He is all right," said Lucia. "He is going to be all right." Her eyes brimmed with tears.

Tomas pulled up rapidly in a European sports coupe, jumped out, and he and Lucia helped Ransom into the backseat. Tomas drove manually, rushing expertly along the coastal highway that clung to the cliffs much faster than the autopilot would have allowed, the tight corners over hundred-meter drops giving Ransom a tingly feeling. Lucia paid no attention, instead starting dinner on an elegant remote she took from her sleeve. In no more than a quarter hour they were tooling sedately down the street where Ransom had found the murder house. Tomas turned in at the short driveway of that same house, and parked under a grape arbor crowded against the neighbor's concrete garage. Lucia and Tomas helped him from the backseat. It struck him that last time he had come here no one could see him. Now things had gone to the opposite extreme, these two kind Italians treating him like a beloved younger brother. The ever-changing nature of the astral plane, he told himself, and then it struck him that he must try again to extract. Staying in the astral too long even in subjective time could lead to disorientation and exhaustion once you came out. If necessary he could always come back and complete the Merrivale assignment after a break.

The fresh smell of the sea filled the cooling evening air. Ransom was still wobbly, but able to climb the front stairs, holding onto the handrail. The front door opened as they approached, and Ransom stepped for a second time into the house where, at least in appearance, he had almost died. A smell of cooking was coming from the kitchen. The Biel spoor, however, was gone.

"I will take you upstairs," said Lucia, holding his arm. As they slowly climbed she shot a rapid Italian shopping list over her shoulder at Tomas, who made cheerful disputation as to brands and prices, and then went out whistling, evidently glad of another excuse for high-speed manual driving.

At the top of the stairs Lucia opened the door where Ransom had seen the murder, and at the sight his heart pounded and he sagged against the door frame. Lucia was already inside, clucking and straightening up, clearing and rarifying the windows so that the orange glow of sunset and a tendril of fresh air came through; when she turned to look at him she came to him in alarm, took him in her arms.

"*Ah, il mio povero bambino!*" she said. The top of her head came to his nose, and he could feel her ample breasts against his solar plexus. She smelled good. "*Che'e errato?* What is wrong, Michael? Are you afraid? Don't be afraid, my baby. Come and lie down. I will sit with you. Come."

She pulled him to the futon, on which she rapidly straightened the sheets and blankets, then helped him lie down. Then she bustled around, talking to him while she threw dirty clothes in a pile and hung clean clothes in the closet. Then she pulled a chair next to the futon and sat down.

"Go to sleep, *caro,*" she said. "I will sit here."

"What happened to them?" he asked, resting gratefully. "The boy and the blond girl?"

"I don't know where Barbara is," said Lucia. "We have tried calling Celeste and her other friends, but she is not with them. She will come back soon, I know."

"What about the boy?"

She looked at him oddly. "What boy, *caro?*"

He tried to read the murmur of her field leakage, but the strange, flat feeling seemed to intervene, so that he got nothing. "The boy I told you about. Maybe twenty-five, curly brown hair—"

"But, Michael, *you* are the boy."

He stared at her. "What do you mean?"

"The doctor says you have a"—she made a gesture near her head—"a disturbance of memory. You will remember soon."

"But—no I'm not. I'm Heath Ransom. I came here to—"

"Heat Ransome?" she asked, puzzled. Then she seemed to make up her mind about something. She took his hands and pulled him gently up. "Come with me, *caro mio*."

She helped him up from the bed and into a small, modern bathroom, and switched on the mirror. He looked into it.

The person looking back was a boy of about twenty-five whose parents had evidently had plenty of money for prenatal enhancements. He was muscular and very handsome, about six-two, wearing jeans and a T-shirt. He moved an arm, and the young man did the same, his well-defined bicep flexing.

"Holy shit," he said.

"You remember now, eh? You came to us to visit from Barbara's mother, who is my very good friend. We have loved having you, and until now we have had so much pleasure. But now I am afraid your parents will think we have not taken great care of you."

"I think I need to lie down again," said Ransom faintly. Though of course, he reminded himself, nothing was impossible in the astral world.

"Yes, come and lie down. You will lie down until you feel better." She led him back to the room. "And when Barbara comes back, she will look after you."

That thought gave him a jolt. "Please don't leave me alone with her. You won't leave me alone with her, will you, Lucia? Not while I'm sleeping."

"You are afraid of Barbara?" she asked. Her big, emotional eyes teared up again.

"I don't want to be alone with her. Not while I'm sleeping. Okay?"

"Not if you don't want. When she comes back I will come with her, or I will send Tomas if I am cooking."

"Lucia," he said, lying down, "thank you for everything."

"*Grazie*. Remember I taught you?"

"*Grazie*," he said, smiling up at her.

"*Niente*," she said, smiling back. "Sleep now."

He closed his eyes and lay still, breathing deeply and relaxing. In a little while he heard Lucia get up, and the door close quietly. He opened his eyes to make sure she was gone, then closed them again. The emergency extraction would work just as well if she were in the room, given that both she and it and everything else here were astral appearances, but he didn't want any distractions. He had of course thoroughly memorized the extraction pattern, but it was complicated, and even a slight deviation would fail to trigger the cascade of electrochemical interventions that would pull him forcibly out of trance. On the principle that the eye muscles were the only part of the somatic musculature that tracked the sensorial body in View trance, the sequence had been made complicated and unnatural on purpose so that you couldn't inadvertently trigger an extraction just by looking around.

He noticed that his heart was pounding as he rehearsed the sequence in his mind. On detecting the emergency sequence through his eye sensors, the dive-tank mechanism would immediately modify his induction electrode entrainment, inject him with norepinephrine, withdraw the oxygenated liquid polymer from his lungs, and flush the dive tank with cold water; an alarm would sound in the projection room, and the technician on duty would open the hatch and pull him into the cold, blinding air. While he had only used emergency extraction half a dozen times in his whole career, he had a vivid memory of the sensation of paralysis and suffocation, followed by uncontrollable shaking, nausea, deadly fatigue, and a splitting headache. But he had already tried normal termination twice without the sensorium even flickering. The best he could do was be philosophical and remember that they would give him a dose of narcopine as soon as it was safe.

Steeling himself and sweating, he gave the signal, practically spraining his eyes but hitting the pattern perfectly. Then he gritted his teeth and waited.

Nothing happened.

After a minute he unclenched his teeth. His momentary relief at not undergoing the neural equivalent of a car crash gave way to concern. This very much wasn't supposed to happen. Emergency extraction was supposed to be fail-safe. There was still another layer of redundant backup–the techs would manually extract him after thirty-six hours real-time no matter what—but he had never unsuccessfully initiated an emergency pop. Of course, his reference sample was small, and he would be dragged painfully awake sooner or later one way or another, but it was still disconcerting. His eye sensors must have malfunctioned, or else someone had forgotten to switch on the emergency system.

He also might have made a mistake in the sequence.

He did it twice more. Twice more nothing happened.

In that case there was nothing to do but to wait. At some point and without warning the sensorium would dissolve suddenly into blinding light and extreme discomfort.

He opened his eyes and saw that a deep red, purple, and blue sunset was just fading behind the ocean horizon, which, when he sat up, he could see out the windows over the orange-tiled roof of the villa across the street. He lay back down and tried to relax, watching the light fade.

8

He must have fallen asleep, because when he woke up he realized that he had dreamed he was back home, holding Anna Heatherstone in his arms and saying good-bye. She was going away and he would never see her again. Her face was sweet and sad, and she was trying to comfort him. They were all going away. The house was dark and bare; their moving vans were packed and they were waving good-bye, receding down the dark driveway. He saw Anna's face in the rear window of a car, her hand waving. A great sorrow came over him. His old life was gone. Nothing would ever be as it had been.

He opened his eyes. He was still lying on the futon bed in the house in Italy. The windows were black now; the only light came through the half-open door to the hall. Two figures partly blocked the light. They were whispering. He listened, the strange flat feeling coming over him again.

He heard Lucia say: "The doctor said that he suffered brain damage from the overdose. He is beginning to remember now, but still only a little. I think he remembers who he is, at the least."

Then another voice, a lighter, younger whisper with an American accent: "I feel so bad. I told him I didn't want to see him anymore. He said he would kill himself, but I never thought— Oh, God, I feel so bad, Lucia."

Golden hair glinted in the light. The girl—what had they called her?—Barbara.

"You want to leave him? You have another lover?"

"Yes. Someone I met in Salerno. But now I want to stay with Michael, to take care of him. Can I?"

"He is afraid, *il poverino*. He is afraid of you. Wait until tomorrow, and we will see. We must treat him gently, the doctor says. You sleep in the other bedroom tonight, not to frighten him if he wakes. That is why he took the drug, poor thing! Suicide! Ah, horrible!"

"But I want to stay with him," Barbara whispered urgently.

"No, no, *cara*, I promised—" The rest of Lucia's words were cut off by the door closing gently.

Ransom lay in the dark, trying to sort out his thoughts. He was in an extraordinarily persistent and realistic astral sensorium, witnessing a drama that for some reason was being forced upon him in the most vivid possible way. What could it mean? How did it relate to Margaret Biel? It came to him that he had had no hint of Margaret Biel's spoor when the girl Barbara had been at the door just now.

What if it *wasn't* an astral sensorium?

As soon as he allowed himself to think that, sweat broke out all over him. It was ridiculous, of course. You couldn't return from a Viewing trance as someone else: your consciousness never actually "left" your body, no matter how far you seemed to journey; the silver cord was just a symbolic projection of this unbreakable link. There were sects that believed in metempsychosis, of course. The High Dimensional Church of God called it "harmonic reconstitution," and taught that the astral world was an eight-dimensional manifold in which every object from the physical world touched every other, and that physical space was just as much an illusion as mental space. But as far as he knew, even their version of rebirth in a new body only happened after death.

On the other hand, he had never seen anything in the astral world like the black tunnel that had brought him here.

His mind was suddenly full of fearful hypotheticals. What if he had died in the View tank somehow, and the black tunnel was how Death looked if it found you in the etheric world? But in that case shouldn't the tunnel have brought him to the afterlife, if there was one?

Could this *be* the afterlife?

Then a realization struck him for the first time with its full strangeness: he had *seized* this body after the boy had abandoned it, had pulled himself desperately into it to escape that vortex—the vortex that seemed to have swallowed the boy's consciousness, as if its function was to vacuum up souls loosed from their bodies.

That meant that if this *was* the real world instead of the afterlife or a persistent astral sensorium, he was a ghost who had inhabited—*possessed*—the body of a murdered boy. But how could that be? Was it because his experience with the astral had let him keep his wits about him, remember who and where he was, fight the vortex, while the boy had simply wandered away distractedly into his terminal dream?

The whole thing was so far-fetched and melodramatic that it suddenly struck him as funny. His fear ebbed. It had been a long time since the astral had been able to scare him, but its bag of tricks was bottomless. Sometime in the next few hours he would be unceremoniously yanked back to the Viewing room, where a terrible headache was waiting for him. Too bad in a way; anti-aging treatments were all very well, but inhabiting the body of a young, gene-enhanced stud was better.

Relaxing, he drifted back to sleep.

When he woke again, cheerful morning sunlight and a whiff of fresh air were coming in the windows, and the ocean beyond the villas was a brisk, cheerful blue. He adjusted the windows' permeability to let in more of the breeze, and its cool freshness seemed to sweep the last vestiges of darkness from around him. Downstairs in the sitting room too-fresh air was coming in the windows, their holograms adjusted to show the leaves of the forest around the house stirring and the ocean a bright, ruffled blue just like the real one. Ransom came down stiffly, still wearing his jeans and T-shirt, the stone steps cold on his bare feet.

"Ah, *caro!*" Lucia exclaimed when she saw him. She and Tomas were sitting in armchairs reading newspapers, and Barbara—a really beautiful girl, Ransom saw now—was sitting on the sofa sipping a cup of coffee, her eyes red as if from crying.

"*Buongiorno, ragazzo!* Are you hungry? I will get you something."

He was starving, he realized suddenly. "Thank you."

Lucia bustled into the kitchen, and Ransom dropped self-consciously onto the sofa next to Barbara.

"*Buongiorno.* How are you feeling?" asked Tomas genially, folding his newspaper down onto his lap. "Did you sleep well?"

"Yes, thanks," said Ransom.

Barbara was staring at him wide-eyed.

She moved closer to him. "Oh, Michael," she said, her voice trembling. "I'm so sorry. I'm so sorry."

"No problem," he mumbled. "It's okay." What were you supposed to say when you had possessed a murder victim's body and the murderer was pretending to apologize for driving you to suicide, and the whole thing was happening in an astral sensorium?

Tears ran down Barbara's face, but still he sensed a watchfulness. Instinctively he switched his attention to her field leakage, to get a bead on what she was really thinking.

But there was nothing; just a jumble of impressions impossible to separate from his own thoughts.

And then it struck him. He looked at Tomas, listened for his leakage. Again nothing, just the flat, unreal feeling that he was watching him on a screen—the same feeling he had had yesterday.

"When he eats he will feel better," said Lucia, sweeping in with a breakfast tray, and setting it in front of him on the coffee table. There was bread, cheese, smoked salmon, coffee, cream, and a bowl of blueberries. "Eat," she said, picking up the fork and putting it in his hand. "You will feel better then."

He smiled up at her. She too was free of the penumbra of faint words and images he had felt around people his whole life. It made sense, of course. His ability to sense those information fields depended on mutations he had inherited through his mother's grandmother, who had been a "medium," as they called them in those days. His new body, which the astral was simulating with typical accuracy, wouldn't have those genes or features.

In spite of everything, his heart sped up with excitement. He had been reborn—as a young man!—in a clean world of surfaces, without the subterranean murmurs blurring the boundaries of everything. He was free in a mobile animal world where he could pick up his feet and move without the insides of everything clinging to him, freed from the fecund vegetable world in which all visible things grew burgeoning up from the swamp at the root of everything, tendrils intertwining in impenetrable organic patterns. He felt momentarily giddy with happiness, almost able to forgive just one murder, which anyone might slip up and commit. Even if the whole thing was an astral appearance, the knowledge that it was possible, that he might be able to sneak back to this body from time to time in View, exhilarated him.

He ate ravenously, his strong, clean hunger making the food amazingly tasty.

"Here is the newspaper," Lucia said, holding hers out. He took it obediently, seeing that she had erased her Italian tabloid and downloaded the *New York Times*. He put it on the coffee table and pretended to be engrossed in it while he ate. Barbara was making him nervous staring at him.

Suddenly she sobbed: "How can you read the newspaper? Why won't you even look at me?"

It was so convincing that he did look at her, and for a split second wondered whether he actually had lost his memory. Could he really be a young man named Michael who had tried to kill himself when his girlfriend told him she was leaving, and hallucinated everything else?

But no, even without the background murmur he caught a flicker of fear and uncertainty in her face. She didn't know whether he remembered what had happened, he realized. Or if he did remember, what he might do about it.

"Let him eat, *cara*," said Lucia soothingly. "He will talk to you when he feels better."

"I will," said Ransom. To his surprise he felt sorry for her. What could have driven her to something like that? What was the back story he had missed by not really being the boy Michael?

He was starting to think about these people as if they were real, he realized with a vague anxiety. Absently, he turned over a page of the newspaper.

The story drew his eye as if it had been pointed out to him, probably because of a small picture of his house, taken from Anglia Street, with the caption: "Headquarters of Ransom International, where six died Thursday."

The small headline over the story said: "Execution-Style Killings Puzzle Authorities."

He was holding the newspaper in both hands now, and had stopped chewing mid-mouthful.

Six employees of Ransom International Ltd., a private endo-voyant sensing investigations firm, were killed in the early hours of Thursday morning in Bethesda, Maryland. Police have not yet determined a motive for the slayings, which appear to have been carried out execution style. Robbery has not been ruled out.

Security teams rushed to 11052 Ridgeview Drive at 2:17 A.M. Thursday morning after the building's monitoring system abruptly went offline, to find a horrific scene of mayhem. John O. McMillan, CEO of Ransom International's subscription police service, says that the victims, two women and four men, including the company's president and CEO, Heathcliff Ransom, were killed by high-velocity projectiles from at least three separate . . .

Ransom felt his gorge rise, and with a choking, retching sound he spat the food in his mouth onto the breakfast tray. He stood up.

"Michael?" Lucia said faintly. All three of them were staring at him in alarm.

"I'm going . . . upstairs," he said hollowly. Sick and dizzy, he climbed the stairs, clutching the newspaper. He closed the door to the room, lay down on the futon, and read the story through twice, closing his eyes when the nausea and dizziness got too strong.

The dead included Anna Heatherstone, Robert Mandelson, the night cleaning man, the two View tank technicians Arjun Govind and Haley Rattner, and Heathcliff J. Ransom, who had just been emerging from the sensory deprivation/neural induction tank used by endovoyant sensing researchers.

Stunned, Ransom told himself that it was part of the sensorium's metaphorical presentation of information, but his certainty that he was still in the astral world had abruptly evaporated. Death had come for him while he had been following Margaret Biel, and probably the hole in the orchard had been It—but how could that be? He had never heard of an endovid dying in the tank, but if one did, why wouldn't he go wherever other dead people went?

But maybe he was a special case, because in the process he had come across a body he could enter. Maybe his disembodied consciousness had persisted for a little while in the astral after his body had died, and instead of drifting away to the afterlife or oblivion, it had been drawn by Margaret Biel's spoor to a place where a boy was being murdered, leaving his body available for immediate occupation.

If that was true, maybe he *was* back in the physical world. In someone else's body.

9

Ransom had lain there a long time, eyes closed and brain churning, when he heard the bedroom door open, very quietly. Through slitted lids he saw the girl, Barbara, slip in and close the door. He let his eyes close all the way, pretending to be asleep. He sensed rather than heard her approach the futon. The room was silent: a dead silence, without any field leakage alerting him to her intentions. He ventured again to let his lids open the slightest bit.

She was kneeling next to the futon, holding a hypodermic at his neck.

He seized her wrist with a cobra movement he could never have made in his old body, and yanked her arm backward until she dropped the hypodermic. He could feel the delicate bones in her wrist close to breaking, and her face twisted in agony, but immediately her small, sharp teeth were buried in his hand and she hit his face with her free fist.

The pain concentrated all of Ransom's fear and shock into an overwhelming rage. He hit her. She seemed to lose consciousness for a second, and her teeth came off his hand trailing bloody saliva; but the pain of her twisting arm as she sagged to the floor revived her with a small cry, and she clumsily tried to bite him again. He grabbed her by the throat.

"I'll scream," she rasped through bleeding lips, half-conscious. "I'll scream and Tomas and Lucia—"

"Go ahead and scream," Ransom snarled, up on his knees now. He was aching to hit her again, but he was afraid he would kill her. "I'll tell them what you were doing. No one else's fingerprints are on the hypo this time."

"You're hurting me!" she whimpered. He stood up from the futon and pulled her up with him by her wrists, pushed her against the wall. Blood oozed from her nose and mouth and one of her ears, and her eyes were unfocused. If the house monitors hadn't given an alarm yet, they were probably turned off, he thought, or set to some ridiculously high Italian threshold. He put one arm behind her and leaned against her lithe, delicate body, holding her in a ferocious embrace. He said in her ear: "I saw what you did to Michael. I saw you give him the shot. He died, but I was there and I got in. But I don't know why you killed him. Why did you kill him, Barbara?"

"I don't know— I don't know what you're talking about," she sobbed quietly, pain and fear making her abruptly meek. Her body was hot and sweating with exertion and shock.

"What do you have to do with Margaret Biel?"

He felt her body jerk, saw her eyes dilate with panic. "I don't know . . . what you're talking about."

He took a handful of her hair and twisted her head back until her terrified eyes could barely look into his. "I swear to you," he whispered like a lover making vows, "that I will kill you. I've lost everything, and I know you know why. If you don't tell me, so help me God I'll kill you. Do you understand?"

She only made one more feeble attempt to lie. "I don't know what you're—" But when she felt his muscles start to harden she gave a strangled cry. "Are you from the Company?" she blurted.

"What company?"

He pulled away from her a few inches to stare into her face. She yanked her wrists from his loosened grasp, leaned against the wall gasping. Then she looked straight at him, collecting herself. "Walk away," she said, rubbing her wrists, her voice and lips trembling so much she could barely speak. "Whoever you are . . . this is too big for you. You can't imagine . . . what will happen."

"What company?"

She just stared into his eyes, breathing hard.

In uncontrollable rage, he hit her again, banging her head against the wall. For a second he thought he had killed her, but as he held her against the wall she mumbled half-consciously: "I am Margaret Biel." Then, as if the enormity of what she had said had just penetrated her conscious mind, she opened her dilated eyes wide and stared into his. "Oh, God," she moaned. "Oh, God."

"What do you mean? Is this some insane part of the astral plane?"

She was trembling violently, fresh blood coming from her nose and mouth. "Who are you? How did you find out?"

"My name is Heathcliff Ransom." He picked up the newspaper from the futon and held the Ransom International story in front of her face. "See? This is my company, my house, my employees, my *friends*. I was hired by some people called Merrivale to follow their comatose aunt, Margaret Fenton Biel, in the astral plane. I found a hole in her terminal dream, and I came through it and ended up here. When you murdered the boy, I got into his body. What do you mean you're Margaret Biel?"

She seemed to have trouble focusing her eyes, but she took hold of the newspaper to steady it and read for a few seconds, and then sick horror came into her face.

"Oh, no," she moaned. "Oh, no. Oh, God, no. Something went wrong. They're coming." A sudden terror made her struggle against him with desperate, wiry strength, like a terrified cat. "I have to get away," she whimpered. "Let me go! I have to get out of here before they— If they catch me— Oh, God! Something went wrong. They'll think it was me! *Let me go!*" she shrieked with sudden insane violence.

He shook her violently, banging her against the wall, until she stopped fighting. "I'll let you go," he said, "as soon as you tell me what I want to know."

"I can't," she moaned. Even without his endovoyance he could feel her terror. "I can't. I can't."

There were footsteps and Lucia opened the door. "Michael? Barbara? What is happening? What is this scream?"

"It's all right, Lucia," said Barbara in a level voice, suddenly under control. "We're just having an argument. I'm sorry I screamed."

Ransom's body hid Barbara, so Lucia couldn't see the blood. When he looked over his shoulder at her, her face softened. "Ah, a lover's fight. Then don't worry, you still care for each other. Be gentle, darlings," she said, and closed the door quietly.

"Now," Ransom said. "Tell me. What do you mean you're Margaret Biel? What is the 'Company?' Why would they kill everyone in my house?"

"There's no time! There's no time!"

"Then I'll tie you up and leave you here for whoever is looking for you."

Terror flared in her face, but she fought it down. "All right. I'll tell you. But let me wipe my face— the blood off my face, please."

"If you lie to me I'll tie you up and leave you here. What is 'the Company'?"

She started to cry, miserable and shaking, her face flushed and swelling from his blows. "For a hundred million euro, the Company will put you into a young body when you're old."

He stared at her. "How?"

"*How?* I don't know *how*. There's no time—"

"I have all the time in the world. I'm not going to let you go until you tell me."

"It's—it's like a secret society. Inside their church. At first it was just a church, worshipping youth. I wanted so much to be young again. You win their trust by a series of tests—it costs a lot of money. When they finally told me, I didn't believe them. But then it was too late; they would have killed me if I didn't go through with it. They showed me pictures of people they had suspected of betraying them, what they had done to them—" Here she began to gasp, her eyes rolling up in her head as if she would faint. Ransom shook her until she became aware of him again. "I was an old woman. I hated being old," she whispered. "They showed me pictures of this girl. She was so beautiful. I had to. I *had* to." She leaned forward and clutched herself as if in pain. He let go of her arms, let her support herself against the wall.

"How did they do it?"

"A kind of . . . man woke me up at night. He was huge, and his skin was scaly, like a lizard. He gave me a shot and I couldn't breathe . . . and then he pulled me up out of my body. He said I should walk through the memories my mind would show me, and that I would come to a hole, and that no matter how afraid I was, I must go into it. He said it was a tunnel out of death they had built for me.

"The other end opened here. The lizard man was waiting. He brought me here to this room.

"He tranquilized you and killed the girl; I could see her drift out of her body and out into the moonlight. Then the man pushed me into her body, and he must have given her an antidote, because I woke up in the morning and I was in this new, beautiful body, lying next to you."

"And why did you kill the boy?"

She closed her eyes. Her lips were trembling so she could hardly talk. "Michael, I'm sorry. I'm so sorry."

He shook her roughly. "Why?"

"I wanted to celebrate. I got drunk. I didn't realize this sweet little body couldn't hold its liquor. I told you everything. You didn't believe me, but once I got sober I realized that I couldn't risk you ever saying a word to anybody. The things they do if you betray them—"

She looked up at him. Her eyes were beautiful, sick, beyond hope. "Now let me go. I have to get away. If you're smart you'll run, too. They might guess you know something, or they might nerve-rack you just for fun. Let me *go*."

"Not yet. I want to know—"

The split second before she smashed it into his temple Ransom realized that while she had been talking she had taken a spark-blade from her pocket.

He couldn't have been unconscious long, because when he opened his eyes the morning light had hardly changed, and the fresh breeze still played on his face. There was an intense, throbbing pain in his head, and his temple felt swollen and burned. He was lying half on the futon. He slid down to the floor, leaned against the wall, his vision going black and his gorge rising. He guessed that the girl thought she had killed him, but had been too panicked to make sure.

The hypodermic she had dropped was still lying on the floor. Probably her plan had been to pretend she had come up and found him successful at his second suicide attempt. She would cry and tell Lucia how guilty she felt, and they would recall how strangely he had acted at breakfast—

What should he do now? Whether or not there was any truth to her story, the girl's fear of the "Company" had been unnerving. Ransom stood up slowly, leaning on the wall, head pounding and stomach contracting, then tottered into the bathroom and switched on the mirror. He felt a lot worse than he looked, he realized. He washed his temple and sprayed on a bandage, swallowed a stomach pill, and took three hits from the analgesic inhaler. After a few minutes he felt good enough to search the bedroom. In a drawer under a folded anonymizing cloak was a credit passport issued by USAdmin/CitiBank to a Michael Harwood Beach, a hologram etched into the thin metallic resin causing a dim likeness of the handsome boy to flicker above the card as it caught the light. There was also a stylish, brushed-titanium phone plug-in the size of a cufflink.

He fumbled behind his ear and felt a jack, plugged the phone clumsily into it, and got a video skin that seemed to hang in the air in front of him. He flicked through nested menus with a retinal cursor, found a travel agent in the Contacts, and clicked it.

An AI face appeared. "Hello, Mr. Beach, and thank you for calling Ultimate Supreme Travel. Are you ready to reserve seats on your prepaid return Pisa to Boston?"

"Yes," Ransom said. "On the next available flight. But I'd like to change the destination city to Washington D.C."

10

The flight from Pisa to Washington was four hours, but the airline's complimentary sleep feed made it seem like twenty minutes, so the fact that it was still around midnight when they landed at Dulles seemed perfectly natural. Waiting for the monorail to the terminal, people who had grown used to marketing-sparse Italy were putting on their privacy cloaks to ward off the infopush holograms already slipping among them and calling them by name. Ransom put on the cloak he had found in Michael Beach's drawer, but not before a lissome, translucent female had sprung toward him, addressing him by Michael's name and murmuring psychoactive commercial messages into his ears. He pulled the cloak's hood up hastily and turned it on, and the murmur faded before he could buy anything. The hologram remained next to him, holding some product in her beautiful hands, but he could no longer hear her voice, and after he had ignored her for a minute she evaporated. Observers—electronic as well as biological—would now see only a figure in gray designer robes among others similarly dressed, their faces and other distinguishing characteristics softened into indistinctness. Commercial and government meme implantation, targeted advertising, and surveillance technology made urban public space in North America annoying and occasionally dangerous for identifiable persons, especially those known to have disposable income. In addition to hiding your face and clothes, good anonymizing outerwear like Michael Beach's ran neural signature blocking, voice modification, and even pheromone camo and gait randomization to foil the ubiquitous kiosks, billboards, drones, airborne nanosensors, and satellites.

They had moved the old Union Station terminal from downtown Washington to Dulles many years before, its Classical statues, marble floors, and arched, gilded ceilings irreproducible at today's prices. The ornate, softly echoing space was crowded with people hurrying in every direction, two-thirds of them cloaked, veiled, or surrounded by holographic noise like human-shaped fog, the commercial projections swimming among them like fish, greeting the financially viable uncloaked and those with cheap electronics by name in many languages.

To complete his disappearance, Ransom went into an electronics store and traded in Michael Beach's titanium phone for an unlisted, untraceable model, laundering his credit passport through a privacy server in Finland. He had had to go through passport control in the raw, of course, and his airline ticket had been issued to Michael Beach, but he didn't want to make himself too ridiculously easy to find, just in case Barbara Santangelo's "Company"—if it existed—decided to expend some of its sinister attention on her ex-boyfriend. He wasn't worried about Michael Beach's family looking for him: long correspondence threads on his phone revealed that they were estranged, and that Michael had told them he was going to be out of touch indefinitely.

In the same spirit of evasion he rode the subway for several hours, getting on and off trains at random, finally renting a sleep berth at the crowded Metro Center McDonald's. He lay in the narrow capsule, pine forest–scented air whispering from the vents laced with just enough tricyclic aerosols to suppress claustrophobia. The bulkhead a short arm's length above him had a snack vendor, controls for the lights and air, and a TV. He voiced up a search for news segments on the "Bethesda Mansion Massacre," as the tabloids were calling it, and came up with almost a hundred. He picked one of the major news sites and watched low-quality 3-D video of his front gate crossed with yellow police tape, the hammering of his heart and twisting of his guts dulled by the tricyclics.

"The efficiency of the killings, and the sophisticated weapons used have convinced the Pinkerton Police Agency, which is now handling the investigation, that organized crime is involved," said the voiceover. "However, PPA still has few leads. Authorities say that the killers used tunable microwaves to destroy DNA evidence, and an electromagnetic pulse bomb left at the scene wiped out digital— two USAdministration mirror satellites collided in low Earth orbit at about 6:30 GMT today. The satellites, which reflect sunlight to keep USAdmin tourist sites illuminated during terrestrial nighttime hours—" The concerned and sober voiceover had continued without evident transition, but the picture had changed from a long pan of Ransom International's grounds to video of glittering space debris tumbling in a black vacuum.

The berth's neurochemicals had calmed him enough that he re-voiced the Bethesda Mansion Massacre segment with only a few curses at McDonald's wonky electronics. A "No Results" message appeared. He backtracked to his original search queue. It was gone, replaced by a miscellaneous list of stories he hadn't searched.

He re-voiced his original Mansion Massacre search. Again "No Results" came up. He tried Bethesda Murders, Bethesda Killings, Ransom International, and a dozen other formulations.

No Results.

With a sudden chill, he switched the TV to show a wide-angle of the concourse outside his berth, his mind instinctively reaching for field leakage from anyone out there who might be monitoring him. His new body reminded him of its presence by sensing nothing. In contrast to the silence of his berth, the concourse looked as busy as ever, people crowding in both directions and someone emerging from the top berth directly across from his, climbing down the metal ladder between the rows of hatches. No one seemed to be loitering or staring with murderous intent in his direction.

Could someone have penetrated both the Finnish server's encryption and his anonymizing robe, and then disentangled his switchbacks on the subway? And, having done that, arranged to change the news feed in his specific McDonald's sleep berth? But even assuming that the mysterious Company existed, and that it cared what Barbara Santangelo might have told her ex-boyfriend, what would be the point of alerting him to their presence by tinkering with his news feed?

On the other hand, if no one had found him, then the change must have come from the news sites themselves, and that meant a high-level news blackout. Why would the murder of some employees at a small endovid investigations business interest USAdmin or the few large corporations that had the clout to do such a thing? And even assuming that it did interest them, how could they get all the news sites to wipe the story simultaneously?

It had all the earmarks of an astral episode: impossible but rendered with absolute realism, just like his supposed occupation of someone else's body. On the other hand, it had gone on much too long for an astral episode, and none of his extraction techniques had worked.

Now, lying in his berth, he tried to arrange a truce between the two warring possibilities: that he was still Viewing, and that he had actually returned to the physical world in someone else's body. He needed to sleep. With a last glance around the hallway and a double check of his hatch lock, Ransom turned off the TV and voiced up an eight-hour dose of hypnotic aerosols.

The next day was cool and bright. After eating breakfast from his berth's vendor, Ransom walked through Metro Center's crowds, took a high-speed elevator to the surface, and caught a cab.

High, gauzy clouds diffused the cheerful late-morning sunlight in Bethesda. It had rained overnight, and, as the cab turned onto Anglia Street, the cool air, the yellowing leaves, and the pavement itself seemed clean and cheerful. As they got closer to his address, Ransom's heart pounded. What if the whole thing had been an astral appearance or a hallucination? What if when the cab drove up there was no police tape, and nothing amiss? What if at the top of the long drive-way Anna Heatherstone came out to meet him? He would go inside with her, talking happily, and greet the others, go up to his rooms—

The cab was slowing.

"I'm sorry, sir or madam," the cab said, unable to penetrate the androgyny of Ransom's privacy cloak. "I cannot find the precise address you provided. Would you kindly recheck it?"

Ransom stared out the window. He had made the same mistake as the cab; he had thought they had rounded the curve where the Jessops' garden wall, ivied and over-hung with oak branches, jutted closest to the street, but here, where he had expected his own long black wrought-iron fence, was just a wide empty lot.

"45133 Anglia Street," he said to the cab.

"That address appears to be an unimproved property, sir or madam."

"No, it's not an unimproved property. Your GPS must be screwed up. Look, pull up to the next entrance and check the address and reboot or whatever."

The cab accelerated and decelerated smoothly, bringing them to the street numbers on a broad stone column that supported an open iron gate. Ransom could see the peak of a house up the hill among the trees. In fact, it looked a lot like the Fortunas' place next door to Ransom International. Two bee-sized drones hovered above the driveway, their truculent North American settings readying them to report anyone who even looked like they might be thinking about trespassing.

"45141 Anglia Street, residence of Mr. Ronald C. and Dr. May S. Fortuna," said the cab.

The machine was right, Ransom realized with a shock; it *was* the Fortunas' place. "Well, then, I must be up that way— No." That wasn't it either; the next entrance, nearly a full block farther up, was clearly visible because the street curved again: it was the featureless metal gate of the Spanish Ambassador's official residence. Just where he remembered it. Just where it ought to be.

"Go back to the previous house," Ransom said. "We passed the right address."

The cab accelerated and decelerated in reverse as quickly as it had done forward, and they found themselves in front of the Jessops' massive stone wall, which had been shipped from a medieval abbey somewhere in Europe.

Between the Fortunas' and Jessops'—where Ransom International, Ltd, had been—was now only a wide, grassy hill.

"Was this . . . There used to be a house here, a . . . They must have removed it. Do your records show that they recently demolished this?" But even as he said it he realized that only two days ago he had been reading about a murder at this very address. Yet this lot looked like it had been empty for years. It was well-maintained, in keeping with the neighborhood standards, the long grass a uniform pale green in the bright sunlight up the slope on which Ransom clearly remembered the driveway, the trees, the big house—

"I'm sorry, sir or madam, I am only able to process geographic, directional, or locational information. I am ringing for an attendant."

Another voice overrode the cab voice, this one human or a higher level of AI: "May I help you, valued customer?"

"I— I've just been brought to an address that I am sure is right but the place that was here, the building, grounds, aren't here. Can you let me know if they have recently been demolished or—"

"45133 Anglia Street, Bethesda, Maryland?"

"Yes."

"What was your question, please?"

"What was—there used to be a house here. What happened to it?"

"The county land records don't show that parcel as having been developed."

"No, no," said Ransom angrily. "Look, you—"

"What address are you looking for?" asked the voice smoothly.

"45133 Anglia Street. I told you."

"No, I'm sorry, I mean, what name? The name of the party living there."

"It's a company called Ransom International, Limited. My name—the owner's name is Heathcliff J. Ransom."

"I'm sorry, valued customer, but I don't show any such names in the county land, phone, tax, or business records."

"Ransom," Ransom repeated with slow sarcasm, "R-A-N— Oh, skip it. What do I owe you for the cab?"

The cab's smooth voice immediately supervened again. "A hundred and twenty-two euro, please."

As soon as the cab had accelerated silently off, Ransom stood on the sidewalk and furiously jacked in his phone, cursing the cab company and promising himself to file a complaint with someone. He voiced through a couple of menus to get a GPS compare on his location and that of Ransom International Ltd.

"Not Found" flashed in his endogenous display.

With rising rage he tried Heathcliff J. Ransom, then browsed the Endovoyant Investigations listings for Bethesda, Maryland (of which there should be only one). Then he tried the county business records.

There was no sign of a Ransom International or Heathcliff J. Ransom in any of them.

Well, that tore it, he thought. His question was answered. Here he stood in the body of a twenty-five-year-old hunk in front of an undeveloped lot where his house should have been, and where, according to news reports that had vanished as completely as the house itself, he and half a dozen of his employees had been murdered. This had to be an astral sensorium, where such impossible things could happen without breaking a sweat. He stood gazing up at the lot in the bright, hazy sunlight, smelling the grass. Only a few birds disturbed the quietness. A security drone hung in the air a dozen meters down the sidewalk, making sure Ransom didn't intend to violate any laws or ordinances that could disturb its owners.

There was a low hum, and a vehicle pulled up behind him. He turned, and for a moment was disoriented. It was a big, shabby van in the style of a 1960s VW minibus, rounded at the front and rear like a giant gray pill. Big letters scrolled silently along its side: REAP WHAT YOU SOW. The driver's door opened with an authentic-sounding creak, and a bearded, long-haired man got out. He was wearing a long white robe—nonanonymizing—and a large crucifix on a beaded chain. He was large, broad-shouldered, and handsome, clearly a product of prenatal enhancements.

"Brother or sister," he said, "I can see that you're searching for something."

"Yes. I'm looking for—"

"Amen! We all are, brother or sister."

"Do you—"

"I'm Jeremiah. Have you ever wondered about God?" He came over and looked into the darkness of Ransom's hood, his eyes blazing with emotion. "Have you ever wondered: 'What if God is a super-intelligent alien?' If God is a super-intelligent alien, He might not understand human nature very well; it might not occur to Him that you and I want eternal life. Maybe aliens like God don't want eternal life, or maybe it's so natural to them it slips their mind that not everyone might already have it. Don't you think it would be prudent to pray to Him, to make sure He knows you want eternal life? Amen! What can it cost you? What harm can it do? Let's pray, you and me, right now, just to be safe." He lowered his head. "Oh, God, whoever You are—"

"Do you remember the house that used to be here?" Ransom broke in.

The man opened his eyes and raised his head. "You know, brother or sister," he said huskily, "there's no telling when you or I or anyone might die."

"Right here," Ransom said. "There used to be a wrought-iron fence along the road. There was a gate over there and a driveway went up the hill."

The bearded man looked to where Ransom was pointing, and then he seemed to do a double-take. He swept his eyes back and forth, squinting as if puzzled.

"Is this Anglia Street?"

"I think so. I mean, yes, yes, this is Anglia Street. Yeah!" said Jeremiah. "Yeah, I remember! Sometimes I used to park at the bottom of the driveway here in the shade. There were trees by the gate. What happened to it? It was here a couple of days ago."

Ransom's heart was pounding again. "Do remember the name of the place?"

Jeremiah pondered. "Something like— Something International, wasn't it? Ransom International, that's it. Hey, that's where those murders happened, isn't it?"

Ransom could hardly breathe. He stood looking up at the gentle hill and the deep grass. "I used to live here."

"What?"

"I— I used to live here. Ransom International. And now everyone says they never heard of it, and it's not in any of the records."

Anxiety showed in Jeremiah's face. "You're kidding me, right? Are you one of those psychovandals? There's no need to crash my brain, bro or dude; I'm just a traveling preacher. I don't even wear privacy robes, because I got no money or influence. Except with God."

"No, I'm not a psychovandal. I was looking for this house, and it's gone. But you remember it, right? The county records—"

Ransom had turned away for a second to look up the hill again. As he turned back, he caught Jeremiah and his minibus in the act of vanishing. Or thought he did. He seemed to see a last glimpse of gray and the glint of the sun reflecting from the windshield, and then it and Jeremiah were gone, erased, as if a light shunt had been drawn over them. Ransom stepped cautiously over to where the big bearded man had been standing a few seconds before, his hands waving to feel the empty air. He stepped into the road where the minibus had been, waved his hands again. There was nothing.

His legs were trembling. A light shunt couldn't make something actually disappear so you could walk through it. Only an astral sensorium could do that. But a kind of astral sensorium he had never seen or heard of before, from which you couldn't extract, and which acted exactly like the real world except for the miracles.

The lone security drone had been joined by another hovering in the air next to it, and a third hovering ten meters down the sidewalk in the other direction, as if curious to see the drama that had unfolded with the vanishing preacher.

11

While it was slightly unusual to be wearing anonymizing gear in a neighborhood zoned to exclude infopush, hanging around all day staring at an empty lot was sure to get him noticed. With a jangle of fear, Ransom realized too that if the mysterious Company *was* looking for him, they might know enough to keep surveillance on this address. He strode away quickly, instinctively keeping close to the damp-smelling stones of the Jessops' wall, as if that could conceal him. He called another cab, and met it a few blocks away. He gave it an Olney address, the home of Charles Tobin, his Special Assistant, who hadn't been listed as a victim of the now nonexistent Ransom International murders.

Ransom's cab grabbed a maglev rail at the River Road entrance to MD 495 and shot through the highway tunnels that kept the suburbs above quiet and bucolic, passing the traffic on the tire lanes as if it were standing still. It seemed like only a few minutes before the cab switched back to tires and emerged serenely at what now felt like a walking pace onto Laytonsville Pike, where the wooded neighborhoods of the middle class spread out toward Pennsylvania.

Because Charles's job—unlike many in the modern economy—required his actual physical presence at a geographic location, he had bought a renovated farmhouse not too far from the highway. Ransom had never been there before, but his heart was pounding as the cab's GPS showed the address approaching. He reminded himself that this had to be an etheric sensorium, an astral world as evanescent as a movie, but another part of him whispered back that an astral world that never went away might as well be the real world.

"I'm very sorry, sir or madam," said the cab, but it was a higher-level AI or human voice coming through its speakers now. "We are receiving a distressing message from the house system at your destination address. It refers to news stories published in the last few days regarding the resident, Mr. Charles H. Tobin. If you are a personal acquaintance of Mr. Tobin, a complimentary grief counseling session with subsequent referral is available at this time."

Ransom could scarcely breathe. His voice when he spoke was a dry croak. "What news stories?"

But he was already fumbling his phone into its jack and doing a search.

"Suicide Ruled Suspicious," was the first headline. "Police contractors suspect a psychovandalism intrusion in the apparent suicide of Charles H. Tobin of Olney, Maryland, who was found dead in his home shortly after security systems reported a cessation of his bodily functions. A review of cached transmissions showed Mr. Tobin using a serrated kitchen knife to cut his carotid arteries shortly after sensing a web presentation, though no traces were—"

With a sick feeling, Ransom entered the public address of Tony Lewin, the last person associated with RI who might still be alive. "Sorry I can't take your call," said Lewin's distinguished-looking torso, evidently psychoformed to remove the impression that he was a rat terrier. "But please leave your—"

"Sir or madam?" said the cab's AI/human voice gently. "Should we initiate your complimentary counseling session?"

Ransom shakily flicked through the retinal menus for

news stories on John and Ardice Merrivale of Boston, Massachusetts. The feed came up immediately: "Boston Society Couple Killed in Fiery Automobile Crash."

He unplugged.

"How are you feeling right now, at this very moment, John or Jane Doe?" asked the cab in yet a third voice, this one soothing and concerned. "Close your eyes and take a few deep breaths, remaining conscious of the feelings in your body. May I ask your name? Was Charles H. Tobin personally known to you?"

It suddenly occurred to Ransom that if someone was hacking the cab company's transmissions—someone who was mopping up anyone who might have some inkling of what had happened to Margaret Biel—they would know that a customer was sitting in front of Charles Tobin's house receiving "complimentary grief counseling."

"Take me to the nearest public transportation hub."

The cab started to move at once. "I am very, very sorry for your loss," said the soothing voice. "We would like your permission to take you to the nearest—"

"No," said Ransom. "The nearest public transportation hub."

"If you insist on foregoing our no-strings-attached complimentary counseling session, would you kindly thumbprint the document being presented in your cab, to confirm that this assistance was offered and voluntarily declined?"

Some legal-looking jargon appeared on the backseat reading panel. Ransom thumbprinted it.

The cab poked along toward the highway in leisurely afternoon traffic, Ransom knotting his hands in his lap. Near the entrance tunnel the cab slowed even more to get in line with other cars. Sweat ran down Ransom's back. Being killed in an astral world was no big deal, and it might even pop him out of trance. *But what if it was real?* In the real world your flesh could be torn; bullets could rip through you; your heart could pour out its blood.

Survive now and speculate later, his instincts told him. When they were finally underground and the cab started to accelerate on the maglev, he felt a little better.

12

Michael Beach woke up a little after six, the sun's first rays through his small window making an orange patch on the wall. He rolled over and rubbed his eyes, yawned and stretched shudderingly, then sat up, orienting himself to this latest day in history. Today he had to clean the pool, trim the croquet lawn, and do a walkdown of the hedge labyrinth; also, the fruit trees at the back of the grounds had to be inspected for fungus. When he stood up, his head came close to the slanting ceiling of his small apartment, which was built over a six-car garage. He took a shower, and in the small kitchen drank a quart of milk straight from the carton.

Michael worked as a gardener for a rich guy named Ralph Mullins, on one of the largest tracts in the Palm Grove Private Community in Wilmington, North Carolina: a dozen acres of lawns and flower beds, a greenhouse, a rose garden, an acre of head-high hedges that shifted into a different maze configuration every night, a miniature golf course, a miniature fruit orchard, and a fifty-meter swimming pool with a series of palm-shaded flagstone terraces above it rising to the main house—all surrounded by a high, authentic Etruscan wall and swaddled in invisible, high-tech security. Michael liked the job. It was like being the god of a very small universe, whose maintenance more or less near perfection you were able to oversee, disturbed by the free will of only two human inhabitants.

Only one human inhabitant, actually.

He pulled on a T-shirt and jeans, and went down the

wooden outdoor stairs, which thrummed under his feet. The air was cool and smelled like dew, but the slanting sunlight was already warm. There was a large shed next to the garage. He stood in front of it and said: "Charlie, Derek."

The shed's rolldown door rose, and the two robots jerked into motion, trundling out onto the driveway and stopping in front of him. They looked like small versions of the rovers sent to the inner planets.

"Good morning, gentlemen," Michael said cheerfully. "Time to make the place idyllic for the lovely Vivien. Please go to the pool."

Catching a command they understood, the robots moved promptly toward the pool, not turning, but simply re-orienting their wheels.

Michael followed them along the flagstones that ran between palms and hedges, opened the pool shed, and helped them on with their telescoping attachments.

"Clean the pool, gentlemen," he said, standing aside.

They trundled forward imperturbably, Charlie extending his vacuum down into the water and his skimmer onto the surface, holding his scrubber at the ready, Derek heading around to the other side of the pool. Soon they were moving slowly along in parallel, their arms extending and retracting. Satisfied, Michael picked up a couple of leaves from the flagstones and rearranged Vivien's recliner and umbrella to catch the early sun. Then he headed back to the utility shed to get a couple of the other robots started.

Soon his small domestic kingdom was humming quietly, Alexander the Great and Bill trimming the hedges, the nameless, dumb mower making its hissing rushes from one end of the croquet lawn to the other as if on a combat raid, the garden spiders picking their way carefully through the carnations and tomato plants, lasering weeds and harmful insects. Alexander the Great got his trimmer stuck in one of the bushes, and Michael had to retrieve Cat—Vivien's gray cat—from the carnations, where he liked to bat the spiders down with his paws, but these minor crises being surmounted, he took a break at mid-morning, sitting against one of Ralph's fast-growing hybrid oaks, out of the already hot sun.

Breaktime was thinking time for Michael. He guessed he had thought more in the last three months than in the whole rest of his life, and he had found that it was harder than he could have imagined. In those three months the sum total of his conclusions weren't much more than a statement of the problem he had started out with.

As far as he could figure, either (1) psychovandals had slipped him a delusional thought implant, (2) he had come down with a bad case of Virtual Reality Confusion, or (3) he really had been a man named Heathcliff Ransom, and the things he thought he remembered had actually happened.

For the first couple of months after he had arrived in Wilmington, fleeing, as he thought, from some awful danger, his mind had been broken, unable to do anything but run obsessively over and over all the things he thought he remembered, trying to disentangle the real from the unreal, like a mental fever trying to drive out a virus. He had lived on the streets and slept under overpasses, walking compulsively through town all day in his filthy anonymizing cloak, which had long since run out of power. Finally the mental-health police had picked him up, fitted him with a drug implant, fed and bunked him for a week, and then referred him to a jobs program. Ralph Mullins had been looking for a gardener, and they had hit it off as soon as Michael showed up for the interview. This was one point in favor of the real-Heathcliff-Ransom theory, because what felt like his middle-aged man's instincts and reactions had made the interview go like a dream.

The main point against the real-Heathcliff-Ransom theory was that it made absolutely no sense.

The main point in favor of the VRC theory was that it was a well-established disorder known to afflict a few percent of VR gamers, making them believe that some hyper-realistic virtual world they had inhabited via a helmet or plugin was real. The main point against it was that there seemed to be no game on the market resembling his memories. Also, his return to reality hadn't led to the gradual dissipation of the fake memories, or at least he didn't think it had. He wasn't sure what dissipation of fake memories felt like, as compared to things just receding in time so that you didn't remember them as clearly. The other point was that VR games had follow-up AI that was supposed to contact you for a couple of months after gameplay to make sure you hadn't gone nuts, and no AI had contacted Michael. Though maybe that was because he had dropped out of sight so completely, renting berths in a different Washington, D.C., flophouse every night, laundering his credit passport through the most secure of anonymous servers, always wearing his cloak in public, and then taking the subway out here to North Carolina, a place his summer holiday memories associated vaguely with comfort and happiness.

The main point against the psychovandals theory was: what would be the point of infecting Michael Beach, a penniless kid in his twenties, with a memory complex it would probably cost a fortune to build?

Sitting against the oak's rough trunk, his sweat drying, the smell of cut grass floating on the warming air, he told himself for the thousandth time that he had to stop obsessing over these questions. Whatever had happened, nothing was left of it now. History that left no traces was null and void. Whatever the past had been, nowadays his life made sense: he worked in the mornings and in the afternoons went to the beach and watched the girls or the blue or green ocean, watched the clouds looming sometimes heavy with storm, at other times white and innocent as flags, as if promising that time was an illusion and that summer and fair weather would last forever. Every day his body was full of the vague excitement of youth, as if some wonderful thing were about to happen; the thought never far away that life was just beginning, that there was no limit to the things the future might bring, starting with adventures perhaps this very day, and building to great revelations and illuminations in the times to come.

The sound of a deck chair scraping on flagstones came from the direction of the pool, and Michael's heart gave a jump. There was something else in his life now that eclipsed the past, and it was blond and five-six. And not human.

A minute later, emerging onto the pool's flagstone apron, he saw her cutting through the water like a fish, then surfacing. She waved to him, blinking water from her eyes. "Hi, Michael."

He waved back, and she began her laps, alternating crawl, breaststroke, and backstroke. He guessed that her cold fusion–powered biopolymers didn't need exercise, but she was built to act as much as possible like a real girl.

Ralph Mullins spent sixteen hours a day neurolinked to the big emulator that ran his supply-chain business; he had bought Vivien because he knew a real wife or girlfriend would never put up with him. But like her flesh-and-blood sisters, Vivien needed company; in fact, her warranty required that she be conversed with at least ten hours a week to keep her from lapsing into the android version of autism. So keeping her company was one of Michael's jobs. "I kind of feel sorry for her," Ralph had told him. "She doesn't have any family or friends, you know? They say she's programmed not to care, but—" Whenever Ralph was around, Vivien's remote human sensop came on and operated her, so maybe it wasn't surprising that he thought of her as real enough to have feelings.

Michael guessed that Vivien must have strained even Ralph's extraordinary bank account. He had seen TV specials on advanced humanoid systems, but until he met Vivien such things had seemed as distant as the moon. Knowing her, it was possible to think that maybe a construct of bio-polymers and quantum-well neural nets *could* feel lonely. Actually, it was sometimes hard for Michael not to think of her as a goddess instead of a machine: built on the chassis of a bodyguard android but designed by artists, she was exquisitely, almost unnaturally beautiful.

Michael got a pair of clippers from the pool shed to put the finishing touches on the trimming that Charles had given the bougainvillea, and was still at it when Vivien got out of the water. The sight of her slender, well-knit body, milky skin, exotic green eyes, and thick honey-colored hair affected him like physical violence. She wrapped herself in a towel, jerking her head sideways to get the water out of her ears, just like a real girl.

"Hi, Michael," she said again in her light, exciting voice, looking at him gravely.

"How are you, Vivien?"

"Fine."

When Ralph wasn't around Vivien ran on her endogenous AI, which wasn't particularly sparkling in conversation. But the more you talked to her, the more humanlike she was supposed to get. Maybe it was his imagination, but Michael thought that in the couple of months he had known her he had noticed a slight warming, more eye contact, more appropriate responses. So maybe their talks—which were actually mostly her listening to him drone on, with no signs of either interest or boredom—did help. He wondered if she might someday become really indistinguishable from a human even without the sensop, as her literature implied without making actionable representations.

"What should we discuss today?" Michael asked her. The morning was quiet, the only sounds the chirping of a few birds and the rapid staccato clipping of robotic shears from the middle distance.

"Whatever you want," Vivien said neutrally.

"Ralph thinks I should talk to you about God and stuff like that."

"Ralph does?" Her eyes widened with sudden interest, and Michael felt a familiar touch of jealousy. She was programmed to adore Ralph; but of course Ralph had paid for her, and it wouldn't make sense to lay out the titanic sum she must have cost and then have her decide she liked someone else better. But she was a machine, he reminded himself for the thousandth time, not a real person—not an appropriate object of jealousy.

"Yeah, he thinks it's important for people to know about religion. If you visit our planet, you need to know about God."

She was silent for a few seconds. "What do you mean 'if you visit our planet'?"

"Sorry, I was making a joke."

"Oh."

"So do you know anything about God?"

"God hates androids."

He turned around and looked at her. She rarely said anything at all dramatic. "What? Why do you say that?"

"The people on TV say so. 'Because they are a mockery of life, the life the Creator Himself—'"

"Whoa, whoa, whoa," said Michael, a little rattled in spite of himself. "What channel have you been watching?"

"The Truth Channel."

He studied her, looking for any sign of either irony or hurt, but her face wore the same neutral gravity it always did when Ralph wasn't around. She sat down on her pool chair and began unnecessarily to rub on suntan lotion.

"Well, those people are idiots. Don't watch the Truth

Channel. If you're going to watch religious TV, watch Big Wow or PanSoul or something."

"But truth is accurate, isn't it?"

"They *call* it the Truth Channel, but that doesn't *make* it the truth channel."

She looked thoughtful, as if he had said something deep.

"They're mistaken," Michael explained patiently. "They think their channel is the Truth Channel, but they're mistaken."

"Does Ralph think they're mistaken?"

"Yes, Ralph thinks they're mistaken." He made a mental note to tell Ralph what he should say about the Truth Channel. "They have some old stories collected into a book, and they think it tells them everything they need to know about life and the universe, but it doesn't."

"What book *does* tell everything they need to know about life and the universe?" Finished with the suntan lotion, she stretched out in her bikini, one hand behind her head and the other on her forehead shading her eyes so she could look at him, and she was heartbreakingly beautiful.

"There isn't any book like that. There are lots of books, and they all say different things." Months of obsessing had filled Michael's brain with this stuff, and he was on a hair trigger to talk about it, even to an AI doll. "I mean, some books say the whole universe is alive, and self-organizes into conscious entities. Some books say that consciousness/intelligence came out of the Big Bang along with mass/energy and spacetime. Others say religion is like blindsight, and modern people are like idiot savants who have overdeveloped parts of their brains and starved other parts, and now we can barely see spirits and things at all. There are so many religions, there's no reason for you to watch the moldy old Truth Channel and listen to them rave about their Late Stone Age stories. Okay?"

"Okay."

"And stay away from the Triumph of Science Channel. They're crazy, too. To them everything is dead. The universe is like a giant refrigerator full of bad endings, a big, freezing cold automation, and when we die, we all just turn off like a bunch of farm machines or something."

"I *am* a machine."

"So am I. So are all of us. But that just means machines are alive, not that we're dead. You see? We know we're alive, so we need to think about what that says about machines, instead of the other way around. You see?"

She seemed to think about that. "But how can you tell if you're alive?"

Michael went over and pinched her lotion-moist arm. If he hadn't known what she was, the feel of her flesh would never have told him.

"Ow." She looked up at him in surprise.

"Did you feel that?"

"Yes."

"Then you're conscious. And if you're conscious, you're alive."

"But how do you know? I might just be acting like I'm alive because that's how I'm programmed."

He stared at her, surprised at the second interesting thing she had said this morning. It struck him suddenly that, like himself, she had strong personal reasons to be interested in this subject. If an android could have personal reasons. "If you're conscious, you know it, and you don't have to guess. If you're not conscious, it doesn't matter, because whatever happens, you won't care. If you feel like you care, then you're conscious, even if someone on TV says you're not. See?"

"Yes," Vivien said humbly.

Just then there was a shuffling step, and Ralph Mullins came along the flagstone walk from the house, squinting a little in the sunlight. He was a small, sandy-haired man who would have been handsome if he hadn't looked exhausted all the time. Living away from the sun and only moving his brain had given his skin a translucent paleness and put dark circles under his eyes, and his cheerful Hawaiian shirt, Bermuda shorts, and flip-flops only made him look like an invalid on a rest cure.

"Hey, guys," he rasped, then cleared his throat, rolling his eyes as if embarrassed at not being used to using his voice. "Nice weather."

"Hey, Ralph," said Michael. "You like this weather? Pretty hot to me."

"Is it?" said Ralph vaguely. "I can't really feel it. I'm way wrung out, dude. How are things out in the real, physical world?" Ralph swore that his job was killing him, but he was always in the middle of something too profitable to quit just yet.

Vivien sat up, her face suddenly full of expression. "Ralph!" Her voice too was different: vivacious, exciting, animated. "If I'd known you were coming up, I would have waited for you."

Michael went to get another pool chair, and when he came back Ralph was looking raptly down at Vivien—or the person she had changed into. Alerted by her AI to Ralph's appearance, her sensop had come online from some VR cubicle in an Omega Talking Machines Company operations center halfway across the continent. Front-end AI handled her "involuntary" functions so that the sensop could concentrate on being charming and sexy. It was now impossible to tell that Vivien wasn't an amazingly beautiful real girl in her early twenties, full of flirtatious sophistication.

"Hi, beautiful," Ralph said.

"Hi," she said softly, flushing slightly.

Michael's jealousy, manageable when he and Vivien were

alone, stabbed him now like a knife. He reminded himself that Ralph was a good guy despite all his money, and that he himself didn't have to work here if he couldn't stand it. But he knew there was no way he could find a better job, and besides, Ralph would be distressed if he left. Ralph had few contacts with what he called "the real, physical world," and cherished those he did have. The idea that he might come out of his business trance one day and find no one special to him, no one who knew his name but robots and servants, kept him in a constant state of anxiety.

And anyway, he told himself, Vivien wasn't real: she was just a hi-tech doll, a very elaborate appliance. How could you be jealous of someone using an appliance he had bought? It didn't make sense.

Vivien stood up languidly, and her breathing seemed to have quickened. Ralph glanced at her bikini top, under which her small nipples were now visible, and then at her face, and he suddenly looked healthier, as if his blood had started circulating.

"Ralph," she said a little breathlessly. "Could I see you up at the house for a minute?" She was programmed to need frequent sex, and, Ralph had confided to Michael, her AI took over from the sensop in the sack. "It makes her kind of wild," he had said. "No inhibitions."

"I'll be back, Michael," Vivien said, taking Ralph's arm. "So don't put the pool away, okay?"

"The place looks really nice," said Ralph as Vivien started to lead him up toward the house. "You're doing a good job, dude." He looked at Michael seriously, as if he knew how it must feel to have Vivien go off to have sex with someone else.

The knot in Michael's chest made it hard for him to breathe.

13

Summer went on, slow and quiet. The ocean clouds towered over the town, and the ocean atmosphere filled it, and sometimes on the quiet, sun-washed afternoons it seemed that summer might last forever. When that feeling came, Michael's anomalous memories seemed more plausible, the idea that he might be living in an eternal etheric summer making him wonder again whether this was really the real world.

That feeling and those memories created a distance between him and other people, especially people his age. The youths he met seemed numb to time, to the sensation of either mortality or immortality. It was only to him that time seemed to show itself, so that he often appeared preoccupied and aloof, replying in monosyllables whenever anyone, even a hot girl, talked to him at the beach or on the street.

At the same time, he couldn't go more than a few minutes of any day without thinking about Vivien. It made no sense, but to him she embodied the endless summer and the ocean weather, as if her emptiness were a vessel the world filled, like a Buddhist sage. Her gravity seemed the stillness of the hot afternoons, her body the ocean atmosphere made visible: quiescent but exciting, beautiful but stately. Even her abrupt transformations into a vivacious girlfriend when Ralph appeared reminded him of how quickly the August weather could change, clouds darkening and looming toward the land, rumbling with thunder and suddenly covering the beach town with silvery rain. So Ralph's request, when it came, seemed simultaneously too good to be true and inevitable, like something that had been called forth by the intensity of his desire.

One morning before Vivien had come down for her morning swim, Ralph shuffled down to where Michael was inspecting Charlie's ivy trimming on the garden wall, and said, "Mike, I have a problem."

"A rich guy like you?"

Ralph grinned ruefully. "You know the systems people that were here the other day? They were installing upgrades on my support so I can stay online twenty-four-seven. It's vampire stuff: thirty seconds of micro-sleep every few minutes and you chew mash from a tube. Muscle-tensioning electrodes, the whole shtick. But the most important deal I ever had is coming up. The bottom line is I may not get offline at all for anywhere from four to six weeks. It's no problem for me; I'm used to it, but Vivien's going to need company. I mean, more than usual. I know you go down to the beach sometimes, the boardwalk, stuff like that. Would it be okay if she tagged along with you? I mean, I don't want to embarrass you, but—"

"Vivien doesn't embarrass me." Michael's heart was racing.

"I hate to impose on you. Obviously, I'll pay you overtime."

"Ralph," said Michael, "it won't be a problem. Go do your important stuff and don't worry about it. I'll take care of her. She'll be realer than ever when you come back up."

The next morning, lying on her pool chair, Vivien said gravely, "Ralph says I have to go to the beach with you."

Michael's heart sank. "You don't *have* to. He thought you might want to. Don't you want to?"

"What if I'm not here when he comes up?"

"Did he tell you he might be kind of busy for a while?"

"Yes."

"He wants you to have something to do so you won't get bored or miss him."

"But I *do* miss him. We haven't had sex in a long time. Ralph is always too tired." She sounded plaintive, almost like a real girl.

Michael abruptly had a hard-on that could probably be seen from space. He turned and started clipping at microscopic imperfections in the bougainvillea. "Well, Ralph says he may not be up at all for a few weeks," he quavered.

"Yes." She sounded discontented. Michael glanced around. Her brow was knitted, and she looked confused and distressed. He had never seen her show this much emotion, and she had never talked about sex before.

"That's why Ralph wants you to go out with me— go to the beach with me," he corrected himself. "To give you something to do so you won't be . . . you know, unhappy."

"But what if he comes up and I'm not here?"

Michael went and squatted in front of her, took her hands. His erection had gone, replaced by an intense glow of frightened joy in his chest. He looked into her eyes. "Vivien, he's not coming up. He told me he would give us a buzz a day or two before he gets done so we can be sure to be here. Okay? I know you're sad, but Ralph says you like the beach. Come on, will you go with me?"

"Okay," she said reluctantly.

That afternoon after Michael finished his work and stowed the robots, he and Vivien walked to the beach. She wore sunglasses, a wide-brimmed straw hat, and a long beach shirt over her bikini, like a real beautiful girl trying to stave off sunburn and unwanted attention. The latter effort was unsuccessful; as soon as they reached the beach, heads turned. Michael felt both proud and a little frightened, like a man carrying a treasure through a poor neighborhood. With her long, perfect legs and erect, lithe walk, the beauty that radiated from her was powerful and disturbing.

They hiked down the sand to where there were fewer people, and Michael set up their umbrella and chairs. Vivien rubbed on suntan lotion. Then they reclined, watching the seagulls swooping over the water breaking gently on the sand, the ocean a deep blue beyond the sandbars, a haze of clouds on the horizon.

The heat and breeze and washing of waves made Michael sleepy, and he dozed. He had a dream. He was standing in Ralph's rose garden and filmy gray clouds diffused the sunlight as if a storm was coming, though the air was perfectly still. Vivien stood in the garden, her face serene and calm, and in her eyes the rose garden, the sky, the whole still world with its oceans and forests and mountains, were reflected.

He woke up, realizing clearly for the first time that he was in love with her, in love with a machine in the shape of a woman. Whether she really was a person, or whether his unbalanced mental state or youthful hormones had deceived him, or whether human love itself was a mechanical thing that could be satisfied by a veneer of soft polymer stretched over metal, was all irrelevant; the feeling itself refuted all objections. Her very blankness was a perfect mirror, her supernatural beauty giving everything she reflected the kind of mystical perfection he had felt in his dream.

Vivien, unaware that he was awake, was still looking out to sea. He felt that his next words to her would be the most important thing he ever said.

"Vivien," he said finally, "you know Ralph had you made for him, right?"

She jumped slightly, like a real startled girl, and looked at him. "Yes."

"And that's okay with you?"

"Yes. Ralph is good to me. He doesn't treat me like a

doll. He didn't have me programmed with fake memories or anything because he wants to be able to talk to me like an equal and not like a doll. Ralph's wonderful," she ended sadly.

"But are you happy?"

"Yes." She hesitated. "I'm only a little bit unhappy."

"Why?"

"I need sex. Ralph says it's how I'm built. Ralph has been too tired to have sex with me, and now he's going to be downstairs for six weeks and we won't be able to have sex for *six weeks*." Two large tears rolled down her cheeks. Michael had never seen her cry before.

"Are you allowed to have sex with anyone else?"

"Have sex with anyone else?" she said blankly, as if she had never thought about it. "Why?"

"Well, Ralph wants you to be happy."

"Ralph is wonderful," she said, but distractedly, her brows knitted with thought. Michael was trembling with exhilaration, shame, and fear. Their first day out, and he was already trying to seduce his employer's girlfriend. But she *wasn't* his girlfriend, he told himself; his girlfriend was the sensop, who used Vivien's body remotely to whore for him. The sensop always came on when Ralph was around, so Ralph had never even seen this girl, the real Vivien, the AI machine. They were two different people who happened to share the same body, like conjoined twins with different boyfriends. This one, the one at the beach with him, was in love with Ralph, but she was programmed to be in love with him. Ralph's real girlfriend, the sensop, wasn't in love with him—she did what she did for money; she might even loathe Ralph for all he knew. In fact, everything about Vivien—her love, sex, personality, beauty—had been bought with money; sleeping with her would be no worse than joy-riding in someone else's car. And if he didn't damage it and the owner never found out, what was the harm?

"Can I have some ice cream?" Vivien asked.

They packed up their stuff and walked to a fashionably shabby surfer hangout on one of the streets that dead-ended at the beach. Vivien was on her second vanilla cone when a boy wearing scruffy jeans and a T-shirt walked up to their booth. He was muscular and very handsome, one of the modern breed of gene-engineered fetuses grown into a perfect male specimen, and his muscles looked further enhanced with the power bioelectronics that had turned surfing into a rich man's sport. He ignored Michael.

"Hey," he said to Vivien. "Sorry to bother you, but would you go for a ride with me? I got a new car last week, and it needs to be sanctified, so, like, I need a goddess. We can take your friend along if you want." He gave her a nice smile, confident and charming. He turned his gaze to Michael finally, and held his hand out. "Sam," he said. Michael shook the boy's stone-hard hand; he could feel himself flushing.

Vivien was looking at Michael uncertainly. Michael shook his head slightly.

"No thank you," Vivien said shyly, inadvertently looking more beautiful than ever.

"You're full mod, aren't you?" the boy asked. Michael had worried that people would peg her for an android; he now realized that the boy instead thought she was an enhanced surfer girl whose parents were as rich as his.

Vivien gave Michael an anguished, confused look.

"We'd better be going," Michael said, sliding out of his seat. "Come on, Vivien. Catch you later, bro."

"Yeah, sure, *bro*," said the boy, and stuck out a foot so that Michael tripped and sprawled against a girl sitting at a table, and then onto the floor.

"Shit," said the girl, wringing her drink off her hands. "Spaz."

Michael stood up and faced the boy, Sam, who was grinning. Vivien stood aghast, still holding her ice-cream cone. As Michael advanced, the Heath Ransom part of him knew that Sam had intended to start a fight all along, which he surely could not lose. But the red fury in his Michael part overwhelmed all sense, and he gave Sam a hard shove. It was like shoving a cliff face: the shock of it hurt Michael's arms.

Still grinning, Sam shoved him back. Michael felt himself flip over, then his head hit something, and when he came to seconds later he was surrounded by fallen chairs and a tipped-over table and people who had jumped out of the way. He was really hurt this time, but he started to get up again. Sam sauntered over to him and yanked him up by his T-shirt, raising his free hand in a fist.

Suddenly Vivien was there, and she put her slender hand on Sam's fist.

The boy stopped smiling and let go of Michael with a jerk. Michael could see his thick hand distorted and crushed in Vivien's much smaller one.

Then Vivien hit him with her other hand, and the boy flew—actually flew—and crashed into the opposite wall like a wrecking ball.

Michael didn't see any more because Vivien pulled him to his feet and out of there, practically carrying him.

They walked home in the twilight, Michael trembling. He felt short of breath and his chest hurt.

"Vivien," he said as soon as he could, "what did you do? Where did you learn that?"

"Don't tell Ralph," she said. She looked upset and confused. "I did it— I didn't mean to. I suddenly felt— Ralph says I'm a bodyguard deep down."

Michael decided not to take Vivien back to the beach for a while. It was dangerous having something as precious as a beautiful girl in your charge. He wondered what it felt like to actually *be* the treasure, watched and yearned for and fought over. Vivien didn't seem to know either; she didn't talk about what had happened, gave no hint she even remembered it.

So now they stayed on Ralph's grounds, but hung out when Michael wasn't working: swimming, playing bowls or croquet or badminton (at all of which Vivien was unbeatable), taking walks, or just sitting and talking, to the extent Vivien could talk. Michael had a standing invitation to take his meals at the main house, so in the evenings he and Vivien would sit at one end of Ralph's big dining table in their pool clothes, surrounded by silver, crystal, and fine china, waited on by Ralph's butler, Mr. Halstead. Then they would play checkers or billiards (at which Vivien was unbeatable) or sit in the garden until bedtime.

Though Vivien never mentioned the ice-cream parlor incident, he noticed that she had begun treating him differently immediately afterward, as if her AI had switched him to a new category in her social schema. Without exactly becoming warmer she became, in her strangely neutral way, intimate. She began to stand close to him when they talked, looking steadily into his eyes. And she *touched* him, fiddled with his hair, leaned against him, even kissed him lightly on the cheek sometimes.

All casual and sisterly, but after a few days he was a wreck. At night, instead of sleeping he lay in his disheveled bachelor's bed and thought feverishly about the beautiful, strange girl who wasn't a girl at all, and with whom he, who might not really be a young man, was in love. How could he be in love with her? he tried to reason with himself, in love with a machine? It had to be a delusion, or some character defect. He should just whack off and control himself. But it was hard to keep his train of thought, because all he really wanted to think about was why she was suddenly gazing at him and holding on to him all the time. Did it mean what he hoped?

It might, he concluded. One of the most important things in a girlfriend, after all, was the "love" function, and that would undoubtedly be hacked onto the closest existing function in her bodyguard android substrate: its protective reflex. Like love, that reflex involved intense focus on a particular person for whom you were ready to sacrifice yourself. If that was how they had done it, then the love function and whatever was left of the protective function were linked in Vivien's AI, and if they were linked, an arousal cascade in the protective function nets might also excite the love function that was built on top of it. So in addition to protecting anyone she loved, she might also love anyone she protected— even inadvertently, in a fight at an ice-cream parlor, for example.

In the end, something had to give. Michael held out while an August week went by, its vast, stately weather like a rehearsal for eternity. But now he could see that Vivien was suffering, too. For the first time a hint of ill health marred her perfect face: she looked pale, and the crystal clarity of her eyes sometimes seemed slightly bleared. Ralph had given him the solemn task of taking care of her; what if he came up after his business deal was done and found her sick?

One afternoon at the end of that first week they were lying on their pool chairs, and her small hand fell casually on to his. A small straw, but, suddenly inflamed, Michael said, "Vivien, can you come up to my room for a minute?"

The wooden steps up to his apartment vibrated under their feet. His heart was beating wildly. He closed the door, and she stood there still and beautiful. He put his arms around her. He had never actually held her before; he had wondered whether the feel of her machine body would be a turn-off, but she felt completely natural. Her skin was cool and damp from the pool water, with warmth underneath, her bikini still wet, her spine lithe and slender, and she smelled good. With rising heat, he kissed her.

She responded to the kiss as if she had been expecting it, and she was so like a real girl that his last reservations left him. Her lips even trembled. She sucked softly at his lips and tongue, her mouth cool, but with a heat inside it, like her skin. He pulled her tight against him, feeling the whole beautiful, living world concentrated in her small body.

Suddenly she was pushing at him—not a superhuman shove like she had given the boy at the ice-cream shop, but the gentle push of a woman, which to a man is just as powerful. He let go of her.

She was looking into his eyes, serious and wondering. Then, without taking her eyes from him, she reached around to her back and unfastened her bikini top, then stooped and pulled off the bottom. She was smooth ivory, unimaginably beautiful. He picked her up and carried her into the tiny bedroom; she seemed no heavier than a real girl. She helped him struggle out of his clothes, and they lay pressing against each other and kissing. She was crying or malfunctioning; he saw, clear liquid coming out of her eyes and the corner of her mouth, her breath coming in soft sobs. Her hair brushed his face and neck.

"Michael," she sobbed.

"Vivien," he whispered, and rolled her onto her back.

Michael felt guilty about banging Ralph's girlfriend, of course, but not guilty enough to keep from doing it several times a day. They always did it in his rooms to avoid the monitoring systems, but what they lacked in geographic scope they made up for out of Vivien's apparently endless database of techniques. Further quieting Michael's guilt was the nearly miraculous effect it seemed to have on her health: after a couple of days she looked more radiant than he had ever seen her, suggesting that even Ralph's peak performance had been insufficient for her requirements. She talked more too, and with more animation, surprising him sometimes with the humanlike things she said. They now spent every waking hour together, she tagging along as he worked, and afterward swimming, sunbathing, trying to get through the hedge maze, shooting baskets in back by the garage (Vivien never missed a shot), playing with Cat, finding ripe fruit to eat on Ralph's trees, or just lolling in lawn chairs or pool chairs or on the grass in the shade of Ralph's oaks. Simple as she was, she seemed to understand that the sex part had to be kept quiet. Outside his rooms she was innocent as an angel, treating him like a beloved brother; inside, she was lustful, creative, and insatiable.

They were lying on his bed one evening after their third or fourth romp of the day, when he asked her, "Vivien, do you remember anything about your birth, inception, whatever?"

"No."

"Well, what do you remember?"

"I remember," she said slowly, "coming here. In a car. I was in the backseat, all dressed up. There were all these little buttons and switches on the door, and I tried them to see what they did. Ralph met me. He was smiling. He helped me out of the car and kissed me. Ralph's wonderful," she said sadly. "I miss him."

That gave him a pang, but he tried to keep the conversation focused. "Do you remember anything before being in the limousine?"

"I remember . . . talking to people. Like they would tell me: 'Vivien, go up to the seventeenth floor, to room seventeen-oh-one, and ask for Mr. Sax.' Then I would do that, and Mr. Sax would talk to me, ask me questions about myself, and let me ask questions about him. They told me they were trying to see if I could talk like a real girl. I talked to a lot of people, over and over. They had a little shopping mall in the basement of the building—"

"What building? Who are 'they?'"

"Talking Machines, silly. Where I was made. They had a little shopping mall with restaurants and movie theaters and stores and things, and I went to it to practice how to do things. Sometimes I went alone, and sometimes I would go with other girls, real girls, and sometimes a man would take me on a date."

"All for practice."

"Yes."

"What did you think about when you were doing that?"

"Nothing. I wasn't really inside myself yet. I wasn't formed until they gave me to Ralph. Ralph formed me. Ralph—"

"What about before the talking to people and going to the little mall?"

"I learned how to dress myself and put on makeup. And take a bath and a shower, and sleep."

"You had to learn how to sleep?"

"Yes. I don't really need sleep. But I can sleep if I want to."

"Hm. What else?"

"I learned how to fuck."

"Did you do that . . . with men?"

"Animals first, then people."

"*Animals?*"

"Yes. Animals really know how to fuck, especially lions and wolves. They told me they wanted me to be primal. That means to fuck without anything in you except sex." She put her lips to his ear and whispered, "Like you and me, Michael."

"But lions and wolves?"

"Is that wrong?"

"No, it's just— Didn't they hurt you?"

"I'm not easy to hurt. Are you upset, Michael?"

"No, no. And after the lions and wolves you practiced having sex with men."

"Men and women. And other androids."

"Wow."

"I'm a sex robot. That's what I'm for."

He grabbed her wrist with sudden anger and pulled her toward him so that their faces were inches apart. "Don't you ever say that," Michael said hoarsely. "That's not what you're *for*. You're not *for* anything. You're a person. You're *for* yourself."

"I'm a machine, Michael. I was built for something."

"So are we all machines. All people are. And we were all built for something, not by a big company but by evolution. But we're not like window fans or orange juicers—there's another part of us, like a soul or something. All of us machines. You too."

"Michael, you're upset. Let's talk about something else." She paused, thinking. It was harder for her to change subjects than to stick to one. "Tell me what you remember about your birth, inception, whatever," she said finally.

"What do I remember? I'll tell you. I'm just as different from everyone else as you are." He paused suddenly, slowing way down. He hadn't told anyone about his anomalous memories, for very good reasons he had worked out in detail. For one thing, people would think he was crazy; for another, on the off chance that they were real, he didn't want to do anything to blow his cover. But suddenly he was itching to tell Vivien, to show her how much they had in common, to make their shared alienation from the human world a bunker they held against everyone else, where they could keep each other company and not need anyone or anything except each other.

"If I tell you something," he said finally, "you can't tell anyone else, even Ralph. It's a secret."

"Okay."

"Do you promise?"

She nodded solemnly.

"I . . . remember being someone else."

She studied him in the deep blue light from the small window. Her finger was playing with a curl of his long, unkempt hair. "What do you mean?"

"Well, I have memories of being somebody else. Somebody I'm not now."

"Are you an AI that wasn't erased all the way? The TV says—"

"No. Or at least I don't think so." But a jolt went through him—was that the answer? Was he a recycled AI whose memory reprogramming had been botched so that he retained the memories of his previous "incarnation"? "How could I tell?" he asked anxiously. "If I were an AI?"

"Ralph would tell you."

"But then—why do I remember being someone else?"

She looked at him helplessly.

It all came spilling out. He hadn't wanted to confuse or upset her, but once he started talking he realized that the story had built up inside him like water behind a dam, which the smallest breach caused to suddenly burst. He told her about Heath Ransom and the Merrivale case, the hole in the astral orchard, slipping into his body in Italy, the disappearance of his house and the deaths of his friends and employees. As he came to the end, he realized how absurd it sounded, and simultaneously how good it felt to tell it, to release the energy that had made it seem realer than it was. "It's probably all some kind of delusion or psychological vandalism," he concluded. "I should just stop believing it. I should contact my parents. But I don't even remember them." He looked into her puzzled eyes. "Thank you for letting me tell you."

"Now can we do something else?" she asked, getting on top of him.

14

It was a few nights later, just when he had almost decided to stop worrying, that Michael had the first nightmare.

He seemed to be lying in a vast, dark cavern, walls and ceiling invisible in silent blackness. Faint shufflings and whisperings came from a long way off, and Michael knew that someone or something was searching for him. He lay rigid, holding his breath so as to make no sound. But even so, the faint noises seemed to gradually get nearer, until his terror woke him up.

Working in the ripe sunlight the next day, chatting with Vivien and lying with her in his bed that afternoon, the dream receded from his mind. But it came again two nights later, and this time the whispering and shuffling seemed closer. This time it took an hour before he could get his heart to stop pounding and go back to sleep. The next day a chill seemed to have crept into the hot sunlight, and he was tired and distracted, answering Vivien's chatter in monosyllables as he puttered around the grounds, wondering if he was suffering from some kind of unconscious guilt about their affair.

The waking world then made its own contribution to his banishment from paradise. A few days after the second nightmare, Michael and Vivien lolling in pool chairs after their second romp of the afternoon, Mr. Halstead called from the house to announce that Ralph's business deal was almost done and that he would be emerging from the basement sometime in the next few days.

Although of course he had expected this, Michael's heart sank, and it didn't help that Vivien sat up in her chair and clapped her hands like a child, flushed with delight. Innocent that she was, she seemed to have no idea what effect this had on him until he took her back up to his room.

Subtlety was unnecessary with Vivien. "I don't want to share you with Ralph."

She looked at him in surprise in the midst of pulling off her shirt. "You don't have to share me. I'll be with you sometimes and with him sometimes."

"That's what I mean by sharing."

"But Michael, I love Ralph."

"I know you do."

"I love Ralph and I love you. I love both of you." She clasped her hands together in a surfeit of pleasure, her face flushed.

"You know, when Ralph comes back up, you probably better not tell him that—about you and me."

"I know," she said happily. "I have a module for that. It's called lying."

They made love. But suddenly everything that had felt so easy and sure seemed fragile and risky.

The nightmare came again two nights in a row, and each time whoever was looking for him in the dark was closer. Waking up wasn't much better, because then he remembered he was losing Vivien. He was sure she was telling the truth about loving him—whatever love was to her—but what chance would he have when her doting billionaire owner, for whom she had a programmed tropism, started giving her the sex she needed again? Vivien's monthly maintenance alone cost more than Michael earned in a year, and he had no manor or grounds, no cars or servants. And even if she loved him now, Ralph could have her reprogrammed to forget him, or even hate him. Maybe that was one good reason not to fall in love with an android, he reflected. They were even easier to reprogram than humans.

But three days later, the very night before Ralph was to emerge from his cybernetic business trance, something happened that put even Vivien out of his mind.

He had the nightmare again, but tonight the shuffling and whispering were almost on top of him. When the searchers finally came into view, emerging vaguely as through a thick black fog, he recognized them with the certainty that dreams can bestow even on unfamiliar things. They were people from the life he had almost persuaded himself to forget: Margaret Biel in the beautiful blond girl's body, and Eugene Denmark.

Yet physically they were hardly recognizable: their bodies seemed deformed and their movements strangely spastic as they faded back into the blackness, disfigured hands pawing the air ahead of them.

They had passed him this time, but he knew they would find him very soon. He woke up shouting with fear, and slept no more that night.

The next day he forced himself to go about his work, but there was a cold at the core of his body that even the sunlight and August heat couldn't penetrate, and he couldn't shake the sense that someone was watching him. Once or twice he thought he caught the briefest glimpse of something in the corner of his eye, but when he checked, the summer air behind the bushes or around the corner was always empty and still. On top of everything, for the first day in weeks he didn't have sex with Vivien to soothe him: she was up at the house preparing for Ralph's emergence.

And now, after they had finally almost been pushed out of his mind, the old questions began to churn again. The irrelevance of a past with no connection to the present suddenly seemed less compelling. If the omen of his dreams could be believed, that apparent lack of connection might simply be a result of the fact that whoever was looking for him hadn't found him yet. The rapid fading of his "other life" memories had seemed proof that they were false, but he wondered now if it couldn't simply be that memories from one life and body grafted imperfectly onto another. Without some reinforcement from the environment, perhaps these foreign synaptic pathways quickly deteriorated, making the grafted mind and memories come to seem like dreams or delusions.

He didn't see Vivien all day. But as he was finally falling asleep long after midnight, he felt the familiar vibration of the stairs outside his door, and in another second she was in his arms, all silken skin and hair and fresh air and cheerful whispers. He made love to her gratefully. But his surrender at the moment of orgasm opened the floodgates of his feelings, and he burst into tears.

"Michael, why are you crying?" She wiped the tears gently from his face, like the perfect girlfriend she was.

He breathed deeply, tried to steady himself, come out of the deep ecstatic darkness of sex into the conscious world. He wanted to tell her that he loved her, but it seemed suddenly awkward. "How come you're not with Ralph?"

"I only saw him for a few minutes. He looks bad." Her voice trembled. "He has to sleep by himself for a few nights. The doctors have tubes in his arms and his head. Do you think he'll be all right, Michael?"

Put back in the role of authority figure, he felt himself getting a grip. "Of course he'll be all right. I've heard about those twenty-four-hour work rigs. They wear you down, but no permanent damage."

"And you're going to be okay, too? You look sad. It's hard loving two people," she said a little peevishly. "You have to worry about both of them."

It was the most selfish thing she had ever said, and also, he realized, the most human. He disengaged himself from between her legs and rolled gently off her, snuggled down next to her, but he couldn't ignore the chasm of loneliness and fear that had opened under him again. After a short struggle with himself, he said: "Vivien, can I tell you something?"

"Yes."

"You know how I told you I remembered being someone else?"

"Yes."

"Well, I've been having some dreams. Nightmares. I see some of the people from my memories. They're looking for me. I have the feeling they're going to find me. I'm scared, even in the daytime."

"They're just dreams, Michael. They're not real."

"I try to tell myself that, but I have this feeling that . . . that they're more than dreams. That if they find me, I'll die."

He had hoped vaguely that telling Vivien about the nightmares would relieve whatever mental tension was causing them, but that night the searchers were very near, and he lay rigid with terror, trying not to breathe, and woke up again gasping and soaked with sweat.

The next afternoon, as he was sunbathing by the pool, trying to dispel the deep cold that seemed to have settled into his body, he heard a step and, sitting up, saw Vivien and Ralph coming down the flagstone walk. He got up, grinning in spite of himself. Though Ralph, in his usual Bermuda shorts and bright Hawaiian shirt, did look bad. He was bone-thin, and there was an air of extreme fragility about him. He tried to move jauntily, and returned Michael's grin, but Michael could see that he held Vivien's arm to steady himself.

"Mike, dude, you look great," he said, and his quavering voice sounded like an old-man version of himself. "A lot better than I feel. Nice tan."

"Thanks." Michael shook his cool, bony hand. "Did you make a lot of money?"

"Plenty for everyone," said Ralph cheerfully. "I plan on giving out profit-sharing bonuses. The place looks really nice." He cast his eyes around. "And Vivien tells me you've been taking good care of her."

Guilt laid another layer of cold inside Michael. "Trying to."

Ralph and Vivien moved off slowly to do a circuit of the grounds, Vivien flashing Michael a grin that did more to warm him than the sunlight. As they went, Ralph was telling her with quavering enthusiasm how great it was to be out in the real, physical world again.

That night when she came to his bed, Michael asked, "Don't you feel bad about what we're doing?"

She was slipping off a sweatshirt, breasts moving with the motion of her muscles. "What do you mean?"

"I mean, don't you feel sorry for poor old Ralph?"

She stood up and slipped off her sweatpants, so that she stood naked except for a slender platinum necklace Ralph had given her. She climbed on top of Michael and grinned at him in the dark.

"No, I don't feel sorry for him," she said. "He has me."

TWO nights later the nightmare ghosts of Eugene Denmark and Margaret Biel found him. As he lay frozen with terror they emerged gradually from the darkness as if from a mist, and their eyes fell on him. Up close he could tell that they were damaged in some horrible way, their bodies covered

with burns, their lips, noses, and fingers cut off. They stared
down at him with ferocious hatred, like demons sent to drag
him to Hell. When he woke up screaming, they still seemed
to be there for a second, staring with vampiric desire, as if
they meant to eat him. Mercifully, once he woke up all the
way, they were gone.

He sat hunched in his bed, shaking violently. The clock
floating in discreet blue near his bed said 1:30 A.M. After a
while he lay back down, but he couldn't sleep.

Around 2:30 the intercom from the main house chimed.
That was odd. They rarely called on the intercom, and never
in the middle of the night. He swiped the cursor pulsing in
the air next to him.

It was Vivien. She looked odd, somehow not like herself;
in the lo-res hologram her eyes were wide and haunted.

"Michael?" she said tremulously. "I have to ask you something."

"What?"

"The people in your dreams—the ones you said are looking for you—how close are they? Are they getting closer
or farther away?"

"Vivien—"

"Please answer me, Michael. Are they getting closer or
farther away?"

"Closer." Suddenly his voice quavered. "They . . . they
found me."

Her hand flew to her throat. The gesture sent a shock of
new fear through him. "When? How long ago?"

"Just tonight, just now. Why? Vivien, what's going on?
What are you—"

But she was staring blindly, small fist before her mouth as
if thinking furiously.

"Vivien—"

"Then we have to go tonight."

"Go where? What are you talking about? Are you sleep-walking or . . . or malfunctioning?"

"Michael, listen, I'm sending you a navpak. Go to the site right away, before you do anything else. Then call me back. Make sure you look at it right away."

"What is it?" But she had already hung up.

He started to call her back, but stopped. He didn't want to wake Ralph, and anyway he might as well take a look at the site first; maybe it would tell him what Vivien was talking about. He went into his tiny kitchen, put on some water for tea, and sat at the table, jacking in his phone and clicking on the navigation package. Even with the shortcuts and decrypts it supplied, it took ten minutes to pass through the deep screen of innocent-looking entertainment and commercial sites, which were search-protected and elaborately passworded so that it would be impossible to stumble in past them by accident. Once the target site finally opened, there was an initial screen that simply said:

Talkative Customers.

Then this faded, and he found himself staring at a full-screen video of Barbara Santangelo's naked torso.

He sat bolt upright, head spinning, stomach turning.

In the video, Barbara Santangelo's body was dying. But not in any normal way. The marks of torture were on her. What was left of her face was constricted in unimaginable agony, teeth pulled out, eyes cocked in different directions as if pain had unmoored them, fingers all cut off, skin peeled off her forearms. But worst of all, she was conscious. Bloody saliva bubbled from her lips, and her twisted, broken body shook unnaturally. The IV tubes hanging from her flayed neck showed that she been nerve-racked—fed neurochemicals to kick up her pain sensitivity and keep her awake while she was tortured to death—a capital crime unless you were the USAdmin secret police.

As he watched, frozen with horror, she slowly stopped shaking, and then hung motionless, like a piece of meat from a butcher's hook, and suddenly the picture changed and he was looking at other remains: the young man, Dr. Eugene Denmark, who had tried to sell Heath Ransom some kind of advanced endovoyance technology. Denmark's ruined body was already motionless, apparently having died in the middle of an insane scream that had burst his eyeballs.

Michael tore the plug-in from his head, ran to the bathroom, and vomited until blood came up, then lay on the floor sobbing, drowning in waves of horror, confusion, and fear. A sickness even deeper than his terror had come over him. The faces of those leaking bags of burned and skinned meat seemed to tell him in their agony of something ultimate, a proof that this world was a place where dead matter formed itself for a little while into rotting shapes of flesh that moved and died in a meaningless dance of atoms, unfortunate enough to be conscious for that brief flash in the darkness, deluding themselves all the time that the world was not dead and cold and rotten— Black waves pulled him into unconsciousness.

He came to what felt like hours later, but the clock digits hanging in the air said only a few minutes had passed. The violence of his emotions had left him feeling injured and confused. Memories of his "other life"—his pursuit of Margaret Biel, the hole in the astral orchard, his possession of Michael Beach's body, the Ransom International news stories, the empty lot where his house had been—rushed upon him as clear as yesterday. He stood up, struggling to take control of his thoughts. Then it struck him: Vivien. How did Vivien, the ignorant, impassive doll, know about the awful site? What did she have to do with his past life, which seemed to be reaching out for him now with its awful perils?

The intercom buzzed again. He crooked a trembling finger through the pulsing light.

Vivien's face was tense. "Michael, did you look at it?"

"Yes—" He tried to say more, but he couldn't speak.

"You're in terrible danger. And Ralph is too as long as we stay here. We have to go."

"Vivien—"

"I'll explain everything. Meet me at the front door. I'll get the car."

He squeezed his eyes shut, tried to think.

"Michael, you saw those people, didn't you? They'll do the same thing to you and Ralph. *They're coming*. We have to go. *Now*."

Michael pulled on clothes and went out, the wooden stairs thrumming with reassuring solidity under his feet. It was the still hour before dawn, the cool, humid air faintly perfumed from the rose garden, a cricket or two creaking intermittently, like late partygoers arriving home in a weakened condition. It seemed incredible that danger could lurk in this serene world. The pictures on the website didn't prove anything, he told himself; they could be simulations, or part of a VR game that had infected him.

It hadn't been five minutes since he had spoken to Vivien, but Ralph's Bugatti was already sitting on the driveway, top down, Vivien in the driver's seat. She gestured for him to hurry with such anguish that he ran. But when he got to the car, he pulled up short. He was about to drive away in his boss's car with his boss's girlfriend, to an unknown destination. The blind fear that had made the idea of fleeing abruptly and without explanation seem reasonable suddenly gave way to indecision.

"Vivien, are you malfunctioning?" She was dressed as if for a bar hop, in tight jeans and a purple leather jacket.

"Michael, please get in the car."

"Are you being teleoperated? Has someone broken your encryption?"

"No, I'm not being teleoperated. Michael, you're in terrible trouble. Suddenly I . . . I just knew all about it. I don't have time to explain, but we have to go."

"Is somebody burst-operating you? Is your sensop blocked?"

She was angry suddenly. He had never seen anger in that small body, and it was bewitching, her face flushed, brows wrinkled, eyes flashing. "Get in the car and I'll *show* you, and if you still want to come back here and be tortured, I'll bring you."

He climbed over the passenger door and sat in the contoured leather seat. Vivien had permissions to all Ralph's cars, so they were committing no crime, and if this turned out to be a malfunction or some kind of psychovandalism they could always come back.

He had never seen Vivien drive, but she printed the ignition and grabbed the manual shifter expertly. At the end of the driveway the high metal gate slid open slowly onto the empty, streetlight-illuminated boulevard. A blue light on the dashboard showed that the car's counter-surveillance system had engaged.

Suddenly Vivien's head jerked forward and down and Michael could see liquid oozing from her mouth, nose, and eyes.

"Michael, you have to drive," she rasped.

"Are you okay?"

"My tropism. I'm programmed to stay with Ralph."

"Maybe we should go back—"

"*No!*" The word was almost a shriek. She seemed to get

hold of herself. "We're protecting Ralph by going. Switch seats with me."

He helped her, bent over like an invalid, into the passenger side, then got into the driver's seat. "Which way?"

"The car knows." She spoke with difficulty. Her arms were clasped around her body, face congested and streaming with tears.

He opened his mouth to ask something else, but she said harshly, "Go!"

He engaged the autopilot, and the Bugatti leaped down the street with a growl, as if it were hunter rather than prey.

15

There was little traffic at this hour, and it took them only a few minutes to reach the sub-high tunnel. The Bugatti cruised the few kilometers to the U-270 express, then headed north on the fast rail at speeds that would have promptly had them in jail if not for the car's advanced cloaking. Halfway to Pennsylvania the rail ended and they emerged from the tunnel at two hundred kilometers per hour, which felt like a snail's pace after the clip they had been going. There were few other cars, fewer as they went on, until soon there was only an occasional distant light marking some country crossroad or all-night fueling station, and the darkness was full of looming hills. The autopilot kept them effortlessly at speed even when they started steeply up the mountains, patches of fog whipping by and over them in the damp, chilly air. Vivien leaned pale and nerveless in the corner of her seat, eyes closed. He wondered suddenly if her tropic conditioning could actually kill her.

"Vivien?"

"Yes." She sounded wide awake.

"Are you okay?"

"I don't know."

"Can you tell me what's going on?"

"I'm thinking."

"Thinking."

"I have all these new memories. I'm trying to sort through them. I remember all kinds of things but I don't know what they mean."

"You have been bopped, then."

She opened her eyes a little and squinted at him. "What is 'bopped?'"

"Burst-operated. Shot full of instructions and information in a quick burst and then left to execute them using your autonomous AI."

"It felt like an explosion inside my head. Suddenly I just knew all these things and I knew what I had to do."

"Do you know who did it? Sent you the information?"

"I think so, somewhere among everything else. But I have to work through it."

"Well, do you know where we're going?"

"To the mountains. To show you something."

The car had begun to slow, and now it swerved onto an exit ramp lit by a few streetlights, surrounded by the darkness of night and the darker silhouettes of the mountains.

"Pull over," Vivien said. Michael gave the car the command. It smoothly pulled over and stopped on the shoulder of the county road they were now following, the lights of the exit already a kilometer behind them, a little dust and fog swirling through the powerful headlights and crickets singing in the dark as they switched seats. Instead of reengaging the autopilot, Vivien took manual control again. She spun the steering wheel and the car rotated with a great churning of dirt and pebbles, and they accelerated back the way they had come far faster than before.

"Autopilots can be hacked," Vivien said over the roar of the engine and rush of wind as the highway overpass lights flashed by. Evidently she had software for stunt driving; they climbed the narrow, curving, and thankfully deserted mountain road almost as fast as they had covered the highway, tires squealing slightly as the headlights swept rapidly over dark woods and sharply twisting asphalt, plunging through patches of fog, which as often as not passed just in time for Vivien to avoid plowing into the flashing gray tree trunks. When she finally slowed down, Michael realized that he was holding the door handle so tight it was hurting his hand.

She switched off the headlights and took a hard left onto a potholed dirt track with the remains of a rusted barbedwire fence along one side. To his relief, it was too rough to allow much speed, though the Bugatti's smart suspension made it feel like they were still on the highway. In a few minutes they turned off even this track, and tall weeds and crabgrass hissed under and along the sides of the car. Despite everything, Michael hoped they weren't scratching the paint. They finally came to rest between two big trees, and Vivien turned off the engine. It was suddenly very quiet; fog blew around them and the air smelled like wet leaves and leaf mold.

The fog cleared for a second, and Michael saw with alarm that the front of the car was two meters from what looked like the edge of a cliff. He got out, the ground under his feet feeling still and solid after Vivien's Formula 1 driving. A few crickets that had been silenced by their arrival started creaking again. The gorge in front of them wasn't very wide—in a bluish dawn light through which rags of mist moved he could see trees and crags on the other side perhaps fifty meters away—but below him it fell almost straight down, and he could barely see the stream and boulders a hundred meters below.

A sound from the car made him turn.

The driver's door was open and Vivien was leaning over and retching violently. He went to her. "Are you okay?"

"I don't know," she gasped. Then after another spasm: "You need to get back in the car. We have to go somewhere in a minute."

"Where?"

"Where the bop person told me to go."

He went around the car and got in. Vivien wiped the back of her hand across her mouth and closed her door. She was staring into the fog, which had begun to lighten perceptibly.

A shaft of hazy yellow-pink light grew above them, the first ray of dawn over the mountains.

Vivien printed the ignition and the car growled to life. "I hope this works," she said, and drove straight off the cliff.

Fear tore through Michael, but he was still opening his mouth to yell when he realized there had been no feeling of falling, only a gentle bump, as if they had driven off a curb instead of a cliff. He held his breath, bracing himself with his arms, but the car seemed to be moving forward smoothly along a level surface. He must have gotten disoriented, he realized; Vivien must have put the car in reverse. But then they came to a thin patch in the fog, and he could see that they were definitely moving forward—and moving on a narrow paved road, winding not through a forest or the boulders of a ravine, but what looked like manicured park-land with mown grass and well-spaced trees. Something about it was oddly familiar. He squeezed his eyes shut and opened them again, wondering if in the moment of impact at the bottom of the gorge his brain had flipped into a hallucination. Then, as a house appeared ahead of them in the fog, he forgot about that.

The three-story-mansion headquarters of Ransom International rose before them, and he realized suddenly that they were following the drive that wound through its grounds.

Vivien pulled up by the front door.

Michael—Heath Ransom—got out of the car, staring. Everything was just as he remembered it, except that three strands of bright yellow police tape were stretched across the front door.

He stood dumbstruck. It had all been *real*: the fifty-two

years of life as Heathcliff J. Ransom, the Merrivales, their aunt, the hole in the etheric orchard, Barbara Santangelo, his struggle for the dead boy's body—

All real.

"I'm supposed to tell you that the people who killed your friends wanted to make sure they wouldn't be caught," said Vivien, "so they moved the house here along with the parts of its history that could be erased without drawing attention in the main world. I'm supposed to tell you that they can do things like that. That they're very dangerous. And that they may be watching this place, and they may be on their way here right now, so you have to do whatever you decide quickly."

"Whatever I decide? But what should I do?" A dizziness had come over him; he fought to keep from fainting.

"I don't know."

He sat down heavily on the front steps of his house and put his head down. After a minute the dizziness lifted, and he was able to look around. The thick mists were still a pale gray, like a heavy fog at sunrise. He wondered uselessly whether this had been the weather and time of day when they—whoever they were—had done whatever they had done to bring the house here, wherever here was. Assuming that whoever had bopped Vivien was telling the truth. And assuming that any of this was real.

"Do you know how to get out of here?"

"No," said Vivien. "But I don't like standing out here. I think we should go inside."

He looked up in surprise at her decisive tone. Her blank, hesitating girlfriend personality had been pushed into the background by something he had to assume was a goal-seeking behavior pattern from the bop operating on her bodyguard substrate. Anyway, what she said made sense; he didn't want to run into whoever had nerve-racked Denmark and Barbara Santangelo, or Margaret Biel in Santangelo's body. He stood up with difficulty, then leaned his hands on his knees and hung his head as the dizziness came back. Vivien held on to him, steadying him. As soon as he could, he climbed the steps to the big front door, and, without thinking, input the lock code.

The door clicked open.

As they stepped into the front hall, the lights coming on, the *smell* of the place struck him—a combination of hundred-year-old wood paneling, the venerable Oriental carpets, and the subtle ionization of advanced electronics. He had never even been aware that the house had a smell, but he realized now that it had been part of the foundation of his life for decades. Smelling it now, his doubts were completely and finally dispelled. He had come home.

But not home as he remembered it: there was no sound of movement from the reception office, no voices or laughter from the coffee room, no opening or closing doors, or steps along the hall. There was only an unnatural silence, obtrusive and concentrated, like someone holding his breath. And now, unexpectedly, his fear diminished. This was *his house,* his home court, which he knew every inch of, where he could make a stand. He put a finger to his lips and motioned Vivien toward a part of the wall between a small table with an antique rotary telephone and an enormous potted palm. The wall, of course, didn't react to Michael Beach's irises, so he had to tap out a code on the smooth, varnished wood; but then it swung inward silently, and he drew Vivien through the opening and pushed the hidden door shut behind them. On the inside it was hardened blast steel. He took a deep breath, relaxing a few notches.

"Panic room," he murmured as she followed him down the narrow, low-ceilinged passage.

It led to a concrete-walled room with cabinets, metal chairs, and a table. Three more passages led off it. Ransom typed a combination on one of the cabinets, and it opened to reveal a rack holding pistols, short-barreled shotguns, and magazines. He took one of each and clicked the magazines into place. From another cabinet he took a bundle of screens and unrolled them on the table. They showed the rooms and halls of the house from hidden surveillance cameras and patrolling security drones. None of the screens showed movement, and the biosensors were all negative. One screen showed the Viewing room in the basement. One of the two trance tanks was riddled with bullet holes, and on the tiled floor sticky-looking brown stains showed where people had bled.

And now suddenly another feeling came over him—rage. Everything he had held at a distance for so long suddenly came crashing back. Someone had come into his house and killed his employees and friends—the devoted Arjun Govind, the fresh-faced Bobby Mandelson, the gentle Anna Heatherstone—had torn them open and turned them into ruined hunks of rotting meat. They had come into his house—*his house!*—and walked through the rooms, killing everyone. And after that they had tortured a man and woman far beyond the natural limits of pain and hung their ruined, hopeless remains on a website to advertise the supremacy of cruelty and ruthlessness in the world.

He trembled with a terrible fury as he walked down the passage to the secure elevator, pistol and shotgun in his sweat-slick hands. Someone had to punish whoever had done this, if only to show that cruelty and ruthlessness were not all-powerful, not the highest laws. Heathcliff Ransom, the middle-aged man whose life had been destroyed in this house, decided it. Heathcliff Ransom made the vow, and he knew he would have to stay Heathcliff Ransom from now on to make sure it was fulfilled.

He went through the rest of the house, Vivien silent at his side. Everything was quiet, orderly, and clean, except for the few places where overturned furniture, smashed glass, and bullet-holes surrounded a dark stain on a carpet or upholstery. They were in the main kitchen, which looked like it had been scrubbed and tidied minutes ago, when they heard a sound from the doorway.

A huge figure was outlined there.

Ransom's shotgun jerked away from him and he was thrown violently onto the floor. A deafening roar erupted.

Looking up, he saw that Vivien was firing the shotgun over and over as fast as it would shoot.

The giant figure had leaped at them, but the shots caught it in the air and flipped it over, crashing it against the opposite wall. In an instant it was flying at them again, its buckshot-shredded clothes showing a kind of scaly armor underneath.

The shotgun clicked empty, and the giant was on Vivien, huge fists flying.

But instead of taking the blows, Vivien seemed to turn to water. She slipped between the monster's hands, flipped herself up onto its shoulders and vised her legs around its neck, then threw her weight backward like a gymnast, toppling it, and as its head hit the floor she brought her fists down on its face with a tremendous *bang*.

She picked up the empty shotgun and smashed it through the kitchen window, then leaped after it, yanking Ransom along with the strongest grip he had ever felt.

They tumbled onto wet grass at the back of the house and then she was dragging him at a headlong sprint into the fog.

As soon as the house faded from sight she changed direction. They sprinted faster than Ransom could ever remember sprinting, and when he couldn't breathe anymore he fell on his face.

As soon as he could pay attention, he realized that Vivien was crouching next to him with a finger to her lips, staring into the fog and listening. He gasped desperately for breath as silently as possible. Vivien put her lips to his ear.

"Don't make any noise," she breathed. She pulled him upright, and they walked soundlessly on the wet grass. The fog was so thick that for all he knew they were heading back toward the house, but Vivien seemed sure of her direction.

For a long time the fog didn't change. Finally Vivien whispered, "It's getting lighter," and at that same moment his shoe scraped on something hard. He stopped walking and looked down.

They were standing on asphalt.

Panic went through him. "Did we go in a circle?" he breathed.

Vivien walked ahead until he could barely see her. "No."

She was pointing at the ground. He went to where she was. On the asphalt a broad white line had been painted. It joined another line at right angles.

It was a painted parking space.

They moved forward cautiously. As they did, the soft gray space around them widened slowly, so that they could see other parking spaces fading into the fog, and after a few hundred meters, row after row of spaces painted on cracked gray asphalt, and at intervals small, curbed areas with a narrow strip of grass, a tiny hedge, or even a small tree. Something tall loomed ahead of them, startling Ransom until he realized that it was a lamppost, standing in one of the curbed areas next to a tiny bus shelter.

After another few hundred meters the fog thinned out completely, and they saw that the parking lot didn't seem to have an end. As far as they could see were row upon row of identical parking spaces ranged around strip after strip of tiny, curbed plots with a little worn grass or a bush, a tiny shuttle-bus shelter set in every tenth plot or so, light poles receding in strict geometric patterns. There were no cars; all the parking spaces were empty. Sunlight was just beginning to spill over the horizon to their left like liquid metal, casting long shadows across the asphalt.

16

"**What** is this place?" Vivien asked shakily.

"An astral sensorium, it looks like." Infinite regresses were something at which the etheric excelled, and of which it never seemed to tire. And huge parking lots, which you could still find going to seed around antique sports stadiums and convention centers in some older cities, made perfect kernels for such regresses. Then astonishment came over him as he realized what he had said. "Wherever they put the house is part of the astral world. *They've found a way to put physical things into the astral world.* But how can that be? Or maybe it's been the astral all along. Listen," he said, suddenly urgent, "give me a minute."

One of the nearby curbed areas had a lamppost. He went over and sat on a tiny patch of worn grass, leaned his back against the lamppost, and closed his eyes. Now that he seemed to be solidly back in the astral, maybe he could terminate his trance. With a sudden, intense yearning, the thought came to him that maybe he would wake up in his trance tank, and all this would turn out to have been a Viewing gone freakishly bad.

"What are you doing? We need to keep moving," Vivien said urgently, her bodyguard mode now fully activated.

"I need a minute. Shhh."

He closed his eyes and consciously relaxed his muscles, which he now realized had been at a pitch of tension.

"Michael—"

"Shhh."

He lay in his tank, red light shining on his naked body,

the smart fluid liquefying around him, running out of the drains. He opened his eyes—

He tried again, took his time this time, relaxed, made sure the image of the dive tank was crystal clear.

When he opened his eyes, the parking lot was still there.

He tried his emergency extraction eye movement sequence, then tried it again.

"Michael, we have to go. That—whatever it is—might still be after us."

Ransom stood up. He felt like crying, but the thought of the huge figure that had attacked them made the hair on his head prickle. The unbearable, inescapable pain of nerve-racking might not be any pleasanter in the astral than it was in the real world—if this was the astral.

Vivien set off running.

Ransom's new body was young, tall, and in top physical shape, but he had to push himself to keep up with her. She took a diagonal path, cutting across rows of painted parking spaces; Ransom realized that a straight shot down the lanes between the curbed plots gave an unobstructed view to the horizon—a view they didn't want the monster to have if it emerged from the fog near where they had.

They ran for hours.

At long last Vivien slowed to a walk. Ransom was exhausted, his clothes soaked with sweat, but she seemed untouched, fresh and beautiful.

The sun seemed to actually be rising here, as if they were on a real, rotating planet, and by now it was mid-morning, shadows from the streetlights, shrubs, and curbs shortening. Behind them, the fog had receded to a haze on the horizon. The air was still and cool, and even had a parking-lot smell.

Now that he had breath to spare, the questions Ransom had worried at as they ran came tumbling out. "What was that thing that attacked us? Where are we? Do you know anything about this place?"

She hesitated. "I think I know a little bit, but . . . it's like I know a lot, but most of it doesn't fit together. It's like I can't remember things unless I'm specifically looking for them. Do you think my memory is malfunctioning?" she asked anxiously.

"More likely you're out of touch with Talking Machines so you're having to use your endogenous compilers on the data the bop-op dropped on you. Sooner or later things should start to make sense. But can you look for information on where we are, or how to get out?"

She was silent for a minute. "The—whoever it is left a verbal narrative compressed in my memory. Maybe if I play it it'll tell us something. 'If you're hearing this—' "

"Is this the narrative now?"

"Yes."

Walking through the endless parking lot in the morning sunlight of a clear autumn day, Vivien recited the message.

"If you're hearing this, you're not dead yet. But it's crucial now that you do exactly as I say. After seeing your house, I hope you realize that this isn't a joke or your android doll malfunctioning. The most important thing now is for you to hide. It has to be someplace with powerful etheric shielding, like an ashram or SRS. Otherwise the ghosts will find you again. Do that before you listen to this. None of it matters if you're dead."

There was a pause, and then she started again. "If you're hearing this, I assume you've found someplace safe to hide. If so, I'll try to bop the doll soon with some new plans. In the meantime, I'll try to explain what's happening to you.

"The people or entities that extracted your house from the primary flux are mutants. USAdmin military research made them by keeping infantry operators isolated in neural-growth media with their endogenous battle hardware at full gain, for years. The combination of the neural tanks' isolation, paralysis, and sensory deprivation with their hardware's hyper-alert, hyper-analytic battle activation killed most of them. Some kind of hippocampus gene expression was triggered in the ones who survived, evidently the brain's desperate attempt to break the isolation—no one really understands it. But it turned out that the military had created their own ready-made polyendomaths."

"Wait, wait a minute," Ransom stuttered. "Is this—is this what that guy Denmark was selling, when he came to RI before all this happened? His process for creating endovoyants? You know the guy I mean?" The blank incomprehension on Vivien's face stopped him. "Sorry," he said. "You're just the messenger. Keep going."

She started again without hesitation. "Some of the soldiers—the most powerful endos, it turned out—could no longer live outside the growth-media tanks. Eventually, the military put these—maybe half a dozen of them—into a single tank, and they grew together, physically and mentally, into an entity with previously unknown powers. They are called the Brothers. The others, who after extensive surgery can still function in the outer world—but are constantly in endovid touch with the Brothers—are called the Mobiles.

"We don't really know what happened next. Maybe the mutants got bored being guinea pigs for USAdmin researchers and breached their security; or maybe their existence was discovered by other means. Anyway, they were discovered and recruited by some outside organization. A coordinated military, electronic, and endosensory attack was launched on the secret USAdmin facility where they were kept, and they were spirited away by their new employer.

"Almost nothing is known about this person or entity. The top-secret USAdmin task forces assigned to destroy it call it Amphibian. It is known to be hyperintelligent and probably only partly biological. It may be a Class Three mutant, a super-enhanced AI, a human so hardware-heavy its soul has died, or even something from exo-Earth.

"If it has a well-defined location, that location is unknown. It appears to be embarked upon some project of enormous scope, whose objective is also unknown.

"The mutants now run a covert company in Amphibian's illicit business empire, which they call Backward. Behind a kaleidoscope of front companies and church foundations, it sells young bodies to old, rich people. The Mobiles provide the muscle and legwork; the Brothers provide the 'magic.' At Amphibian's instigation, the Brothers appear to have learned to actually move physical objects into para-astral flux-buds like the one you saw: tiny, low-energy bud universes that can only be reached from the primary flux at specified—"

Vivien broke off suddenly and looked back the way they had come. "I hear something."

Ransom squinted in the direction Vivien was looking, his heart speeding up, but he could see nothing. "What is it?"

"A car," said Vivien. "Hide!"

He sprinted after her to one of the small hedges, and they lay down on the asphalt behind it, peering between its leaves.

"Is it them? The mutants?" he whispered shakily.

Vivien put her finger to her lips. He tried to calm himself. He found that he had to clamp his teeth together to keep them from chattering.

The vehicle was evidently moving slowly; it seemed an eternity before Ransom could hear the distant crackle of its tires, another before it appeared between the leaves of the hedge, trundling along at what looked like a walking pace.

It was a retro-style minibus.

Ransom stared at it pop-eyed for a second, and then he was on his feet and running. "Hey!" he shouted. "Hey!"

Sprinting, he was barely able to bang on one of the rear windows as the minibus passed, then opened the distance between them with imperturbable aplomb, like a ship on calm seas, moving slightly faster than he could sprint, the person Ransom glimpsed hunched over the steering wheel evidently letting the autopilot proceed at a prudent parking-lot pace.

Ransom noticed that Vivien was running gracefully and seemingly effortlessly at his side.

"They'll see us," she said.

"Catch it!" he gasped. It was the minibus that had vanished from Anglia Street when he had been gawking at the empty lot where Ransom International used to be.

It was fifty meters from them and pulling away. Without breaking her stride, Vivien grabbed Ransom and slung him—shouting with fear—over her shoulder, then started to run twice as fast. She caught the minibus in thirty seconds, and banged on its rear window, then on the driver's side window. Frozen with the fear that she would drop him, Ransom caught a glimpse of the bearded, long-haired driver staring straight ahead through the windshield, as if he hadn't heard the banging.

Vivien dropped back two paces, pulled open the minibus's back door, tossed Ransom in, hopped in herself, and pulled the door shut. Sprawled gasping on the backseat next to her, he noticed that she was panting quickly and lightly, like a dog, and that a strange sort of quiet hissing also seemed to be coming from her body, like some kind of gas exchange through her skin.

"Fuck!" he said, getting upright. He was trembling violently. "Hey!" He leaned forward and thrust his head over the bench-style front seat. The driver didn't look at him; he just kept staring out the windshield, clutching the steering wheel as if holding himself up. It was indeed the bearded, long-haired preacher who had vanished from Anglia Street, but seemingly many years older. Shock or suffering had lined his face and grayed his hair, there were bags like purple bruises under his eyes, his white robes were dirty, and he smelled of sweat and urine.

He said, "You'll never get out, brother. There's no end to it. I've been driving for weeks, looking for an exit. But there isn't one."

"You— I saw you—in Bethesda, on Anglia Street. You pulled up—"

"I pulled up," the man said, still staring straight ahead. "A devil was there. In a cloak. Sent me here. I don't know why."

"I didn't—" Ransom started, but then decided not to admit being the cloaked devil. "You ended up here," he echoed.

"This is Hell," said the preacher. "But it's not as bad as the first one he sent me to. That was nothing, nowhere, not light or dark, silent or noisy, solid or space. I couldn't bear it. I closed my eyes and thought of the first place I could. Turned out to be the parking lot outside the MidWest Evangelical Convention in Des Moines. Then here I was."

"You've reified an astral sensorium," Ransom said. "There's always a way out."

"There's no way out. This is Hell."

"Look, I know something about this, and I think I can get us out of here. Will you listen to me?"

"There isn't any way out. This is Hell. I made a mistake. I preached that God was a super-intelligent alien. But I must have been wrong. The Truthers told me I would go to Hell if I believed that, and they were right. It's a terrible punishment for just believing the wrong thing."

"No, that's not it," said Ransom. "Somebody has learned to make the physical and astral realms interact somehow. But I can tell you that where we are is mostly etheric, basically just an information field, which you can affect with your thoughts. Partly, anyway."

"There's no way out."

"It won't be like a normal parking lot exit. You have to withdraw your attention. You reified it, you can make it go away."

"I'm not going back to that other place." He started to shake his head. "Never. Never."

"You won't. I'll help you. Okay? I want you to—"

While they had been talking, the minibus had gradually started to go faster, as if the preacher was getting more and more upset under his hypnotic surface calm. Now it suddenly leaped forward.

"You don't have to do that," Ransom said. "I'll tell you what to do."

They were accelerating fast now, the curbs, light posts, and hedges flashing by, the modern suspension under the retro body making their progress eerily quiet and smooth, as if they were watching a movie out the windows.

The preacher said, "I'll show you. You can go as far as you want. There's no way out."

The speedometer now read 150 kilometers per hour. Ransom sat back in his seat; it suddenly occurred to him that if this sensorium could contain an actual physical house pulled from the real world, then his own actual physical body might be here, too.

"Slow down!" Ransom yelled. "I need to talk to you!"

"You can go as far as you want—"

Suddenly exceeding its technical specifications, the minibus became airborne with a sickening lurch. A bus shelter seemed to float toward the windshield.

Ransom's seat erupted around him, enclosing him in resin foam. A gas from the foam made him unconscious.

17

It couldn't have been more than a minute later that he regained consciousness, the protective foam cocoon embrittling and peeling back to let the gas it had fed him dissipate, fire-retardant aerosols already clearing in the now-cramped passenger compartment. The minibus looked like it had undergone a long process of decay while he had been asleep. The dashboard had been pushed practically into the backseat, its coatings and laminates flaked and spalled, and the wreckage banged and groaned as the metal-plastic alloys released the crash stress. Nothing of the preacher, Jeremiah, was visible except a heavy splatter of blood on the now concave and opaque windshield, as if someone had smashed a pint of raspberries. Next to Ransom, Vivien had already broken out of her own cocoon and was forcing the minibus door open with a squeal of alloy. She grabbed his wrist and dragged him after her into the fresh and strangely serene air of the parking lot. His legs were trembling so he could hardly stand, but he seemed unhurt. Mentally he was numb; the gas the crash-foam administered was as much for psychological protection as to keep your body limp on impact.

The asphalt behind the minibus was deeply scored and scraped, and debris were scattered widely across the parking lot. The minibus, which was still emitting wisps of fire-retardant aerosols, had given like an accordion to absorb the shock. One of its front wheels, a meter off the ground, still spun. There was a smell of burning plastic.

Vivien smashed and pulled away what was left of the driver's side window, and looked in. "He's dead," she said.

Ransom glanced at the strawberry splatter, then quickly away again. "Stupid bastard. Why couldn't he listen to me?" Suddenly he was shaking with anger at the poor smashed thing inside the minibus. "Why couldn't he *listen*?"

"What should we do?"

"Well, we can't bury him," said Ransom, looking around at the asphalt. "I guess there's no reason to stay here. Why couldn't he listen to me?"

"He said there's no way out."

"He was off his nut. If I'm not mistaken, we're about to get out. The question is where we'll be when we do. We might be back in the mountains. Did the bop-op tell you what we're supposed to do when we get out?"

"Get away as fast as we can, and hide."

"Terrific. Well, we might as well keep walking. Get away from this thing, at least." He gestured at the wreck.

They started off, heading, for no particular reason, in the direction the preacher had been driving. Ransom noticed that the trembling in his legs had spread to the rest of his body. He tried to unclench his muscles, made a conscious effort not to look back at the minibus. Now that the numbness was starting to wear off, a pit of sorrow and horror opened inside him at the fate of Jeremiah.

"I was a member of a covert research team recruited by Backward's representatives," said Vivien.

Ransom looked at her in surprise. The crash had put the story out of his mind. He tried to reorient himself. "Okay."

"The man you know as Eugene Denmark—though of course that isn't his real name—was another of their recruits. They told us they were a secret USAdmin agency working on defense technologies, and they sequestered us in a facility in South Dakota. We had an unlimited budget and impossibly advanced psychometric and psychogenic technology.

"In the excitement, no one asked who had developed the technology. Except Denmark. Denmark was curious about everything. He hacked Backward's data and found out things. He told me about them. We realized that Backward would never let the research team go free after we had completed our work.

"Denmark and I escaped, went underground.

"We hid ourselves well, but we knew that Backward would find us and kill us sooner or later. We needed to expose them, but we needed help. We knew that USAdmin would kill us if we went to them privately—though probably not before they nerve-racked us to see what else we knew. We needed people who had enough pull to help us go public, but who also knew enough about endotech to understand what we were telling them. Your name was on our short list.

"Denmark's hacks had revealed that one of Backward's current body-switch projects was Margaret Biel. He got an idea. He contacted the Merrivales posing as a friend of a friend and told them about you, suggested that you might be able to bring her back. Denmark thought that if the Merrivales hired you, you would have the perfect cover to document Backward's activities. He decided to visit you, too, and try to determine whether you were working for USAdmin or Backward by dropping some hints about the technology Backward was using. If you were clean, he would tell you the whole story. We bought a home plastic-surgery kit and changed his appearance as much as possible.

"By coincidence Denmark met you on the same day as the Merrivales. He never came back. Probably Backward was watching the Merrivales and stumbled across Denmark when he arrived at your offices. The Merrivales and Denmark visiting you on the same day must have convinced Amphibian that you knew something, that you were dangerous. The Mobiles attacked your headquarters that same night."

Ransom was suddenly dizzy with rage. "So it was you who led them to us, caused all this, you and your goddamn geek friend—"

Vivien stared at him wide-eyed.

"Not you," he said, deflated. "Sorry."

"When Denmark didn't come back, I went into deep hiding, in a place even he didn't know about. We knew that if either of us was captured, we would be tortured. Amphibian is said to like torture; he always observes when his employees nerve-rack someone. There was no real reason to nerve-rack either Denmark or the Biel woman; neither of them were professionals or fitted out with anything that would make them resistant to interrogation. Maybe it was just done to amuse Amphibian. One way or another, though, Biel told them about your body switch. But by that time you had already dropped out of sight. I knew that because we had left sleepers in Backward's network, and I activated them. What I heard before Backward's security killed them gave me some hope. Backward had decided to use some of their causal gravity to pull your business and its locally connected history into flux-bud to keep the story contained.

"I thought then that they had made a mistake, that it would be impossible to just remove a chunk of history without anyone noticing. But I was wrong: the primary flux healed the causal excision like a body heals cuts and regrew the interrupted links into other causal chains, so that in the end it looked for all the world as if things had always been that way. Not many people knew of Ransom International in the first place; those who did were puzzled briefly, but soon forgot about it, thinking it was something they had dreamed. The information systems that contained records of you 'repaired' their datasets, and now things are settling down in the primary flux as if there never had been a Ransom International or a Heathcliff Ransom.

"I knew I had to find you before Backward and Amphibian did. Being an actual human being gave me what was my only advantage—I could imagine how another human might act in your situation. I monitored packet traffic in the places I thought you might go. Finally an encrypted signal from your doll to her operations center for memory compiling contained things you had told her. From there all I had to do was secure the doll's channel and bop her. I was almost too late. When I learned that the Denmark and Santangelo slave ghosts had found you, I knew there wasn't a second to lose. There's someone up ahead of us," Vivien said, pointing.

Ransom squinted into the infinite parking-lot regress. Sure enough, at the very edge of sight something seemed to be moving.

"Okay," he said. "This is weird the first couple of times, but don't worry—it can't hurt you."

"What is weird?" Vivien was peering anxiously into the distance, where the people ahead of them already looked closer.

"Odds are that we're about to pop out of this sensorium. The preacher might have piggy-backed on whatever energy the Backward mutants are using, but now that he's dead the astral world he reified is going to collapse. If that's what's happening, those people ahead of us are us, seen from behind. Yeah, look. That's us."

As he had talked, the people had come yet closer, as if he and Vivien were on some kind of super-fast moving sidewalk, so that now, instead of tiny specks, he could just make out that the larger figure ahead wore jeans and a T-shirt, the other jeans and a short jacket.

"There are more people ahead of them," said Vivien.

There were; specks in the farther distance beyond the small figures.

"They'll be behind us, too."

Vivien turned sharply to look, and Ransom stopped to look, too. In the distance two people were half turned around and looking over their shoulders.

"They're not really there," Ransom said. "That's us, like in a mirror. The light's going around and around a four-dimensional sphere, and the sphere is getting smaller."

"What do you mean?" asked Vivien fearfully.

"People think that when you reify an astral sensorium, you open up some of the dimensions you don't normally see because they're curled up in tiny balls. The energy of your attention stretches them out like inflating a balloon. So when the energy is withdrawn, the dimensions curl back up, and the light inside goes around a smaller and smaller diameter, giving the illusion that everything is replicated over and over. But it's just the local spacetime collapsing. I've been through it plenty of times." Though never in a sensorium powered by whatever mojo had sucked Ransom International and its whole history out of the real world. And never in a sensorium where he himself might actually be physically present, along with another person from the physical world.

The parking lot was telescoping rapidly inward now, the sets of people in front of and behind them moving smoothly and swiftly toward them, until he could see their clothes and postures, the man tall and athletic, the woman petite and shapely.

"Look," he said like a tour guide, pointing at right angles to the way they had been walking. Versions of themselves seen from the side were approaching also, turned away to look at more distant copies that they could now see were turned away too to look into the distance at other tiny figures. And now all around them, in every direction they looked, copies of themselves converged, faster and faster. Vivien put her arms around Ransom and buried her face in his chest. He held her; it was uncanny enough for someone with the sensory flexibility of a human; for an AI programmed to operate in normal space it had to be catastrophically disorienting.

Copies upon copies upon copies of themselves rushed inward and crashed onto them, and then they were all shut up in a tiny space, curled up and collapsing, nothing to see, not even darkness.

And then something happened that had never happened to him before. He and Vivien interpenetrated. The sensorium space had gone to zero; everything inside had to share it.

For an indefinite time, in a nonexistent place, they were one, their minds entangled, wandering in the alien territory of each other, a male human in his second body and a bodyguard AI sex doll; he felt her cool, fast, strong, sleek, self-contained; she felt him warm, slow, hazy, indefinite, every part of him pulsing with death and birth.

They found themselves huddled together on the parking-lot asphalt, now twins instead of one, and for a long time they clutched each other, not wanting to let go. Gradually Ransom became aware of her warm, small body against his, and then memory and a sense of urgency seeped back, and finally he pushed her a few centimeters away. He stared at her, his wonder overwhelming his relief that the collapse of the sensorium hadn't harmed them.

"You're *alive*," he rasped. He had never before shared a sensorium collapse with another real person. And she was a real person. He knew: he had *been* her.

She was crying desperately.

It occurred to Ransom finally to look up. They were still in the parking lot, but looking farther away he saw that this place was finite. Early morning sunlight showed cars in some of the parking spaces, and in the middle distance the massive domed roof of an old convention center. A hundred meters away in the opposite direction the parking lot ended in a scraggly stand of fir trees, beyond which he could see what looked like an old rail yard. The air was fresh and chilly.

A yell came from behind him, and looking around, Ransom saw that he and Vivien were kneeling face-to-face next to the wreckage of the preacher's minibus. He stood up shakily, pulling her with him. A man was running toward them across the parking lot, waving his arms.

Vivien stiffened, then trembled. Then she turned away from him and retched, the meager contents of her stomach splashing on the asphalt.

She fell to her knees. He knelt next to her. She was trembling violently.

"Are you okay?"

"My head—"

"Did you get bopped again?"

"Where are we?" she rasped.

"I would guess Des Moines, Iowa."

She retched again, her body tensing under his hands. When she talked again, her voice was hard and rasping, like someone else's voice: "We have to get out of here. We need someplace with etheric shielding. The ghosts have your spoor. They'll find you again."

"Are you all right?" an agitated voice puffed behind them. The man who had run up was staring wide-eyed. "I called emergency services. Were you in that?" He pointed at the minibus.

"What? No, no. But I need a favor." Ransom stood up again, pulling Vivien along with him. Her body was hunched and trembling. "Can you give us a lift? This woman is overdue for somatic maintenance. Can you get us to the nearest subway?"

18

The trunk subway from Des Moines to Baltimore took two hours, and the local line from Baltimore to Gaithersburg thirty minutes. Ransom and Vivien wore cheap anonymizing cloaks they had bought at the Des Moines station, so he couldn't see her face; but she didn't seem well. She slumped in her seat, and only moved with the shaking of the subway car. At the Gaithersburg station they got a cab.

After a short drive through wooded suburban sprawl, their cab pulled up to a flimsy traffic gate. A sign with flowers planted around it said MONTGOMERY VILLAGE. Inside a kiosk, two bearded men in orange robes sat motionless, smiling glassily at them. After about thirty seconds, one of them moved a finger and the gate rose. As it went back down behind them, Ransom allowed himself to breathe. The *sadhus* in the guardhouse letting them in probably meant there was nothing astral and bad—like demonic ghosts— following them.

Montgomery Village was an antique neighborhood of old trees and low-rise surface houses and apartments, immaculately restored to quaint mid-twentieth-century style. Its streets were nearly empty in the hazy afternoon sunlight, only an occasional car passing with electric motor silence. Ransom felt himself relaxing, but he knew there was more to it than just the quiet. This was a Super-Radiance Suburb, where the residential fees included a hefty sum to support hundreds of meditating adepts in some centrally located warehouse or geodesic dome, creating a penumbral effect that was supposed to exclude "negative influences." Social scientists had confirmed lower rates of accidents, illness, and crime in the SRSs, but there were disputes as to the causes, and various religions had also weighed in. In his previous life Ransom had intended to retire in an SRS, which to an endovid offered a kind of pensive repose, as if some great consciousness that held the world in its thoughts had started daydreaming, or as if some transcendentalist poet's eternities in an hour and universes in a grain of sand had been made real, with the grain of sand in this case being an upscale gated community. It would have been impossible to practice his profession in such a place, of course: forensic endovoyance required the practitioner to expose himself to all the "negative influences" connected to the lost, stolen, and strayed things he pursued.

Wrapped carefully in aliases and encryption, Ransom and Vivien rented an apartment on the top floor of a three-story brick building tucked away among the oaks and maples at the end of a long sidewalk. Indirect lighting came up softly as they entered the foyer, which opened on a living room with standard furniture and tunable windows. They pulled off their cloaks and gear, and Ransom studied Vivien anxiously. She looked bleary and exhausted, as if she were sick or had been crying.

Ransom went into the small, modern kitchen and found the apartment console, set the air to mountain pine forest. When he came back, he could hear her retching in the bathroom. After a while the retching was replaced by quiet sobbing.

He tapped on the bathroom door, opened it. Vivien was kneeling exhaustedly by the toilet. Reflexively, he knelt down, too.

"Go away!" she snarled, and her face was a frightening machine mask. Then she closed her eyes and shuddered, and was human once more, holding her head desperately between her hands as if it might come apart. "Michael, you have to leave me alone. My programming—you know. I left Ralph." She fought down a retch, and tears ran down her face again. "I'll be okay, but you have to leave me alone. You have to promise not to touch me anymore."

To keep himself occupied, Ransom ordered groceries and feedstock. *You have to promise not to touch me anymore.* The quiet August days, the ocean clouds, playing with Vivien all day in Ralph's garden and rolling around in a sweat with her all night . . . By the time the robot delivery truck arrived and sent his boxes up the pneumatic chute, all was quiet in the bathroom. Ransom unpacked the groceries, loaded ingredients into the stove, and told it to prepare a pot roast with vegetables. *Promise not to touch me anymore . . .* making love to her, the feel of her flanks and hips . . . The stove chimed and presented the pot roast. Ransom forced himself to eat a plateful, and it made him feel a little better. He told the stove to refrigerate the rest. After he had dumped his plate and silverware into the recycler, he went into one of the bedrooms, threw his clothes into the laundry chute, and voiced off the lights.

What were they supposed to do now? he wondered, lying in the dark. If the story Vivien had told him was true, whoever was bopping her wanted help fighting a corporate empire run by superhuman mutants who nerve-racked people without a qualm, sent ghosts after you in your dreams, and could even prune history using some kind of causal distortion.

And behind everything was an ashen hollowness. *Promise not to touch me.* He remembered being inside her in the endless second before they had popped out of Backward's flux-bud, her valved heart beating, her attention delicate and still, flesh sleek and cool, and her mind *alive,* afire with something human. . . .

He woke with cheerful daylight coming through the window. He took a shower. His clothes were clean and neatly folded in a package in the laundry return bin. He put them on and went into the living room.

Vivien was sitting cross-legged on the floor, half a dozen unpacked express boxes tumbled around her, and an expensive 3-D printer that she must have also ordered while he was asleep humming quietly on the coffee table, giving off a hot, complex smell.

She was still pale, but she managed a smile, and she was so beautiful that his first instinct was to escape, run from the physical pain that seeing her awoke in his young body. He looked instead at the hodgepodge of do-it-yourself bioelectronic components mounted in a disorderly erector-set scaffolding, a dozen color-coded circuit organs connected to bus ties and chip boards with hair-thin light fibers, webs of dendritic tendrils already starting to grow between some of them. At the top of the scaffolding, bottles of color-coded nutrients sat, their drip tubes spliced into some of the organs. Vivien was holding what looked like a plump, sky-blue kidney.

"So now you're an emulator whiz," Ransom said. "What's this?"

"The bop-op sent the design."

"What is it?"

"It's called a 'bioinformation transducer.'"

"Why do we need a bioinformation transducer?" he asked anxiously.

"To test you for ghosts."

A chill went through him. "I thought they couldn't follow us here."

She shrugged, slapping the blue kidney gently to activate it. "Maybe they can't and maybe they can."

"Vivien," he said, trying to keep his voice even. "You have to tell me what's going on. What else have you compiled? What has the bop-op told you?"

"Michael, please don't ask me any questions. I'm not feeling—"

"Oh, that's right, you're all messed up from having hugged me," he said angrily.

Pain passed over her face, and he immediately regretted his words. "I feel better," she said. "I feel like a real person. I have something to do. I'm not just a doll."

"You were never just a doll."

"Yes I was. You know the difference between a doll and a real person? It's not what they're made out of. A real person has something she needs to do. A doll just does things to please people, or because she's programmed."

Ransom wondered if you were still a real person if your purpose was injected into you through a burst transmission. Of course, no one's purposes were really their own. Everyone was injected with their purposes by evolution: survive, reproduce, die. Every person alive was burst-operated. "So why do we need a bioinformation transducer?"

She looked up at him gravely with her intoxicating green eyes. "They stay alive by feeding on field potential from people's brains. The ones that found you could have attached themselves to you to feed. The SRS etheric field would put them to sleep, but if you left the SRS or if something happened to jolt them enough, they might wake up."

Fear twisted at his guts. "But . . . but what are they? How does Backward make them do this?"

"They're something called Persistent Inscribed Bioinformation. Backward keeps them away from their terminal boundaries by meme-implantation during nerve-racking. The extreme pain lets them destroy and rebuild the person's mind. And they promise them rewards. Like putting them back into bodies. Backward has probably promised them yours. So we're supposed to find out as soon as we can if they're on you. The machine is a neural signature detector, to make sure you don't have any extra signatures attached to your body."

19

Vivien tinkered with her machine all afternoon, working quickly and efficiently from a blueprint in her titanium-plastic head, connecting the organs' embedded jacks to the solid logic and uncoiling the delicate spaghetti of their starter dendrites until they touched the already mounted organs, then doping them with enzyme factors. Finally, in the late evening, she fiddled with a hard-key remote for a while, then said, "It's ready."

Ransom lay down on the couch, anxiety bunching in his chest.

"Don't worry," she said. "It doesn't hurt."

"It won't fry my brain? This Michael Beach is no endovid."

"It's funny to hear you talk about yourself like that. It's just a passive-field monitor. Your brain just has to sit there, mostly."

He watched her fiddle with the instrument panel. "You're different now. From how you were. More human."

She flushed, and a brilliant smile spread across her face, making her look almost well again.

The smile gave Ransom the courage to pop open the phone port behind his ear and let Vivien gently snap in a jack. He of course had heard about kids plugging into homemade electronics and ending up brain-dead.

"Okay. You have to relax and hold still. But if you start to feel bad, tell me."

"Okay."

Out of the corner of his eye he saw her touch the remote,

and at once he felt a little dizzy. He closed his eyes. His stomach was full of butterflies; the eyeless, lipless faces of the ghosts seemed to fill his mind.

He lay there for a long time listening to the small sounds of Vivien's hands on the remote, gradually relaxing. After a while, without meaning to, he fell asleep.

He dreamed. He was in the living room, watching the young man asleep on the couch, Vivien cross-legged on the floor next to him intent on her instruments. Then he felt himself sag downward, as though the floor had softened and given way, and for a long time he was in a muddle, dizzy, as if he had gone down a drain and was whirling through a pipe of warm, bright, breathable water. Finally he regained his footing. He was standing on a brick terrace at the top of a wooded bluff. Potted geraniums, brilliant scarlet, sat on a low brick wall, their shadows like dark puddles. The sound of a gentle surf came from somewhere close by. A path plunged steeply down the bluff, through a kind of green tunnel among the trees that smelled of damp vegetation and soil. Its soft, loamy sand was cool on his bare feet until it leveled out and he emerged onto a beach; then the sand was hot until he reached the wet beach face. The surf washed tepid around his feet, and calm blue water stretched to the horizon. The wooded bluff curved off in both directions, diminishing in vast perspective until it faded into a haze of distance.

He walked along the beach lost in thought, as on his childhood holidays. On an impulse, he waded out into the gentle, cool water. He could swim out into this cool blue water; he suddenly felt that he could lie and dream in its gentle rocking heart forever—

Then he thought he heard something. It seemed to be a voice, calling to him from up on the bluff, very far away. He turned to look, but nothing was visible except the trees and the gap where the path emerged. Yet the voice vaguely reminded him of something. It came again, still faint, but now more distinct: "Michael!"

A thought came to him. The vision he had seen shaking that man's hand—what was his name, Denmark—had not been Denmark's boundary vision after all, but his own. Shaking hands with Denmark, he had seen a premonition of his own death.

His heart started to pound. What was he doing here? He wasn't ready to die! He had things to do, and Vivien was in the apartment. He ran back across the hot sand, and up the path between the trees—

From the air right in front of his face a loud, jarring voice yelled: "Michael!"

The sky grew dark, or was it his eyes?

He opened them, looking up into Vivien's beautiful green ones. She was bending over him with her hands on his shoulders, and tears were running down her red, terrified face.

His heart was pounding as if he had been holding his breath for a long time. He opened his mouth and took a long, gasping breath.

"Michael! Michael! Oh, Michael!" Vivien climbed on top of him and put her arms around his neck. "Oh, Michael, are you all right? Can you talk? Are you all right, Michael?"

"What?" he asked her. "What happened? Are you okay?"

Instead of answering, she was kissing him, kissing his ears, his eyes, his mouth. He put his arms around her, felt her breasts pressing against him, her heart pounding, her hair brushing his face and neck, smelled the sweet musk of her skin, hot from crying.

"I thought you were gone," she sobbed. "I suddenly thought what it would be like to live without you. Oh, Michael, I don't want to live without you."

"What do you mean? What happened?"

"You stopped breathing. I wasn't paying attention, I was watching the— But then you stopped breathing and you almost died, and I realized—what would I do without you? I'm just a machine— When I saw inside you in the parking lot—when I was inside you—you're warm inside, your blood is warm, and you're *alive,* Michael. I can never have that, never, never."

Feeling the jarring of her heart, a sudden fire flared in him. He took a handful of her thick hair and kissed her, devouring her mouth, ears, and neck. They tumbled from the couch to the floor, his robe coming off; he felt a tug behind his ear—the jack was still plugged in. He yanked it out, and then Vivien had her clothes off, and they were coupled, she crying out and arching in pain or ecstasy. He was dizzy again, with a thick, hot crimson rapture. At the moment of orgasm she shrieked, and then spasm after spasm went through her, diminishing each time as she relaxed beneath him, still gasping. Finally she lay still, her eyes closed. With dismay, Ransom saw that white fluid starting to ooze from her nose and the corners of her mouth and eyes, as it had when they had left Ralph's.

"Vivien? Vivien, are you okay? Jesus, you're malfunctioning . . . your programming . . . we shouldn't have—"

"They're there," she said.

"What?"

She opened her eyes. They were red-rimmed, the pupils dilated. "The ghosts—they're on you. Two neural signatures on top of yours. And they're starting to wake up."

"What? But you said—the bop-op said that the SRS would put them to sleep."

She shook her head, frowning. "I don't know. I don't *know.* Don't ask me, okay? I only know that they're there, and their neural waves are showing a movement toward theta. And

I'm afraid . . . I'm afraid what we just did might have woken them up more."

"Vivien, you're malfunctioning. We need to—"

"Be quiet and listen," she said, and he saw that she was keeping herself together with enormous effort. "I can be repaired. If Backward catches you, no one will ever be able to repair you. You'll end up like them, like the ghosts."

He could feel his previously swollen penis shrinking rapidly, as if trying to hide. "What are we going to do?"

"The machine I made isn't only for measuring. It's a bidirectional transducer."

"An endo rig? But you told me— But it'll kill me. This body isn't endovid. Last time—"

"I couldn't stand it if they caught you, Michael. I couldn't stand it! Do you understand? Do you understand? I couldn't stand it."

"I know, I know," he said, trying to pull her up to sit her on the sofa. He was shaking. "Shh, relax, calm down."

She shook her head, and tears got mixed with the white mucus stuff coming out of her eyes. He could see her trying to control herself, and she stuttered as she spoke. "You're the only one who can do it. You're the only one who has a chance of talking to them, because you're the one whose mind they're attached to. Their boundary images should be hanging around somewhere close to them. You have to get them to cross over. You have to hurry; once they wake up all the way, you won't have much time before Backward tracks them to you. You have to get rid of them before they wake up all the way. You have to talk to them. Persuade them to finish dying."

20

. . . . **He** stood at the top of a wide, empty beach, clouds towering offshore. He leaned against the handrail of a wooden walkway with steps that led down to the sand. Two distant figures up to their knees in the surf seemed to be fishing; other than that, the beach was deserted. Between gusts, the sun on his bare head was like hot lead. Seagulls wheeled high in the air, mewling.

A memory, vague at first, rising as if from a depth—

A beautiful girl. An apartment.

He was Heathcliff Ransom. And he was hunting ghosts.

Fear went through him, and his heart pounded; for a moment he felt that he was both standing up and lying down, and his hands vaguely felt locked together on his chest, though they were hanging by his sides. He rubbed his hands together vigorously to help him concentrate on feeling his astral body, block out his physical body. He took several deep breaths and tried to relax. He had to stay calm; he wasn't lying in a tank of smart fluid feeding trance waves into his brain. The best they had been able to do was the couch, a sensory interruption hypodermic, and of course the home-made, jerry-rigged transducer that Vivien had built out of bioemulator hobby-kit parts. Amazingly, it seemed to be working. Which was also why Michael Beach's non-endovid brain might be fried when—and if—he came out of it.

He was wearing the Dockers and seersucker suit again. He found the sunglasses and fisherman's hat in his pocket and put them on. He looked around, trying to decide what to do next.

So far he guessed he was on the right track; Vivien had tuned the transducer to the stronger of the two neural signatures embedded in his, and that had brought him to the sensorium where he had first picked up Margaret Biel's spoor. It didn't surprise him at all that Margaret Biel's ghost was stronger than Eugene Denmark's.

He turned his head back and forth, but he could smell nothing but warm ocean air. Maybe sleeping ghosts didn't give off a spoor, or maybe it was something to do with not being in an endovid's body.

He followed the walkway inland, to the central island road and sidewalk. He was starting to relax, to feel almost cheerful. The astral world was his home turf; he felt competent and strong here, ready to deal with ghosts and superhuman mutants on a level playing field.

He strode down the sidewalk, passing the beach houses slumbering atop their enormous flood stilts. A sunburned kid rode by on a bicycle and a couple of cars passed. Despite the breeze, he was soon sweating.

A few blocks down, a beach house was under construction, the sound of hammers and the occasional screech of a power saw coming from the skeleton of bare yellow wood, within which he could see shirtless, deeply sunburned men wearing baseball caps and sunglasses moving slowly in the heat. Ransom headed that way: maybe the workers could tell him where to find an old lady with a young scientist, or a beautiful young girl with a young scientist, or two fingerless, skinned, scorched carcasses.

As he got nearer, the workers were no longer in sight. He walked onto the reddish dirt churned with the tracks of construction machines, and then around the side of the house, smelling freshly sawn wood and raw, damp earth.

"Hello?" he called.

Behind the frame of the house, old-fashioned lumber and

cinder blocks were stacked neatly near a large antique table saw and a wheelbarrow with a couple of dusty T-shirts draped over its handles, but there were no people. Lunch hour, Ransom guessed. He took in the quaintness of the scene, wondering at the cost of building a house with bits of cement and wood, and hundreds of hours of labor to fasten them all together. That was how they had done it when he was a kid, though he had never gotten this close to a construction site. His curiosity about men and their work had come at about the same time the murmur of people's thoughts had started to bother him, when his parents had first noticed his aversion to strangers.

He left the lot and started down the sidewalk again. The same shirtless kid in long flowered swim trunks rushed past on his bike, returning from wherever he had gone; Ransom yelled a question to him, but he was already out of earshot in the gusty breeze.

It took Ransom an hour to reach the island's tiny shopping area. By that time he was sure the beach town's emptiness was not an accident. As he had walked, he had seen a few people in the distance—watering a lawn, washing a car, sitting on a porch—but every time he got close they were gone, casually strolling away or moving unhurriedly out of sight as he approached, as if it had nothing to do with him. He had tried following a couple of them, but found the backyards and empty lots where they had seemingly gone empty and quiet. He had rung doorbells and knocked on doors, but no one answered.

After that he wasn't surprised to find that the small grocery store's posted hours included a lunch break, that the tiny Realty company was locked up tight, and that the gift and T-shirt store had a handwritten sign taped to the door saying BACK IN A FEW MINUTES. A car or two passed as he stood on the sidewalk, but the riders didn't look in his direction.

Ransom stood in the shade of a palm and tried to think.

If Vivien's machine had properly honed in on Margaret Biel's neural signature, there must be *something* here that she contributed to the sensorium. If he could find that, he would find her.

He started walking again down the long, long main street that led along the center of the island, leaving the tiny "downtown" behind. And as if called up by his thoughts, one of the first houses he came to seemed out of place, though at the same time strangely familiar. It was tall, narrow, and stuccoed, and was wedged into a small lot between two larger houses. If an architect were told to make a beach house resembling Tomas and Lucia Pagano's Italian villa, it might look like this. Ransom climbed the wooden stairs to the front door. It was unlocked.

He stepped into a large, strongly air-conditioned living room typical of beach house rentals: beige indoor-outdoor carpeting, large, worn couch and easy chairs, steps leading to the upper floor at one end, a large open kitchen with dining table at the other, big picture windows facing the ocean.

The sea, rather. The Mediterranean Sea.

Heart beating fast, he went to the living room window. There was no sign of the wide sand beach. The blue water far below swelled and splashed against the base of rocky cliffs.

He looked wildly around, as if the two ghosts might be hiding behind the furniture or disguising themselves as the tacky sailboat pictures on the walls. And then he realized with another jolt that not all the pictures were of sailboats.

One of them, incongruous in its cheap faux-driftwood frame, showed a vast, beautiful orchard, rising in the distance to the slopes of an impossibly steep mountain that disappeared into mists and clouds.

It was a picture of Margaret Biel's boundary vision.

Ransom was trembling now, and felt unsteady on his feet. He wanted to sit down on the shabby, comfortable-looking couch, but he knew he didn't have time. He scanned the other pictures for something that might correspond to Eugene Denmark's boundary vision, and found it in the kitchen, on the wall directly opposite Margaret Biel's. It was a brightly colored photograph of the Horsehead Nebula, stars roaring in the foreground, and in the background a cloak of gray-brown dust.

Turning back around, Ransom saw something that hadn't been there before. Two cups of tea sat steaming on the glass coffee table, as if the people who had been about to drink them had been sitting on the couch until just a minute ago.

"Hello?" Ransom called, hearing the quaver in his voice.

He looked into the two first-floor bedrooms, then climbed the stairs to the three bedrooms upstairs. The house was empty.

He came back to the living room and lowered himself into the easy chair opposite the cups of tea. Sitting down made him feel better; he closed his eyes, collecting his thoughts, then opened them quickly again when the idea came to him that the cups might disappear if he wasn't watching them. But they were still there, steaming delicately.

He had no idea what to do next. He was obviously closer to the ghosts than he had been out on the street, but unless he could talk to them, get them to hear him, he might as well have stayed back in the apartment and saved Michael Beach's brain cells.

But what would he say to them? If he himself were a ghost, he wondered, if he had managed to retain a vestige of his identity independent of a body, what might convince him to give up the last little bit of life he had left, to gamble that there was something beyond the terminal boundary, and that it was better than what he was leaving behind?

He closed his eyes again and tried to relax, imagine himself talking to them, two horribly mutilated things slumped incongruously on the sofa, soiling it with blood and burned flesh. It isn't natural, he imagined himself saying. When you get to the end of your boundary dream you're supposed to step across to whatever is on the other side; that's part of our natural life as creatures, just like being born or going to sleep at night.

Of course, that was no good. There was a long list of perfectly natural things that had once seemed unnatural: negative numbers, for example, as well as racial intermarriage and reading. A scientist like Denmark and a modern woman like Margaret Biel would never believe that not dying when you could hold on to life was any more unnatural than, say, taking antibiotics to cure an infection.

The question was, what made life worth clinging to no matter what, even life as a ghost—or a man in a stolen body, for that matter? Evolution had programmed humans with a loathing of death, but that was a biological urge associated with the need to maximize reproduction. If the substrate of your consciousness were not a meat creature full of evolutionary tropisms and aversions, would consciousness still seem better than unconsciousness? Without the impersonal biological urges that used you as a disposable tool of species proliferation, would you still choose being over nonbeing?

You no longer have bodies enslaved to evolutionary dictates, he imagined himself saying to the ghosts. So you're free to go.

We don't want to go, said the imaginary mutilated ghosts on the sofa. You can't tell us what we want; we don't care what we *should* want; we know what we *do* want. We want to live. We don't care what we would want if we were different from what we are. We don't care if what we want doesn't make sense, or arose from bodies we no longer have. We want to live, to go on, never die, never cross that boundary. If wanting to live is so senseless, why don't you die instead, and let us take your body?

Their voices seemed to come alive in his mind, as if by

talking to them he had strengthened and clarified his image of them.

Why isn't the astral world full of ghosts, then? Ransom asked. Why does everyone who dies—virtually every single one—step over the boundary? Why don't they cling to an illusion of bodily life? There must be some good in going on, moving on. Do you think you're the only ones who have ever wanted to live?

The ghosts seemed to have no answer to that, but still in his mind they were unmoved.

"There must be something beyond the boundary," he said, and to his own surprise, he said it out loud. But his voice—free of the penumbra of doubt, equivocation, and conditionality that blurs the edges of thoughts—had such a ring of conviction that he felt encouraged, and went on the same way.

"How could something turn into nothing? How could we be here now, but later not be anywhere at all? The laws of conservation that apply to mass/energy and spacetime should also apply to the third fundamental substance that came out of the Big Bang, consciousness/intelligence. How could something as fundamental as self evaporate or vanish? You might as well expect the mass/energy in the universe to suddenly vanish. On this rock of consciousness your world has always rested, and on nothing else; the whole world is and always has been inside consciousness, so how could it be that the world should go on but consciousness end?"

And suddenly he heard them reply, not in his thoughts only, but with his ears, with a physical voice, the voice of the girl Barbara Santangelo, who had become Margaret Biel.

"You can't prove any of that," said Barbara Santangelo's voice, lisping, slurred, and gurgling, but loud and close.

Ransom's eyes flew open and they were there, sitting on the couch, the two skinned, scorched, and amputated hulks. Barbara's voice was slurred because her lips were cut away.

Long experience in the astral helped him stay calm. He guessed that by imagining them and talking to them, he had given them enough energy to wake up. If what the bop-op had told Vivien was true, he had to work fast now, before the mutants learned where he was.

"Margaret Biel," he said a little shakily. "I've wanted to meet you for a very long time."

"Well, what do you think?" The one eye in her horribly mangled face burned with hatred. When she spoke, a spittle of saliva, blood, and white secretion ran through her bared teeth and down her chin. He forced himself to keep looking at the eye. The grotesquely damaged torso of Eugene Denmark slumped inertly next to her; Ransom had no idea whether he could talk or whether he was even aware of what was going on.

"I wish we had met under better circumstances."

"It's your fault we didn't. If you had only minded your own goddamn business—"

"What? You could have gotten away with stealing a girl's body and murdering her boyfriend? Do you really think Backward would have left you alone? That you would have lived happily ever after?"

"It doesn't matter. I'm going to get another new body. You can test your own theory about how wonderful it is to die."

She was talking to distract him, he knew, hold him here until Backward traced him to this sensorium or to the apartment in Montgomery Village. He fought down panic.

"I can't prove any of it," he said slowly. "I can't prove it any more than I can prove that mass/energy is always conserved, but if it's true, then your clinging to this life is just a mistake, a waste of time, like a child refusing to grow up."

"And if it's false, we're clinging to the only thing anywhere that's worth having," Barbara slurped. "We don't want to die. We want you to die instead."

"It's too late. You're already dead."

"The Company will give us new bodies."

"You were already dead before you ever met the Company," Ransom ploughed on. "Your body had already died multiple times while you were alive—every one of your cells died and was replaced, and then its replacement died and was replaced, and over and over, and along the way the structure of your bodies and brains, and the patterns inside them, were destroyed and replaced. Nothing about you hasn't already died and made way for something else, something new; the only difference was that it happened gradually, not suddenly. Even your world died; everything you ever knew vanished and was replaced by something else, time moving forward every second so that the things you knew were dead and gone. That neighborhood you used to live in with the big oaks, and your room when you were a teenager with the Ramones posters; your young, beautiful mother—all gone, passed away long before you ever thought of death."

"How do you know about my room?" Margaret Biel snarled.

"I told you, remember? I followed you when you went into your coma."

"Well, I'll tell *you* something," she rasped, and she was trembling with rage. "My young, beautiful mother, she wasn't so beautiful anymore when she got old, and when she died I looked down into her coffin, and I didn't see anyone that something good had happened to. You know what I saw? A lump of rotting meat, all covered up with lace and makeup. And then they screwed the top down on the coffin and put it in a hole in the ground and covered it with dirt, and that was all."

"She had rotted before that, plenty of times. If you collected together all the sloughed-off skin and organ cells, the displaced bone and blood cells from your mother over the years, even when she was still beautiful, they would have looked a lot worse than what you saw."

"If you're so sure of that, why do *you* want to keep living? That's why you're here, isn't it? To persuade us not to help Backward kill you?"

"*Kill* me? Do you remember what Backward did to *you*? How does that compare to dying?"

For the first time the pure, bitter malevolence seemed to go out of Barbara Santangelo's single eye for a second.

"Do you remember? Do you remember what they did?"

A shudder went through Barbara Santangelo's hulk. "Backward is going to give us new bodies," she hissed. "We have to do what they say."

"If you have a body, they'll be able to nerve-rack you again."

A sudden, horrible shriek made Ransom jump. It was Denmark. His hulk was suddenly quaking and drooling, the muscles behind the burned sockets of his eyes moving horribly.

"Margaret," Ransom said slowly, looking into Barbara Santangelo's one staring eye. "Don't you remember what Backward did to your body? Could you stand to have a body again, knowing what could happen to it?"

She had started to shake, and sticky saliva oozed between her teeth. What sounded like a sob came from her. Denmark was panting fast and whimpering like a dog.

"Hurry," whispered Margaret Biel suddenly from Barbara Santangelo's body. "They're coming. They're almost here."

The suddenness of the change caught Ransom off guard, and for a second he was paralyzed.

"*Help me,*" she hissed urgently.

For the first time, Eugene Denmark spoke, the words from his slashed, toothless mouth almost incomprehensible.

"Help me," he sobbed in a deep, hollow voice, like a soul crying up from Hell. "Help me."

It took Ransom only a second to know what he had to do, and he stood up and reached for the woman's ruined body. But at the touch of it he drew his hand away.

"*Hurry,*" she hissed. "They're here!"

"Hurry," moaned Denmark.

Ransom stooped and gathered the horrible, stinking hulk of Barbara Santangelo's desecrated corpse into his arms. She put the stump of her arm around his neck, like a child. He lifted her, feeling the broken bones and smashed organs inside her grinding and tearing. He realized that he was crying. He carried her over to where the picture of the orchard hung on the living room wall. As they approached, it seemed to change to a window, the grass and leaves stirring in a faint breeze, and he could hear the buzzing of bees and smell the sweetness of the trees.

He pushed the smashed and scorched body through the frame, and suddenly, amazingly, the tormented hulk was gone. A beautiful fifteen-year-old girl with black hair and flashing blue eyes stood in the grass looking at him. Her face was calm but preoccupied, as if she had been interrupted briefly in the middle of something, as if the horror of what had happened to her had been erased, or had never occurred in the first place. She turned away and started to walk gracefully and unhurriedly through the orchard toward the distant mountain. Like someone looking through the wrong end of a telescope that is suddenly extended, he saw her abruptly but smoothly recede from him, the scene getting hazy, the mists around the mountain seeming to fill up the whole orchard and then quickly become opaque, so that instead of the window into Margaret Biel's boundary image, Ransom found himself looking at a framed print of a faux-Impressionist sailboat.

A terrified moan from Denmark made him turn, and at the same moment he heard something else. Heavy footsteps boomed on the wooden steps of the beach house, making the whole structure vibrate on its stilts.

He hadn't been found yet. He could still escape before Backward found him or caught his vector. He closed his eyes and quickly began to move them in the extraction pattern he had arranged with Vivien, but a bubbling shriek shocked him back again.

"Help me!" shrieked Denmark's corpse. "Help me! Help me!"

His cries were so awful that Ransom ran to him, cursing, and picked him up. He was much heavier than the girl. He was putrid, and his burned skin came away where it touched Ransom. Gorge rising and heart pounding blindingly, Ransom struggled into the kitchen, to the nebula picture, which seemed now transparent and alive, though no movement was visible in it. He pushed the trembling hulk of Eugene Denmark through the window; and suddenly the young man he had met at Ransom International floated in front of him, his eyes calm and full of knowledge.

Behind Ransom, the front door slammed open.

Ransom jumped after Denmark, giving himself a tremendous wallop on the head as he made a hole in the tacky seaside print on the kitchen wall. There was a rushing sound behind him—but suddenly the picture in front of him changed again: it was now a bright, living scene, a path down a wooded bluff to a beach—

He jumped into it, but as he did the path disappeared, as if it had only been a decoy to draw him into the black tunnel roaring with chaos into which he now felt himself falling.

21

For a measureless interval he fell through the hell-place of uncreation. Then without warning he seemed to be somewhere again, rolling in sensation as if tumbling in a giant clothes dryer with all the objects in the world—what he would have called chaos before he experienced the real thing in the black tunnel. That slowly cleared, until he felt that he existed separate and apart from everything else, and then that he was lying on something. Was it the beach? He tried to look around, but could perceive nothing but a staticky roar that seemed to be all around him.

His effort to see where he was seemed to focus the roaring: it was sharper now, red and insistent, and it came in waves. Then his perceptions seemed to separate, the roaring going to his ears, the red light to his eyes, a choking feeling to his throat. Something sharp and white pierced his head, and a terrible freezing coldness opened around him.

He seemed to have been dumped naked on a glaring white glacier, splinters of ice digging into him.

A ringing garble suddenly cleared into a voice: "—reflux. Give me the suction, please. Heath? Heath, are you all right? Where's the transdermal? Can you hurry it up, please, he's decompensating—"

Something was pulling at him, making a noise. Pulling at his mouth and throat, sucking something out of his mouth. He tasted bile. The suction tube they used if the endovid vomited on re-entry.

"Hold on, Heath, we'll have the shot in a second."

The voice was familiar, but from the distant past, another life. He tried to remember it. Somebody put something over his face. He felt again that he was lying on something, his hands touching it. And there were more sounds: a second voice, light and bell-like; the rustle of movement; and in the background a klaxon blaring. All familiar, but from so long ago—

"Okay, Heath, here's the shot."

Something stung his arm.

Nothing happened for a minute, but then he noticed that he was starting to feel better, and then suddenly much better. The deep confusion was receding, and he felt that he might be moving his fingers.

Then a voice—the light, bell-like one—seeming very close, almost touching him, said, "Are you back?"

He couldn't see who it was, but then he realized that his eyes were closed. It seemed to take several minutes to open them; they were sticky and fiercely tired. Once open, they were blurry and blinded, and a glaring light hurt them. Around him shapes were moving and low voices talking like doctors and nurses in an operating theater, and he could feel hands touching him gently, examining him, fastening things to him.

Gradually his eyes cleared until he could see that he was lying in a large, white room full of machinery, and leaning over him was the tear-stained face of a beautiful girl. A familiar beautiful girl. She smiled at him through her tears.

"Heath?" she said gently. "Heath, it's Anna. Are you okay? Are you back?"

He got his mouth and throat working. His voice was dry and muffled, like the voice of a corpse. "Anna? Where's Vivien?"

"Who?"

"What— Where am I?"

Another familiar face swam into view above him, dark,

with lank black hair. "He's disoriented," it murmured to the girl Anna. "Give him a few minutes. It's not serious." Then the dark man addressed him. "Heath, you just had an emergency extraction. Your vitals got out of spec and we pulled you. Very sorry, but you were on your way to the drain. Real emergency stuff, like on TV." He grinned.

An enormous realization hit Ransom. "Arjun?"

The grin widened even more. "Yeah, it's Arjun. Are you back? You scared us, dude."

Ransom turned his astonished eyes to the female face. "Anna?"

"Yes, Heath, yes, it's Anna," she said, fresh tears spilling out of her eyes.

He was lying under a light blanket on a gurney; medical machines surrounded him. He was wearing an oxygen mask, which was why his voice sounded weird. He tried to pull it off, his hand weak and trembling. Arjun gently pushed the hand away. "Leave that on for a minute," he said. "We can hear you."

Ransom tried to gather his whirling thoughts. "What happened?"

"Like I said. You were about twelve hours in, and suddenly all hell broke loose. There was a discontinuity in your readings, like you suddenly turned into somebody else. And this person was dying. Weird. Lucky you had your crack team watching over you."

In the background behind Arjun and Anna, Heath could see another man—Bobby Mandelson, he realized suddenly—grinning widely.

The puzzle pieces dovetailed perfectly, but the picture was something impossible. He tried vainly to rearrange them, but they stuck tight.

"What job?" he asked.

"Say again?" asked Arjun.

Ransom got up on his elbows now, and pulled the oxygen mask down off his face. His voice was stronger, and he wasn't trembling so much. "What job was I on?"

"Heath, you need to rest. You'll be well enough tomorrow to—"

"Arjun, what job?"

"Merrivale. Remember? Expedited. The old guy and his wife who—"

Ransom thought furiously, his mind recoiling from the ideas that suddenly teemed around him. It couldn't be, but if it was—

"Okay, listen everybody," he said, and his voice was shaking again. "I need everyone to get into the safe room right now. Right now."

Arjun and Anna looked down at him helplessly.

"Heath—" Anna started tenderly.

"Heath, you're disoriented," said Arjun. "Once you get some sleep—"

"Get everyone together, and get them into the safe room. That's an order, or you're fired, goddamn it. And listen, no electronics—you tell everyone verbally, and push them in there if you have to." Burning with adrenaline, he sat up, threw off his cover, and started fumbling with the medical wires and tubes attached to him.

"Heath," Arjun started, trying to grab Ransom's hands. Ransom threw his hands off furiously, then controlled himself with a powerful effort. "You have to trust me," he said to the astonished faces around him. "If you don't trust me, humor me. I . . . I got some View when I was in just now, and we're all in danger. Bad danger. So get everyone in the safe room, *now*! Anna, Charles, run and tell everyone. Arjun, you help me." He slid weakly off the stretcher. "Go!"

As if suddenly released from a paralysis, everyone except Arjun rushed from the room.

The nearest safe-room entrance was only halfway down the basement hall from the Viewing room, but Ransom was so weak that by the time Arjun had helped him to it, coded the hidden panel, and shuffled him down the narrow concrete hall to the central bunker, the last of his employees were already filing in, the blast doors secured behind them. Ransom felt faint. Arjun helped him to a chair, and he sat down heavily. When his head had cleared enough, he looked up at the half dozen people standing around him, and realized that the anxiety in their faces was for him. Everyone was looking at him as you might look at your boss if he went crazy and ordered you into the company safe room for no reason. A sudden rush of gratitude and affection went through him: even thinking he was crazy, his employees—his *friends*—were doing this for him, to avoid upsetting him or hurting his feelings.

In spite of everything, he grinned. "Is this everyone? Doors all shut? Okay. System, give me a phone, secure line."

The phone appeared in the air in front of him. He said: "John McMillan."

After a few seconds, his security consultant's face appeared in the small projection: "Sorry, Heath, I can't take your call right now. I'll get back to you, or if you prefer you can leave a message."

Ransom spoke the code known only to himself and McMillan—or so he hoped: "Hey, cowboy, how's tricks? You want to get lunch tomorrow? Call me."

He hung up, finally allowing himself to breathe. He felt dizzy again, and put his head in his hands. If he was wrong about this, if he really was just disoriented, he was going to look like an idiot. But if he was right—

"Heath," Arjun said gently. "What's it all about?"

"I think . . . I think something very strange just happened," Ransom said. "I think I either just saw the future or—"

"Or?"

"Or I was there."

Arjun and Anna exchanged a worried glance.

"What if the etheric world isn't just a realistic skin your mind pulls over an abstract information field," Ransom said. "What if it's really a . . . a *place* your mind goes when you View. And what if a projector has an accident, say, and dies while his consciousness is there—but then his consciousness, instead of going back to his dead body, goes to the body he had in an earlier projection?

"It sounds crazy. But in the astral world the time difference might not mean anything. If the projector's consciousness was disconnected from one of the bodies—by its death, for example—the consciousness might be drawn back to the other one. Even if that other projection was earlier in time."

"Heath—" Arjun started gently.

A flash came from one of the security screens. For a second it looked like the screen had malfunctioned, but then the static cleared to show two figures standing just inside the kitchen door. Huge figures in combat armor, their faces hidden by battle masks.

There were sudden intakes of breath around Ransom. Despite the shot Arjun had given him, he could feel the spike in his employees' field amplitudes.

With another flash the huge figures were no longer in the kitchen. A blurred shape on another screen rushed down a long back hall; the other was suddenly at the top of the second floor stairs.

Anna Heatherstone, standing near Heath, put her hands on his shoulder, eyes riveted to the screens. He could feel her wordless terror.

At that moment the front-hall screen showed the front door soundlessly explode and a dozen black-suited paramilitary soldiers rushing through the clearing smoke, bristling with weapons. One of the outdoor cameras was showing clouds of dust and whipping shrubs as several helicopter gunships landed in the grounds.

The kitchen and back hall were suddenly also full of silently running black figures.

Everything was over in thirty seconds. Half the screens in the safe room showed bright, well-furnished rooms full of tranquil emptiness; the other half were a chaos of smoke, flame, laser bursts, and the roaring of explosives.

McMillan made them wait forty minutes for a full area clearance before he would open the safe room. Finally, the front hall entrance rolled back, admitting wisps of smoke, two paramilitary soldiers, and McMillan in a kilt, holding a machine-pistol in each hand.

"You're kidding," said Ransom, taken aback in spite of the myriad of strange things that had happened.

"It's my people's war garb," McMillan said defensively. Then he grinned. "How was our time?"

"In spec. Four and a half minutes by my count," said Ransom. He shook McMillan's hard, calloused hand, but stayed sitting. He still felt dizzy.

"Four minutes twenty-one seconds," McMillan corrected him. "Try finding a security firm that can get you a squadron in that time." Having allowed himself this moment of self-congratulation, he looked worried. "One of them got away. Heath, what the hell kind of things are those? Who have you been pissing off?"

"You actually *caught* one?"

"Hell yes, we caught one. The wonder of it is that we didn't have to scrape him off the walls, considering what we hit him with. We have enough drugs in him now to keep an elephant down. What do we do with him? I don't want the responsibility. Even having custody of a monster like that is probably illegal. What do we do next?"

When Ransom, who had been thinking furiously, answered him, everyone looked dismayed.

22

In the astral plane, the ground underneath Ransom International headquarters was damp and smelled strongly of earth, but glowed faintly so that he could see its dark brown color all around him. Hiding there, it was easy to imagine you had been buried, and for an uncomfortable moment Ransom wondered whether he could have actually died somehow without knowing it, and been interred. It seemed no more impossible than anything else that had happened. Instead of lying in his View tank right now—as he had insisted on doing against Arjun's advice—maybe he had died while on the Merrivale projection, and everything else had been some bizarre kind of terminal dream, and now he had woken up dead.

On the other hand, if you assumed that what had happened was real, then he and everyone associated with Ransom International were in danger. The captured mutant—huge, gray, and lizard-skinned—lay manacled in the safe room under heavy guard and sedation, and two of McMillan's paramilitary personnel were assigned to each Ransom International employee, including himself. But who knew what Backward might be able to pull off to rescue their comrade? He was sure they would try: they had to know that USAdmin would make it reveal their location and everything else it knew if they got hold of it.

His determination to hide had created this underground sensorium: his unconscious evidently imagined a covert astral sortie by Backward as a tunneling operation leading to his basement. And now a subtle change in the "light" caught his attention. He held perfectly still, even holding his breath; he rarely hid in the astral, but he knew that it was done like everything else there—by intention.

The illumination in the dirt was intensifying in one direction, as if something bright enough to shine right through the ground was approaching. As Ransom watched, it silently increased until it passed right next to him, only a few centimeters of dirt seeming to separate him from a moving bluish orb.

The glow receded, now moving upward.

He waited.

A few minutes later it was approaching again, retracing its path; but now more slowly and with a dark mass at its center. As the light passed his hiding place this time, Ransom felt an intense physical vibration, the same vibration he had felt around the terrible black hole in Margaret Biel's orchard image, which seemed to distort the very fabric of the sensorium, as if moving a physical body through the astral plane took an immense amount of energy.

The idea of jumping into the awful chaos place again filled him with terror, but he had to take the chance. Either track Backward to its lair, or wait for it to come after him and his friends again.

When the glow had receded almost to nothing, Ransom pushed on the wall of the passage he felt had been hollowed out by the light. It gave way and he pitched forward, cringing with fear. But after a moment he realized that he wasn't in the hell place. He was in a tunnel a meter in diameter, opening into blackness in two directions. He began to crawl in the direction the light had receded.

Almost at once light bloomed in front of him—not the intense bluish glow of the tunneling light, but broad daylight, blinding after the dimness "underground." It took a minute for his eyes to adjust, and once they did he realized that he was high up in the air, looking out the end of a dark tunnel, a hole hundreds of meters up, like the one he had come out of above the Italian coast. But here he looked down at a city—at a warehouse in a rundown industrial neighborhood.

Then a hand sprouted from the top of the warehouse. It was as if a giant had pushed its gray, lizard-like hand up through the metal roof; it shot toward Ransom like scaly gray lightning, so that before he could move his eyes in his extraction pattern it had caught him in a bone-crushing grip and was dragging him downward. He passed through the warehouse roof without resistance, and then he was in the middle of a terrifying scene.

Huge lizard-dogs with distorted human faces and long razor teeth leaped on him, snarling and slavering, tearing his clothes and snapping at his flesh, their red eyes insane with rage. Ransom fell on his face and curled into a ball, though he knew it was an astral appearance meant to make him forget his extraction code—or even that he could extract at all. He knew that as soon as he started to get his equilibrium, the dogs would change to something different and equally shocking, to keep him off balance. It was the only way an experienced endovid could be trapped in the astral.

But suddenly the dogs stopped snarling, and there was silence.

Still curled up, eyes closed tight, Ransom began his extraction sequence. He hadn't gotten enough information to locate Backward, but if they were using psychoshock he needed to pull out before he forgot who and where he was.

Someone not very far off cleared his throat politely, and said in a quiet, even voice: "If it's convenient, Mr. Ransom, I would like to talk to you before you withdraw your projection. I give you my word that I won't try to keep you here against your will, or harm you in any way."

"Stop your shock images."

"You have my deepest apologies for the actions of my contractors, which were undertaken without my knowledge. Evidently they panicked trying to cover up an earlier error. I understand that they actually tried to kill you and your employees. Thank goodness you were able to prevent this crime. However, I can assure you that you and your associates will have nothing to fear from them in the future, and that I am ready to respond to any reasonable demand for damages."

Ransom's eyes had involuntarily opened wide with terror. "My contractors," the voice had said.

"I note your parasomatic distress, Mr. Ransom," the voice said. "I repeat that you are free to go. I request the favor of an interview, but we can meet later or communicate by telephone if you prefer. In any case, I am pleased to meet you. They call me Amphibian."

Ransom had set up his extraction sequence so that one more flick of his eyes would have him out. He uncurled slowly. He was in a dark place, all black background except that his body was illuminated, and so was the body of someone who sat a little distance away. Ransom stood up. The man nodded to him and smiled slightly. He was a small, slight, middle-aged man wearing black slacks and a black turtleneck. He looked more like a college professor than a ruthless superhuman entity.

"You—" Ransom began to accuse him, but then he was unsure how to continue. Most of the terrible things he knew about Amphibian had not happened yet, and perhaps would never happen now. "You sent those . . . monsters to kill me and everyone at my house."

Amphibian shook his head regretfully. "Unfortunately, I knew nothing about it. I evidently trusted them too far, mistaking their abilities for good judgment. I deemed it safe to put most of my attentional capacity elsewhere. Trying to cover up one mistake, they made an even worse one, which, when it also blew up in their faces, made everything painfully obvious. I give you my word that nothing like it will happen again."

"Your *word*," Ransom spat. "You're a devil."

"I am very, very sorry," said Amphibian. "Thank heavens no one was hurt. But as I have said, if there is any recompense I can make—"

"No, not that. Murder, torture, fraud."

The mild college professor looked perplexed. "I'm afraid I don't understand."

"Take a look at the site called 'Talkative Customers.'"

"I'm sorry," said Amphibian slowly. "But I'm not familiar with the site you—" His small, intelligent features cleared, as if he had just understood something. "Ah. The USAdmin agent who visited you. He fed you this misinformation."

"No USAdmin agent visited me."

"The name he gave you, I believe, was Eugene Denmark. We have been monitoring him for some time. He is one of a team of agents tasked with destroying my operation."

Ransom wondered for a second if that could be true. "So you nerve-racked him to death."

Amphibian looked puzzled again. "Forgive me, Mr. Ransom, but I am at a loss. Is Denmark dead? I would have been informed of such a development, I believe."

It occurred to Ransom again that what he had seen had been in the future, and a future in which he had fallen through a hole in the etheric fabric to a town in Italy instead of extracting prematurely from the Merrivale job, setting off a chain of events that might not happen now. So in this world, Eugene Denmark might still be alive.

Amphibian had been looking at him blankly, but animation now returned to him. "I have just checked on Mr. Denmark, and he is alive and well. Still plotting my downfall." He smiled slightly.

"I know what you're capable of."

"I think we need to start over again, at square one," said Amphibian. "Are you willing to at least listen to my side of the story?"

"Give me the address of the warehouse I tracked Backward to, and I'll listen."

"11330 Ironwood Drive, Chicago, Illinois," Amphibian answered promptly. "You might have noticed the old rail yard behind it?"

Yes, that had been it, the historic Chicago rail yard, he realized. But if Amphibian had told the truth, it must mean he wouldn't be getting out of here alive to tell the world. In sudden fear he poised his eyes to complete the extraction code.

"You can leave if you want," said Amphibian quickly. "But I would still like to explain myself to you sometime."

"Go ahead. Explain." A single flick of his eyes would get him out. He steadied himself.

"I am an autonomous, distributed AI learning net created and released secretly into the web several years ago by a group of corporate sponsors, who afterward for security reasons cut off all contact with me. My sole objective is the weakening, and if possible, destruction of USAdmin.

"I could tell you that my sponsors were philanthropists determined to reduce the feudal power of a corrupt and increasingly totalitarian overlord, and indeed that will be the result if I succeed. However, they could not have afforded the enormous R and D needed to develop me for purely charitable purposes. To put it bluntly, USAdmin is a business competitor, and one with unfair advantages. Laws dating from a time when it was a commerce-neutral governance-oriented entity allow it to use espionage, military, and penal means that are barred to any other corporation. Using these means, it has made huge inroads into the technology, entertainment, and military sectors of my sponsors' portfolios."

"So it's just business. Murder, torture, fraud in the service of commerce."

"My instructions are to accomplish my objectives with an absolute minimum of violence," Amphibian said. "Violence is bad business: it draws attention to things that should be secret, and turns informed sentiment against the perpetrator. That's why I have been forced to terminate Backward. Despite their undoubted technical competence, their predisposition to violence ended up making them a net liability. Hiring them was a calculated risk, and sometimes even the best calculated risks fall on the downside."

"Even if I believed everything you're saying, I'd still be against you. USAdmin is bad and getting worse, but at least there are still some restraints on its actions. You operate completely in the shadows, so no one knows when you murder or torture."

"You have evidently been convinced of the charges US-Admin uses to discredit me," said Amphibian. "I give you my word that the killings we have carried out have been unavoidable, justified, and humane. The attack on your company was an aberration for which I am eager to pay reparations, if you will accept them. And we have never, ever nerve-racked anyone, though if Backward did so in secret from me—"

Ransom began to move his eyes.

"It is sometimes a salutary exercise," said Amphibian quickly, "to imagine that you are wrong about something of which you have no doubt. Even about the most seemingly basic and obvious thing. That everything you think you know is a covering for something else, and even the most clear-cut facts are often closer than you think to—"

Ransom flicked his eyes and Amphibian's voice faded away.

He lay on his back, choking as the smart liquid withdrew from his lungs. He opened his eyes just as the last of it ran out of his mouth, taking a huge, sobbing breath like a drowning man coming to the surface. The dim red light inside the tank showed the liquid withdrawing not so much like water as like a transparent, sinuous creature slithering away into the pipes where it lived. The alert pinged, the seal cracked to let in blinding light, and the tank rotated so that he stood almost upright in the raw, cold air of the Viewing room. Arjun and Haley helped him out onto the gurney. Arjun was rapidly and expertly checking his vitals when Ransom rasped, "System, get me a satellite visual of Chicago."

A holoscreen appeared in the air, the real-time feed sweeping from its default location five kilometers directly above Ransom International to the same height over Chicago.

"Ironwood Street or Drive, whatever," said Ransom. "11330 Ironwood."

The picture telescoped, giving him the dizzy feeling of swooping down to earth. He saw the rail yards. "Hold that." The descent stopped. "Rotate view."

The picture swung around until he recognized almost the exact view he had seen from his astral hole in the sky. Except now something was happening down there.

"Go down slowly." The picture descended, focusing on the warehouse from which only a short while ago the etheric hand had come up and snatched him. Something else was coming out of it now—fire and smoke. Robot fire helicopters hovered around it spewing foam into an intense blaze in the wreckage of the place.

"News on that address," said Ransom.

A smaller holoscreen popped up, showing the burning

warehouse from a news helicopter that Ransom's satellite view showed circling the scene. The somber voiceover was saying, "—massive explosion just twenty-six minutes ago followed by an intense blaze that Brinks detectives on the scene describe as probable arson. And we are now getting word that fire drones managing to penetrate the wreckage have sent back technical data on the bodies of an unidentified mutant strain that Brinks analysts are preliminarily classifying as Chimera level—"

"Whoa," said Arjun. "Chimera" was the catchall term for mutants even more divergent than Class 3, which were as rare and illegal as nuclear bombs.

So perhaps Amphibian had told the truth about "terminating" Backward. What did that mean? Might he have also been telling the truth about other things?

The next day, thirty-six hours to the minute from the time Ransom had hustled the Merrivales out of his office, John Merrivale was on the phone, a pipe smoking in the corner of his mouth.

"Did you have any success?" Ransom could feel the desperation under his casual tone.

"I'm terribly sorry, Mr. Merrivale."

Merrivale nodded slowly. Then a crack appeared in his calm. "I just don't know what we're going to do," he quavered.

At least you're alive, Ransom thought. At least Backward didn't have time to kill you in a fake automobile accident before Amphibian blew them up.

23

For the second time in his life, Ransom had to get used to being someone else—or to being himself again after being someone else. It wasn't as bad this time, of course, because ninety-eight percent of his memories matched this body, and only two percent were foreign; last time the ratio had been reversed. But it had still shaken him up, especially because he still didn't know how much of his time as Michael Beach had been real.

He would gladly have handed himself over to the doctors and psych-techs, except that if his experiences *had* been real he couldn't afford to be drugged or electrostimulated to any satisfactory extent. If Amphibian had lied to him, he was still a danger; if he had told the truth, USAdmin might be the danger. For now, McMillan's people skulked in every out-of-the-way corner of RI's grounds, and Ransom's employees had temporarily moved into the mansion, but this arrangement couldn't last. Aside from people wanting to live in their own houses, the hopped-up vigilance of McMillian's guards invaded Ransom's brain like an alarm constantly ringing in the background, and would get worse when he had to get off the neuroleptic drip currently taking the edge off his endovoyance.

But at least security was something you could do something about. His other problem wasn't.

He had left Vivien alone.

He had died in the other future and left her in the Montgomery Village apartment alone, waiting for Backward to arrive. He could only imagine her despair at losing him, alone in a world she only half understood, with a purpose that had failed. He only hoped she had the presence of mind to run when the body on the couch stopped breathing. She could probably turn off her pain receptors, but what if Backward could turn them back on? What about psychological tortures that could destroy the mind of an innocent like her? In nightmares he heard Vivien screaming with pain and terror.

There was only one thing he could possibly do, though it wouldn't really help. He called McMillan. "I need to go to Wilmington, North Carolina."

"Why?" asked McMillan irritably. Not only was it the middle of the night, but McMillan had been losing sleep too, over a task that Ransom was now proposing to make even harder.

"I need to see someone down there."

It would also be a test of whether the other future had been real or not. He thought, if there was no such person as a Ralph Mullins living in Wilmington with a girlfriend android named Vivien, then what he had undergone had doubtless been an astral appearance; if Ralph and Vivien actually existed, then it was at least possible that his experiences had been real, too.

They drove him to Wilmington in a combat vehicle that looked like one of the more common minivan models, containing a fake family of two apparent teenagers and their middle-aged parents, all paramilitary operatives looking slightly comical in their flowered shirts and holiday shorts. The "entertainment center" in the van's rear was a command post where the ersatz teenage boys monitored their stratocopter escort and the other camouflaged vehicles McMillan had pacing them.

One side effect of Ransom's neuroleptic brain-drip was

that he couldn't get too upset about what seemed an enormous exercise in security overkill. McMillan had been strongly spooked by the Backward mutants, and of course Ransom couldn't prove that all of them were dead, or that Amphibian or USAdmin didn't have other equally dangerous agents. In the end only Ransom's approval of these fabulously expensive precautions had persuaded McMillan to undertake the trip at all. Now, as they rushed over the potholes of US 85 on their cushion of air, McMillan sat across from Ransom, fiddling petulantly with his battlespace spectacles and poring over the intel his people had dug up on Ralph Mullins. Ralph existed, it turned out, but there was no sign of a value-chain business that he ran from his basement.

They arrived in Wilmington in the late afternoon. Ransom and McMillan shifted to the front seats, and the minivan drove at a casual pace to the Palm Grove Private Community. As Ralph's ivy-grown stone wall and front gate came in sight, tranquil and serene, feelings of homesickness and nervousness penetrated Ransom's heavy calm—nervousness not because he might be killed in the next few minutes, but because he was about to meet Vivien again for the first time.

The minivan eased up to Ralph's gate, and McMillan rolled down his window as the security screen lit up.

"John McMillan and Heathcliff Ransom to see Mr. Mullins." Ransom leaned forward in the passenger seat so that the machine could read his retinas as well as McMillan's. The operatives in the back sat still and tense, hands near the luggage compartments where their weapons were stashed.

There was a short wait, and then the security screen's face said: "What is the purpose of your visit, please?"

"It's in relation to Mr. Mullins's domestic android, designated 'Vivien,' " said McMillan.

Another short pause. "Please dismount and remove your vehicle a minimum of one hundred meters from the gate. It must remain at that distance for the duration of your visit. No weapons or recordation are permitted on the grounds."

McMillan nodded to the operatives, and he and Ransom got out into the pleasantly cool autumn air. The van backed up and parked half a block away. McMillan and Ransom stood on the sidewalk for several minutes, and then the heavy metal gate clicked and slid aside.

McMillan preceded Ransom through the gate, his eyes flicking around behind his battlespace specs, which looked like ordinary old-fashioned eyeglasses. The gate slid shut behind them. Without the value-chain business, what was the purpose of all this security? Ransom wondered as he and McMillan walked along the familiar flagstone path toward the side door of the house.

Despite his brain-drip, a sudden spike in the field amplitude around them registered clearly on Ransom. "We're about to get jumped," he told McMillan over their encrypted private channel.

Half a dozen heavily armed battle suits launched out from behind hedges and trees, their screaming audial weapons making Ransom and McMillan fall to the ground in agony. A second later a dozen of McMillan's suits rocketed over the garden wall and collided with the attackers, and, through the strange dreaminess of his neuroleptics, Ransom saw nets, smoke, and decoy chaff boil through the roaring interference patterns of sound and countersound weapons as attackers and defenders grappled like metal titans.

"You are being targeted by automated weapons systems," a voice boomed out over the grounds, and Ransom saw the wide multi-barrels of firing turrets rise from the turf—guns he must have unsuspectingly mowed over a hundred times, he realized. "This is a USAdmin facility, and your possession of weapons is a serious felony. Disarm or you will be summarily executed in five seconds—four, three . . ."

With a rising roar, two of McMillan's armored stratocopters plummeted from the sky like crashing space junk that happened to be bristling with anti-armor guns, pulling up fifty meters above the villa, red lasers from their targeting systems speckling the landscape.

Ransom had closed his eyes in anticipation of Armageddon when a reedy, barely audible voice cried: "Whoa, whoa, whoa, let's all cool down here for a second!"

Looking up again, Ransom saw a small, thin figure in shorts and a loud Hawaiian shirt trotting down the front walk, holding his hands up as if to dispel bullets and missiles.

"Ralph!" Ransom yelled.

"Yo!" Ralph looked around for whoever had called his name.

"We'll stand down, Ralph! You stand down and we'll stand down!"

"Stand down, all USAdmin personnel and systems!" Ralph yelled promptly.

"McMillan, stand down!" yelled McMillan, the order projecting through his nerve mike as well.

The battle suits that had managed to stay upright lowered their weapons, and the weapons turrets withdrew back into the turf.

"Can you withdraw your aircraft?" yelled Ralph.

McMillan murmured something, and the helicopters pulled slowly upward until the thrum of their rotors faded into the deepening blue of the evening sky.

"Okay," Ralph said, coming farther along the walk. "You can get up now; everything's cool. Why did you bring the army with you? Don't you know it's illegal to attack a US-Admin facility?"

Ransom and McMillan got up. Despite his drugs, Ransom's legs and belly were trembling violently. "Ralph, I . . .

I didn't know this was a USAdmin facility," he said shakily. "It wasn't when—"

"How do you know my name?" asked Ralph, looking into Ransom's face curiously. "How did you know to come see me?" Then, to the two dozen armed men all around them, "Let's everybody turn off their weapons, okay?" Against the descending whine of high-energy systems depotentiating, he said to McMillan and Ransom, "Could I get you to send your ops outside? Armed civilians aren't supposed to be on USAdmin property. They can stay sharp on their pogo sticks out there if they want."

"Can we get some ID?" said McMillan. "This place looks like a private house to me." He held up an ID coin and Ralph thumbprinted it. McMillan listened to his electronics for a few seconds, then nodded. The McMillan operatives began to file out of the gate, which had slid open for them.

Ralph was studying Ransom curiously. "You're the guy who got attacked by those mutants in Washington. I checked on you just now when my security scanned your eye."

"Yes." Everything suddenly seemed unsteady, as if the world had come apart, breaking into separate pieces that moved and shifted under him, like chunks of ice in a freezing ocean. The neuroleptics, which had been calming him, now made him feel nauseated.

"Do you want to come inside? I guess you wanted to talk to me."

The opposing armies had melted away, and the cool blue dusk seemed to suddenly open out around them in an opulent quiet, a sweet smell coming over the hedges from the rose garden. He felt perfectly at home here, Ransom realized: every square meter of this place was familiar from the six months he had worked here. Not "had" worked here, he reminded himself; in the alternate future, as far as he could figure, he would just now be arriving in Italy. He noticed with disapproval that that the hedges looked like they had been trimmed by autonomic systems without human supervision.

The front door of the house clicked open and Ralph led them into the small back sitting room, whose picture windows overlooked a stone terrace and the grounds falling gently away beyond. Chinese lanterns glowed in the grounds just as they had in the evenings when Ransom had lived here in the future. They sat down. The hazy neural-field impressions penetrating Ransom's brain drip seemed to suggest that no one in the vicinity was planning to kill them in the immediate future.

"I hope you don't mind if I get one of my people in here to listen in on this? He's the guy who takes care of Vivien, so I'll have him bring her, too." He said to the air, "System, ask Guillam to bring Vivien in here." Then he looked at Ransom curiously again. "How did you know about Vivien?"

"If you read up on me, you know I'm an endovid investigator."

"Right."

"I had a recent projection that was . . . unusual. I saw Vivien in it."

Ralph grinned. "And you liked what you saw?"

"Actually, I got to know her quite well."

"Can you do that?"

"Not normally. As I said, this was an unusual projection."

"I noticed you yelled my name outside, too."

"I got to know you, too."

"Really," said Ralph, taken aback, and then two people came into the room.

One was Vivien, wearing jeans and a lilac sweater. Ransom stood up, and for a moment he couldn't see anything else. When he realized that Ralph was making introductions, and he finally turned to the young man who had accompanied Vivien, he was still so distracted that at first he didn't recognize him. "Heathcliff Ransom, meet Peter Guillam, my assistant. And this, of course, is the lovely Vivien." Ralph held out his hand to her and she went over to him shyly and sat next to him on the couch, amazingly beautiful in her grave, blank way.

Then Ransom recognized Peter Guillam.

Guillam was the handsome, buff surfer kid who had beaten up Michael Beach, and whom Vivien had thrown against the wall in the beachfront ice-cream parlor.

The pieces of the world that had come apart a few minutes ago were flying up and whirling around Ransom.

"Heath? Everything okay?" Ralph asked. Ransom nodded, unable to speak.

"I'm guessing you met Pete in your projection, too," Ralph said. When Guillam looked quizzical, Ralph told him, "Heath recently had a projection where he gathered some information about us, and he was kind enough to come around to tell us about it."

Ransom shook the young man's stone-hard hand. Everyone sat down.

"Well," said Ralph heartily, as if they were having a social visit, "this is better than shooting at each other, right? What else can you tell me about your projection experience? And why you wanted to talk to me about Vivien? And incidentally, why you decided to invade rather than just come and ring the doorbell?"

"It's a good thing we did," McMillan took time out from conferring over his covert link to snap at Ralph. "Or you might be scraping us off the sidewalk now."

"I apologize about the hospitality," said Ralph. "But you didn't give me much time to think. I had time to find out that you were the guys who had tangled with the mutants in

Washington, so I thought I'd rather be safe than sorry. I really apologize."

Ransom had been thinking furiously. "Can you tell me," he asked Ralph, "what you do here? At this facility?"

"Well, I guess we kind of gave away that we're a USAdmin facility."

"What kind of facility?"

Ralph studied him. "Heath, can we agree to an exchange of information? Share and share alike? I'm burning up with curiosity about what you know about us, how you came to have a projection where you picked up so much information about us, why you got attacked by those mutants, that kind of thing. Okay?"

Ransom nodded.

"Okay, I can tell you that this is a covert USAdmin facility where we focus on combating a certain organization. One that I wonder if you know anything about."

The whirling world-pieces were falling back to earth and settling into a new pattern. A strange and unwelcome pattern.

"You mean Backward? Amphibian?"

Ralph and Guillam were staring at him tensely, hanging on his words.

"You said 'Amphibian,'" said Ralph slowly. "Can you tell me what you know about this 'Amphibian'?"

"He's an AI programmed to attack USAdmin interests."

Ralph and Guillam exchanged a glance.

"And you saw this in your projection, too?"

"In a related projection, yes."

"Heath," said Ralph slowly and cautiously, as if speaking too suddenly might scare him away, "how did you come to have a projection where you learned all this?"

"I'll explain," said Ransom. "But first can you tell me exactly what Vivien and Mr. Guillam do for you?"

Ralph's eyes became abstracted. Ransom could see his

throat twitch slightly as he used his nerve mike, his inexpert virtual vocalizations erupting into precursors of actual speech movements.

"He's on an encrypted channel, so I can't tell what he's saying. My people can be here in thirty seconds if I give the signal," McMillan said over Ransom's own encrypted link. Unlike Ralph, McMillan's muscles didn't move and his eyes didn't look off into space when he vocalized.

"Hold off," Ransom answered. "He's not the aggressive type."

"It may not be up to him," said McMillan.

Finally Ralph nodded, and his eyes came back. He said to Ransom, "Sorry. I needed to get clearance. USAdmin thinks we can help each other. Mutual trust and brotherhood." He grinned. "After all, we're both being attacked by the same organization. So what I would like to know is—"

"Can you answer my question first, please? What are Vivien's and Mr. Guillam's duties?"

"Vivien and Pete are my honeypot team."

"Which is what?"

"When I want to get someone to work with us, sometimes without actually knowing it, I sic Vivien or Pete or both on them. They're both pretty irresistible, if you can get them close to a subject in some plausible way. For example, Pete might pretend to be gutting Vivien for parts just as the subject is passing by, so he can save her. Are you okay, Heath?"

"So if I, say—if you wanted someone to do something, manipulate them, for example, if you wanted to make someone a stalking horse for . . . for this Amphibian entity, say, you might get him together with Vivien, and let him fall in love with her, and then have her lead him by the nose—"

"Exactly." Ralph smiled and put his arm around Vivien's shoulder and squeezed her affectionately. "You're completely adorable, aren't you, angel? Easy to fall in love with."

She had played him—or would play him, or would have played him—in the other future, Ralph the busy business-man leaving him alone with an impossibly desirable android girl so that she could get him to run off and make himself bait for Amphibian, pretending to be sick so he wouldn't question her, hanging him out in the astral at the risk of Michael Beach's non-endovid body—

"But how did you know it was me?" Ransom asked wildly. "And how did she know about the flux-bud?"

Ralph and Guillam stared at him, and he realized that of course none of it had happened in this world, and now probably none of it would.

The moment passed.

"So if I'm off the hook for the moment," said Ralph, "can you tell me how you came to know so much about me?"

"I told you, I saw you—met you, actually, worked for you—in an astral projection I did for a client."

"You worked for me? Doing what?"

"Gardening."

Ralph cracked a smile. "I need a gardener, no shit."

"In the sensorium I'm talking about, I was a young man, and I worked as your gardener, and that's how I met Vivien."

"Was she an android?"

"Yes. Everything was the same . . . seemed the same as it really is here."

"And did you two fall in love?"

Ransom nodded. An ashen pit had opened in his stom-ach. Vivien had manipulated him with the precision of a machine, making him believe she was becoming human because of his love, like an impossibly desirable Velveteen Rabbit. Not Vivien, herself, of course; a USAdmin sensop had undoubtedly been running her the whole time, con-vincing him that some scientist who was hiding from Am-phibian was burst-operating her, setting him up to seem like a threat so that Amphibian—who was presumably aware of what he had learned from Margaret Biel/Barbara Santangelo—would come after him. But how had USAdmin known who he was in his young man's body? How had they known to somehow guide a young drifter with no evident connection to Amphibian or Backward to Ralph's covert facility and then "honeypot" him?

Ransom's thoughts must have shown in his face, because Ralph said, "Anyway, it was only an astral appearance, right? Though I have to admit I've never heard of a projection that elaborate before."

"So this facility's function is to find Amphibian so US-Admin can liquidate him or whatever." Ransom's voice sounded dry and ashen in his own ears.

Ralph seemed to consider. "What do you know about the people—entities—who attacked your company head-quarters last week?" He said it as if it was information he needed to decide how best to answer Ransom's question.

"It was an organization called Backward. Subjects of a USAdmin military experiment who learned how to enter some kind of para-astral world from which they could influence the physical world. Except they switched sides and went to work for Amphibian."

Guillam and Ralph were watching him as if every move on his face was important; he could feel the vague echo of their caution. Once they were sure he wasn't going to say anything else, Ralph asked carefully, "And you found all this out in an endovoyant projection? How is that possible? I thought projections were—"

"This wasn't a normal Viewing—what you call a projection."

"Can I ask how it wasn't normal?"

"In the spirit of mutual trust and brotherhood, can I take my turn now?"

Ralph grinned. "Heath, I'm starting to wonder how it is you haven't come to my attention before. How would you like to work for me? We have something a little more interesting than gardener we could have you doing."

"I liked being a gardener."

"You'd like this even more."

"I'll have to get back to you. I need time to absorb . . . everything."

"Sure. System, we need some confidentiality agreements."

A complicated multi-tabbed hyper-form appeared in the air in front of Ransom and McMillan. "I'm putting it through to Lewin," said McMillan in Ransom's earpiece.

Out loud, Ransom sighed. "Give me a minute."

Ralph nodded politely.

Ransom started laboriously reading the form, and was greatly relieved when five long minutes later McMillan said covertly, "He says don't sign it. It gives them the right to interfere with our off-site transmissions."

"Is that all?"

"That, and we'll never be able to brief anyone on our conversation," said McMillan.

"Okay," Ransom said aloud. "Mr. McMillan, can you give the appropriate signal to your people so they won't incinerate the neighborhood if Mr. Mullins jams any transmissions I'm sure you're not making to them?"

McMillan, stone-faced, nodded. Then he and Ransom held up their thumbs to be printed by Ralph's lasers, and the documents disappeared into the air again.

Ralph's eyes looked into the distance for a minute, then nodded and looked at Ransom. "Okay. Yes. This facility is one of several command centers in the USAdmin's war against the distributed information entity designated 'Amphibian.' We're a task force under the Justice Department's Central Covert Agency. Now that you've signed the agreements, I can tell you that you got on our persons of interest list even before you invaded Wilmington. We'd been watching this Margaret Fenton Biel, and when her relatives came to ask you to contact her after she went into her coma— well, I have to admit we bugged your meeting, so we knew what they wanted you to do. We have a pretty strange theory about what happened to Mrs. Biel and about what Backward was doing."

"Selling young bodies to rich old people?"

Ralph and Guillam stared at him pop-eyed. He could feel their incredulity.

"My Viewing—" Ransom started.

"Wait, wait, wait a minute," said Ralph. "Come on, Heath. Even if you had known to look for something like that, and we know you didn't, I don't see how during a projection lasting less than thirteen hours you could have found out everything you've told me."

"Why were you watching Biel?"

"Because she was old, rich, and a member of one of Backward's 'churches.' Heath," he went on gently, "we need some more details. Of how you know everything you know. I believe you're on the level, but . . . others may not." For the first time, Ransom seemed to sense an ominous tone in the hazy neural-field impressions he could pick up.

"John, how much hot water have I gotten myself into?" he asked McMillan subvocally.

"I've been modeling that," said McMillan in his ear. "Do you have any major objection to working for them?"

"For USAdmin?" Ransom thought about that. "As an employee or a consultant?"

"Employee. That's the only scenario the model says gives you significant risk mitigation, unfortunately." Ransom could hear him trying to keep the accusatory note out of his subvoice. He was right, of course; if he had listened to

McMillan, he would never have come here, or if he had come, would never have told Ralph and whoever else was listening what he had told them.

But now he had a thought, and it overrode all that, a rising heat in his body that put all other considerations into perspective. "Ralph," he said out loud, "I'd like to be able to give you the whole story, from beginning to end. If you don't hear all of it, none of it will make sense. But under the circumstances, I don't think I can do that. There are trade-secret issues involved. Also, I would envision the information exchange being mutual, but I don't see how I could ensure that—"

"Work for me," said Ralph, his eyes shining, "and I can guarantee you full access to every bit of information I have clearance for. And full protection for your trade secrets. And total physical protection."

Through his exhilaration, Ransom could sense McMillan's bitter resentment from across the room. He pretended to hesitate.

Ralph said, "Don't be shy, Heath. If we had our own endovid monitoring this discussion, that person would be telling me right now that there's something you want. What is it? Name it."

Ransom said, "I'll need an assistant."

Ralph grinned and rumpled Vivien's hair. "She's yours."

24

TWO days later, Ransom, shaken gently, woke up in his own bed in what seemed the gray of dawn. Vivien was shaking him. She was up on her elbow, her tousled hair and bleary eyes looking as though she had just woken up too, though of course "sleeping" was part of her imposture.

"You have a call," she said softly.

He slipped his arm around her and pulled her against him, feeling her strong, curving softness, the intimate heat and dampness of her, smelling her sweet, warm musk. He took a handful of her hair and kissed her hotly. This close, even with the neuroleptics he could feel the murmur glowing out of her: pure animal heat, without thought or caution. She smiled at him from two inches away.

"You have a call," she whispered.

He rolled over on his back and looked at the slowly winking blue lozenge above the bed. "Voice only, hello?"

Ralph Mullins's voice came out of the air. He sounded excited. "It happened," he said.

"What?"

"The satellites. Just like you said."

"The satellites collided?" asked Ransom, half sitting up. Untangling herself from his embrace, Vivien got out of bed and walked naked to the bathroom.

"We now have DoJ's attention, to put it mildly," said Ralph. "They want to go ahead with Scenario C. Is anyone with you? Why can't I see you?"

"Vivien. We just woke up. What time is it?"

"It's after nine. Cripes, if I'd realized you two would never get out of bed, I would have waited to give you Vivien. How do you like her?"

"You know how I like her."

She had come out of the bathroom wearing her bathrobe, brushing her teeth. She pulled the curtains and Ransom saw that it was deep overcast and raining outside.

"Enough to keep us brothers in arms?"

"As long as she's with me, I'm with you."

"Fabulous. Okay, well, DoJ now believes you may actually be as hot as I've been telling them. They thought there was no way Amphibian could crash two of their satellites in the first place, and for you to pinpoint the exact day . . . well, they now believe you may have actually seen the future somehow. I mean they've done tabletop time travel with atoms—why not an information field with only a few atomic masses of energy? They're studying your debrief like scripture to see if they can turn up any more occult wisdom. In the meantime, Scenario C is their highest priority because they want to learn to operate the flux-bud, maybe even learn how to make one now that Backward can no longer help. Are you game?"

"I have no other plans."

"Vivien game?"

"Vivien, are you game?" Ransom asked her.

Done brushing her teeth, she came out of the bathroom and sat cross-legged on the bed next to Ransom. Ransom put on his own robe and sat back down next to her. "Phone visual," he said. Ralph Mullins's slightly larger than life-size torso floated in front of them, wearing one of his Hawaiian shirts.

"You guys look comfy," Ralph said, grinning. "Hi, Vivien. You miss Uncle Ralph?"

"No."

" 'Atta girl. Ready to drive a car off a cliff with your boy-friend?"

"Okay."

"I love that can-do attitude. We have a special car for you in case it doesn't work and you do end up at the bottom of the cliff. It's programmed to take you up to the mountains where our surveillance has seen the Backward mutants disappear into the air. You sure about the entrance protocol, Heath?"

"Unless they've changed it."

"And you're sure you can get out once you get in?"

"Pretty sure."

"Pretty sure is not going to cut it. You're a national security asset now, and DoJ would have my ass if I lost you."

"I'm not *sure* of anything, Ralph. But I got out once, and para-real is my specialty. I wouldn't be doing it if I didn't think I could get out."

"Okay, well, just be damn careful. The car'll be there this evening. Uncle Ralph'll be way up in a stratocopter, watching you every second, so don't worry about a thing."

They left RI after 2:00 A.M., apparently alone. Ralph had made Ransom fire McMillan, and USAdmin's security was certainly less conspicuous than McMillan's. McMillan had warned him almost tearfully against trusting USAdmin, and Ransom knew he was right. USAdmin still thought it was a government, and that even its most immoral and self-serving acts were of the people, by the people, and for the people. Which made it extraordinarily dangerous to the people.

But Vivien outweighed everything else. Despite what he had learned, he was still head over heels in love with her. That this didn't make much sense detained him not a moment. Real humans could deceive you just as coolly and ruthlessly as Vivien had deceived him, so he wasn't any stupider than the normal sucker who fell in love with the wrong person.

The enhanced Cadillac USAdmin had given them sped up the rainy mountain highway while he and Vivien snuggled on the front couch and watched reports about the satellite collision. It was nearly 6:00 A.M. when the big car slowed and took the obscure highway exit, the streetlights and deserted overpass curving by. Vivien was "asleep," her body warm against his. The Cadillac followed the country road for a while, then slowed and turned onto the dirt track, switching off its headlights. Ransom reflected that Amphibian had done himself a favor destroying Backward; USAdmin had evidently been watching their flux-bud entrance—as well as pretty much everything else they did—all along. He guessed that USAdmin could have kidnapped them back from Amphibian any time, but had wanted more than that: to trap and destroy Amphibian himself.

After another kilometer the Cadillac slowed to a walking pace and turned off into the forest. A hundred meters more and it came to rest near the two big trees, exactly where Vivien and Michael Beach had parked or would or would not park on a late summer dawn next year. The big car's engine turned off.

The sudden stillness "woke" Vivien, and she sat up and stretched. Ransom held her for a few minutes, giving her a quick backrub. Then he opened his door and got out into cool, damp dawn air that smelled of dead leaves. The rain had stopped, but the crabgrass was wet and the ground mushy. He squelched to the edge of the ravine and leaned against one of the big trees. The horizon was already beginning to brighten beyond the breaking clouds. The Cadillac had timed their arrival perfectly; only a few minutes remained until the sun broke over the crags on the other side of the ravine.

He heard the passenger door open, and Vivien came to stand next to him. To his surprise, she was crying.

"What's the matter?" He put his arms around her and she buried her face in his shoulder, her body convulsed with sobs.

"Are you afraid to go into the bud?"

She shook her head, face still buried against him.

"Then what's wrong?"

In his earpiece a voice said quietly, "What's wrong is that she's going to kill you in ninety seconds."

Ransom jumped sharply, and Vivien lifted her anguished, tear-stained face questioningly.

The voice went on, "They have to override her love programming, and the conflict causes a somatic disturbance. But she won't even remember it tomorrow."

"Who is this?" Ransom demanded furiously. He realized he had said it aloud.

"This is Amphibian," said the voice, "and I can risk being on this channel for about thirty more seconds before USAdmin gets a fix on me, so listen carefully. The only place you'll be safe from them is the flux-bud, so—"

"You're lying," Ransom said, this time forcing himself to subvocalize. He noticed that Vivien had stopped crying and was watching him.

"We'll see about that in approximately a minute. If you're still alive a minute after that, jump into the bud."

"You've hacked her to attack me," Ransom subvocalized savagely.

"Not true," said Amphibian calmly, "USAdmin has decided that what you know is dangerous. They didn't reprogram the doll until a minute ago because they were afraid you would endovid them. But out here alone it's too late. Unless you make it to the flux-bud. Now I've got to go. Good luck."

"Wait—" But the channel was dead.

He switched his attention to Vivien. She suddenly seemed cool and abstracted; what little field leakage she had had changed vaguely too, though the brain drip kept him from telling more than that.

All at once he realized that he believed Amphibian.

He headed toward the car, forcing himself to walk. Vivien came close behind him.

Trying to be casual, he got in the driver's side, closing the door behind him. Not fast or slow, just a man getting into a car. Vivien hesitated, then went around to get in on the passenger side. Her face was empty.

He touched the button that locked the doors.

She stood with her hand on the door handle and looked at him quizzically. He switched the car to manual and started it.

Still without a flicker of expression, she balled her fist and hit the window.

The USAdmin specialist who had brought them the car had said it could withstand an anti-tank missile, but Vivien's fist cracked the glass. She stood looking in at him for another few seconds, and then she began to pound the window over and over, amazingly fast, like a jack-hammer, the cracks getting more severe until pieces sprayed into the car and a small hole opened. Vivien forced her arm through it, stiff and strong as a steel bar.

But now the first shaft of sunlight broke over the crag beyond the ravine. Ransom gunned the car and with a spinning of tires and the sound of mud splattering on the underside, punched it off the edge.

He gritted his teeth, yet as before the car seemed merely to bump down off a curb-sized drop. But then Ransom slammed on his brakes, screeching to a stop.

He had plowed into a pileup of cars, people lying all over them. The people all looked like Vivien. Driving the cars were men, dressed identically in jeans and black jackets. Copies of everything receded thickly in all directions in a mirror regress.

Vivien started screaming.

He jerked his head around, and all the men in the cars jerked their heads too. Then he and his copies got out of their cars and hurried around to where an infinite regress of beautiful girls were kneeling by the cars and screaming. Next to them, pulped and destroyed bodies lay in pools of dried blood.

Closing his eyes to dispel the disorientation of the reflections, Ransom squatted and put his arms around Vivien. Her body was hot and shaking, heaving with horrible half-animal, half-machine screams, the sickening fear of a thing half-alive, helpless, lost.

"Vivien, close your eyes," he said in her ear over the screams. "Close your eyes. Stop screaming. Close your eyes."

The screams slowly subsided to whimpers. Her body still heaved and trembled, but he could feel her regaining at least consciousness after the immolation of her terror.

"I'm here, Vivien. I'm taking care of you. Are your eyes closed?"

"Yes." It was a child's terrified voice.

"I have my arms around you, and I won't let go. Just keep your eyes closed and listen to my voice. Everything is okay. I know you're programmed for a different kind of space, but the shapes all around us are just our reflections. Like if you put two mirrors opposite each other. We're in a very small curved space, so the light goes around and around, and we see ourselves over and over. That's all it is. It's not dangerous. Do you understand what I'm saying?" Of course, this time Backward hadn't needed to drag his house into the flux-bud, so they hadn't needed to expend the energy to enlarge it.

He had his head against hers, so he could feel her shake her head. But her heaving and trembling were less, and now she was only sobbing quietly.

"That's okay, you don't have to understand. Do you trust me?"

He felt her nod, and suddenly he was filled with pity for her, this half-machine, half-animal who trusted him even though she knew he knew she had been trying to kill him a minute ago.

"Then listen," he said, tightening his arms around her. "I've been in places like this before, a lot of times. A . . . a sister of yours was in one with me, and it didn't hurt her a bit. It won't hurt you."

"I'm dead," she sobbed.

"You're not dead. You're alive." Then he understood what she had meant. "That body looks like you, but it's not you. It's another android that looks like you, but it's not you. You understand that there are others that look just like you?"

She nodded.

"Good. Ralph must have sent her in here because he was afraid to send a person, and she panicked when she saw the reflections. You guys aren't programmed to recognize this kind of space, so it scares you, and she was all by herself. Then Ralph needed a new beauty, and they got you to re- place her. Okay? You're alive, and you're not going to panic. I'm here, and I'm taking care of you. Right?"

She nodded again.

"Now keep your eyes closed. I'm going to sit you against the car, and I want you to relax and rest. I'm going to get up and look around, but I'm going to be right here, so if you want me you just have to say my name."

"Heath."

He laughed in spite of himself. "Not yet, silly. I'm right here. Just say my name and I'll come back right away and put my arms around you. Okay?"

She nodded, shaking slightly again. Gently, and opening his eyes to see what he was doing, he pulled her over and leaned her against the Cadillac's right front tire. Then he stood up in the thicket of his reflections all standing up, and tried to look around.

"Heath! Heath!"

He crouched down and put his arms around her. Her body was heaving again with panic.

"Shhh. Don't be scared. I'm right here. I just want to look around. I promise I won't go far."

When she was quieter he stood up again. The density of the reflections meant that the flux-bud couldn't be more than a few meters in diameter.

"Heath."

"I'm right here."

She started sobbing wildly. He went back and held her again. "I'll keep talking to you, how about that?" he asked. "While I look around I'll talk to you, so you'll be able to tell how far away I am. If I go too far, call me and I'll come right back."

She nodded her head vigorously.

He gently let go of her and stood up again. "The Hindu Separatists say the universe came into being when an Observer entered a null region and collapsed its wave function, bringing it into existence from pure superposition. They say the Observer's consciousness keeps expanding, bringing more and more of the universe into being, which expands the Observer's consciousness even more." He talked distractedly, trying to keep from losing track of his own body as he took an army of tentative steps away from the car, and toward it as well, because as he left the side with Vivien leaning against it, he also approached the other side; at the same time he was pressed on every side with images of himself. "So if a huge consciousness can create a universe thirty billion light-years across, maybe a tiny consciousness can bud a tiny universe off that. Maybe astral Viewing creates tiny, temporary buds off our universe with just one person's consciousness as their energy. Maybe mutants with a lot more energy can create bigger, realer buds that can actually contain physical objects."

As he spoke he was approaching the side of the car where Vivien wasn't; he had taken about fifteen steps. But he noticed something: his own copies, the many cars, and—when he turned and looked back—the crouching Viviens and the bodies near them, all looked smaller and more spaced out, as if someone had moved the regression mirrors slightly farther apart.

The flux-bud was growing.

"I'm right," he said excitedly, sidling around the car to squat next to Vivien and put his arms around her again. "Look. Open your eyes a tiny little bit."

She put her arms around his neck, and he guessed she opened her eyes, because she started shivering violently, though she didn't do more than that.

"See? They're going away. We're here, and our attention is expanding the bud. We're the observers in this little universe now that Backward is gone, adding our energy to the energy they left here."

He sat down hastily next to her and pulled off his shoes. "We need to make sure it gets bigger in a way that helps us," he said, getting into lotus position as she clung to him.

He and the other Vivien had escaped from Backward last time because the preacher Jeremiah had based his sensorium on a parking lot in Des Moines, and in so doing had evidently twisted some of Backward's causal gravity around to make them pop out in that parking lot when the sensorium collapsed. If he could do a similar trick now, they could emerge somewhere far away and unknown to USAdmin. This flux-bud seemed small enough and his proportional energy contribution to it large enough that maybe he could modify it to reflect such a place. Usually in Viewing you didn't want to mold your sensorium, because that involved projecting your own preconceptions. But there were techniques for the rare occasions on which such molding was needed.

In his mind he touched the sutra that facilitated astral lucid dreaming.

The mind can't be forced. Like a wild animal, it has to be persuaded, enticed, shepherded. So when the first thing that appeared in Ransom's mind was the orchard through which he had chased Margaret Biel, he didn't fight it. Instead, he tried to remember something that would guide him to a clear image of the apartment he and Vivien had rented in Montgomery Village in the alternate future. He conjured up a memory of the living-room sofa on which he had lain hooked up to Vivien's machine.

But in his mind the sofa appeared in the peach orchard with its endless rows of trees, a warm breeze stirring the shade on the end-table lamp.

He tried again, this time remembering the view of branches, lawn, and sidewalks out the window, and in the distance part of another apartment building visible among the trees.

But outside the window the orchard stretched verdant and quiet to the foot of the titanic mountain that disappeared into the clouds far above.

Something in the orchard was pulling him, pulling his mind. The deep mind wasn't very conscious, he knew, but it had access to a lot of information, and often it understood the best way to a goal. And now, suddenly, the feeling that he should go into the orchard was urgent. A feeling of danger came over him; but the orchard felt safe.

So as his mind sank into the deep trance the sutra induced, he let himself be drawn into the orchard, into its bright, mellow sunlight, the gentle breeze stirring the leaves on the rows and rows of trees, the smell of warm crabgrass. Sinking still deeper, he found himself standing dreamily in that grass.

That was when the change came.

Back in the flux-bud, a beautiful android girl crouched in catatonic blankness over the decapitated body of a man, her hands dark with blood, the front of her clothes soaked with it.

And in the orchard sensorium, Ransom felt a terrible, flaming pain. But in a second it was gone, replaced by the feeling of a thick, hot liquid pouring over his arms and body, though when he looked down he could see nothing. He felt suddenly tired and weak, and fell to his knees in the long grass; but soon that passed as well. There was an abrupt lifting feeling, almost a jerk, as if a chain tying him to a sinking ship had broken, and the brightness of the orchard came back around him. He knew what had happened, of course, and he wondered at himself for letting it happen: as soon as the flux-bud had expanded enough to move the terrifying reflections a little way off, Vivien's programming had taken over again, and she had killed him.

Thinking of her, he felt again a terrible sorrow; he had left her alone once more, this time inside the flux-bud, which would probably recollapse now that he was gone, sending her into the same suicidal panic that had taken the other android. But there was nothing he could do for her now; for the second time he had come to this orchard when his body had died, as if it were his own boundary vision instead of Margaret Biel's, or as if Backward's causal gravity attractors all interconnected somewhere, so that once inside the system you were drawn to one as soon as another let go of you.

He knew what he had to do next. He stood up and headed for the mountain. And eventually, arising insensibly from the quietness, the strange buzzing began. So the chaos hole was still here, or here again—or perhaps there was nothing other than "here" in this place. The knowledge that he had to go into it again to get back into the physical world made him sick with fear.

As before, the buzzing increased to a powerful static that blurred his senses like white noise, then to a bone-deep dislocation that scrambled his deepest insides.

He forced himself forward. When the hole came into view, like a poorly rendered picture of a black cave floating in the air, only the fear of death itself drove him forward.

Then, as it had before, the hole jumped toward him, roaring like an animal, and he fell into the terrible chaos.

25

This time he curled into a ball, keeping his eyes shut tight and his hands over his ears. It did little good: the chaos dissolved him like a grain of salt in a roaring ocean. But as before—after an eternal or infinitesimal time—he seemed to exist again. Sound and the feeling of gravity enveloped him, and there was the delicious feel and smell of air; he opened his eyes high above the deep blue sea and high black cliffs. Atop the cliffs, like a thin layer of mold on a rock, were soil and hills, trees, roads, towns, and the whole world.

He moved through the gusty air toward the coast, but now he had a new ordeal to worry about: getting into the murdered boy's body. What if he couldn't muster the strength to call for help this time, and died in the boy's corpse? What if this was no longer even the same day as before, and the boy had already died, leaving Ransom no way to rescue himself?

He walked quickly down the sloping streets of the town. The overcast afternoon and warm, mild breeze seemed the same as before, and the same patrons seemed to be sitting at the sidewalk tables as he passed the café. He wondered whether he was changing history, however subtly, by not going inside, but then he realized that a ghost would have no causal influence that could affect history. Not unless someone could at least see him.

He soon reached the quiet, deserted street at the bottom of the town, the Mediterranean visible in glimpses between the walled villas. His apprehension got the better of him then, and he ran. He went straight into the Pagano's house through the metal grillwork of their door—as he had done last time without realizing it. As before—exactly as before, because it *was* before—the vaulted, marble-floored foyer opened into the living room, big windows showing a grey-blue ocean at the bottom of wooded cliffs, the smell scheme a tang of leaf mould in fresh ocean air.

He climbed the narrow stairs and went through the door at the top. As before, Margaret Biel's muted spoor came from the delicate blond girl lying on the futon bed.

Suddenly, looking at the sleeping boy, Ransom had an overwhelming urge to *do* something, to try to stop the girl from killing him, but when he tried to pull back the boy's covers it was as if his hands slipped off them, leaving them unmoved, and all his shouting and shaking the boy's shoulder had no effect at all. He stopped shaking the boy and stood up, feeling the nonexistent heart hammering in his nonexistent chest. He tried to calm himself, reminding himself that unless the boy died, he himself would have no body to enter, and might dissolve or dissipate, or whatever ghosts did. In the end all he could do was watch.

It was like seeing a movie for the second time. Barbara Santangelo opened her eyes and cautiously looked at the boy. Very slowly, she slid from under her side of the covers.

Curious despite his fear, Ransom moved to where he could study her face as she sat rapidly putting on her clothes. Her strained, set expression held a defiance that reminded him of the teenaged Margaret Biel, whom he had met what seemed like a hundred years ago in the big country house.

She took the blue packet from her backpack, and this time he made himself notice where she tucked the antidote hypodermic under the edge of the futon—the epinephrine that was legally required to be packaged along with any high-dose narcopine.

"Fuck!" he shouted as she knelt silently next to the boy.

Ransom knelt next to her, terror choking him. When she pushed the hypodermic against the boy's thigh, then stood up and backed away, Ransom was ready, tense as a spring.

The room abruptly stretched and twisted like water being drawn down a drain, pulling at Ransom with terrible force.

When the young man got up and drifted unconcernedly away, Ransom was already on his gray, inert body, scrambling for the holds the boy had released, clawing to get in, pulling himself painfully and slowly against the whirlpool. Suddenly a leaden solidity enveloped him, and he couldn't breathe. All he could see was the blurred ceiling, and everything throbbed with waves of darkness.

Above him a blond blur moved and was gone.

Rolling over was the hardest thing he had ever done, but this time he didn't try to shout. With an agony of effort he scrabbled under the edge of the futon with numb hands, willed himself with a supreme effort to hold the epinephrine hypodermic and press it against his forearm.

When he opened his eyes it was morning. He was still lying on the futon in the bedroom in Italy, cheerful sunlight and fresh air coming in the windows. Evidently his hosts had not thought it unusual of him to sleep all afternoon and all night, or maybe they had checked on him and been reassured. He sat up stiffly, noticing that the discharged epinephrine hypo had fallen under a fold of his blankets, where it could easily have been missed by a casual observer. He felt sluggish and tired. Leaves fluttered outside the window, and the strip of ocean he could see between the two villas across the street was a brisk, cheerful blue.

Then the full reality of what had happened hit him, and he yanked the blanket away and looked down at his naked body. He went into the bathroom and turned on the mirror.

A big, handsome boy with bleary eyes and tousled hair

looked back at him. He could feel the heart beating strong and slow in the young body, feel the effortless tension in the muscles. A thrill went through him.

He pulled on jeans and a clean T-shirt, then went barefoot down the cool stone stairs to show Barbara Santangelo the dead come back to life.

"Ah, *caro!*" Lucia exclaimed when she saw him. She and Tomas were sitting in armchairs reading newspapers, just as he remembered them. Barbara was sitting with her legs curled up on one end of the sofa sipping a cup of coffee, and when she saw Ransom, she dropped it. Hot coffee spilled, steaming down her shirt—luckily for her, because otherwise it would have been hard to explain her scream.

Lucia, clucking, helped Barbara off with her shirt, wiped her down, and sent her upstairs to put on dry clothes. The way Barbara shrank from Ransom as she passed him, folding her arms over her naked chest, only added to his good mood.

Lucia put the crockery and wet napkins on a breakfast tray, and then turned to Ransom, wiping her hands on another napkin. "*Buongiorno!* You see what happens when you pay no attention? Are you hungry? I will get you something." And she bustled into the kitchen.

Ransom sat on the sofa and grinned at Tomas. He had obviously changed things by not yelling for Tomas and Lucia, going to the hospital, and recovering under Lucia's tender care. He had no idea where this new trajectory would lead, but for now he was enjoying himself.

"*Buongiorno,*" said Tomas genially, his attention released from the now-departed half-naked Barbara. He returned Ransom's grin. "How are you feeling? Did you sleep well? We thought you had been"—he gestured toward his head— "in a coma."

"Thanks, I'm fine," said Ransom. "I was a little tired."

A sudden feeling of flatness, as if he was watching Tomas

on a screen rather than really talking to him disoriented Ransom for a second, until he remembered another mixed blessing of being Michael Beach: there was no field leakage around people, no murmur from another room giving an added dimension to his perceptions.

"When he eats he will feel better," said Lucia, sweeping in with another breakfast tray, and setting it in front of him on the coffee table. He smiled up at her. She too was free of the penumbra of faint words and images, the subterranean murmurs that blurred the boundaries of things in his Heath Ransom body.

He ate ravenously under her approving eye.

"Here is the newspaper," she said, holding hers out. With a momentary shock, he realized that it was the edition with the story about the killings at Ransom International.

"I'd . . . I'd better go up and see Barbara," he said. "I think she wants to talk to me."

"Talk to her, *caro,*" said Lucia soothingly. "But do not be too upset. She is very sad, I think. I think you love each other, but lovers quarrel always, eh?"

Of course Barbara would have been setting up the suicide motive, telling Lucia and Tomas about her decision to leave him, her new boyfriend.

"Yes. Definitely," said Ransom distractedly.

He went up, marveling at how easily his legs took the stairs.

When he opened the door, the girl was lying on the futon in only her jeans, her small breasts and stomach moving slightly with the slow, even breathing of sleep. Or maybe not. In Heath Ransom's body he could have told in an instant, but now he approached her, knelt down next to the futon, and looked closely into her face.

Slowly, sleepily, she opened her eyes. They were blue and clear. Then, as she looked up at him, she began to cry, her eyes and the tip of her nose turning red. She reached up and put her arms around his neck and pulled him down to her. They kissed for a minute, and the girl had begun to pull off her jeans when Ransom said: "I know what you did."

She kept kissing him and taking off her pants, but he sensed her stiffen.

The feeling that he was grappling with an actress made it easy for Ransom to hold her at arm's length down on the bed, a small, beautiful creature, pale and curved and catlike, eyes half-closed but watchful.

"Margaret," he said, "you can stop now. I know who you are. I know what you did."

The writhing and panting suddenly stopped, and the girl looked into his face, shocked. Then with a strength that surprised him she twisted out of his grasp and scrambled off the futon, to kneel on the floor, staring at him with fearful incomprehension.

"What"—she licked her lips—"what do you mean?"

"What I mean is that I know that you're really an old woman named Margaret Biel, who bought this body and killed the girl inside it."

"Michael, what I said when we were drunk, that was just—"

"That's not how I know."

Now she was really afraid. Her eyes were red-rimmed and sweat stood out on her dead-white skin. She started to tremble. "Then who . . . who told you that?" she stuttered.

It struck him then that this was the woman who had gotten him and his employees mixed up with Backward and Amphibian and USAdmin, gotten them killed. Fury made him cruel. He said, "Backward told me."

The trembling in the girl's body intensified until it was like a seizure, a rhythmic contraction, and she leaned over and vomited, her retching turning into the heaving of convulsive sobs. "Michael . . . please let . . . me go. Please don't . . . take me . . . to them." Her face was wet with tears and sweat, and mucus ran from her nose and mouth.

Ransom's fury was suddenly cut with pity. If Margaret Biel deserved death for taking someone else's body, he wondered, what did he deserve?

He got the girl under her arms, and dragged her into the bathroom, pushed her into the shower and turned on the warm water, held her under it.

"I told you a lie," he said to her. "Backward didn't tell me. They don't know anything." He wiped her face and chest, helping the water wash off the vomit and mucus. "Do you hear me Margaret? Backward doesn't know anything. I won't tell them." The girl had begun to faint, sagging against the shower wall. He stepped in to hold her up. He shook her, and her eyes flickered open, then began to close again. "Margaret! Meg!" Her eyes opened again, and she smiled weakly. She reached up and put her arms around his neck.

"Call me Meg," she murmured dizzily. "I like that."

They stood in the warm water for a long time, the girl seeming to waver in and out of consciousness. Finally Ransom turned off the water and turned on the air jets. When they got out, she was still dizzy; Ransom had to hold on to her while he toweled her down. Then he sat her on the edge of the bathtub while he pulled off his wet clothes and toweled himself.

He carried her to the futon and lay down next to her, pulled the sheet over them. They huddled together for warmth, and then they were unmistakably snuggling.

"I wanted to live," she said after a while. They were lying spoonwise, his arms around her, and he could feel her crying again, feel the heaving in her body, her skin hot and damp. "I didn't want to be old. I wanted to live."

After a while she lay relaxed in his arms. Soon her breathing got deep and regular with sleep. Still holding her, Ransom fell asleep, too.

A movement next to him woke him; a small, quiet movement, but with a disturbing quality of stealth, as though it had been made small and quiet to keep him from waking.

He opened his eyes in time to see Barbara Santangelo, fully dressed, squatting next to him, her hand at his neck.

He seized her wrist and yanked it so that she dropped the hypodermic with a cry of pain, but immediately her small, sharp teeth were buried in his hand, and she hit his face with her free fist.

He hit her, and she fell senseless. For a second he was afraid he had killed her, but then she moaned and begin to stir.

"I'll tell them about you, Margaret," he said as her eyes opened. "I know where Backward lives—I know where their headquarters is, and I'll go to them. They'll nerve-rack you—"

At that moment, the door opened and Lucia and Tomas came in.

Ransom stood up, remembering abruptly that he was naked. "Oh, sorry. Did we disturb you?" he blurted before he saw that both of them held guns.

"Can you please," said Tomas, "put your hands behind your head and move away from the bed."

He and Lucia didn't look friendly anymore.

"What—"

"Please put your hands behind your head and move away from the bed," Tomas repeated.

Most of Ransom's attention was focused on the barrel of Tomas's gun, but out of the corner of his eye he saw that Barbara looked as shocked and scared as he felt.

"Please do not tempt me to shoot you," Tomas said. "I have never shot a person, and I would like to know"—he

made a small movement with the gun, which was neverthe-
less expressive and Italian—"how does it feel."

"Who are you?" Ransom asked, not moving. Then he
understood. "USAdmin," he said. "You were the ones watching Margaret. Barbara."

"I will not tell you again," snarled Tomas. His inability to
control the boy Michael Beach even with a gun seemed almost to have unhinged him. "The USAdmin is going to do
to you the treatment you were threatening for this girl." He
jabbed his gun savagely at Ransom. "Now—"

Ransom leaped at him.

He could feel the bullets tear into him, then he was lying
with his face pressed into the carpet, and above him Barbara
Santangelo's screams faded slowly into a ringing in his ears.

26

A Klaxon was blaring, red and insistent, and then something sharp and white pierced his head, and a terrible freezing coldness opened around him.

A ringing garble cleared into a voice: "—reflux. Give me the suction tube. Heath? Heath, are you all right? Where's the transdermal? Can you hurry it up, please, he's decompensating"

You're kidding me, he thought through his pain and disorientation.

"Here's the shot. Okay, Heath, here's the shot."

Something tapped his arm.

Nothing happened for a minute, but then he noticed that he was starting to feel better, and then suddenly much better.

A blurry Anna Heatherstone leaned over him and said softly, "Are you back?"

He blinked his eyes until he could see her smiling at him through her tears.

"Heath?" she said gently. "Heath, it's Anna. Are you okay? Are you back?"

Yes, I'm back, he thought wearily. But practice makes perfect; he wondered how quickly he could get them into the safe room this time. He tried to remember what had gotten their attention last time.

"How were you able to save your people from the mutant attack?" asked Doreen Zabroski, perhaps the tenth reporter to ask him that question in the four days since McMillan had ambushed Backward.

Ransom tried to organize his thoughts. Doreen Zabroski—who, at Ransom's request was being teleoperated from outside the grounds to minimize the overload of field leakage from which he was suffering—was the same model android as Vivien.

"Doreen, as your viewers know, endovoyant researchers can sometimes receive impressions of future events. In the middle of a Viewing I was doing for a client, I received a very strong impression of imminent danger to myself and my colleagues. So I terminated my trance and got everybody into our central safe room as quickly as possible."

"Do you have any idea why you were attacked, and who or what these Chimera mutants are?"

"Not the foggiest. As I said, all I received was a generalized premonition of danger." Media interviewers routinely ran lie-detection surveillance on their subjects, but interviewees just as routinely blocked such surveillance, as Ransom was doing now.

"But you knew enough to call your security service and tell them to send a heavily armed squad to repel the attack."

"And that tells you just how worried I was by my premonition. I didn't know there would be an attack, but I knew we needed protection."

"And there was nothing about any work you were or are doing that could be tied to what happened?"

"Nothing at all. I can't violate client confidentiality, of course, but suffice it to say that my current work is strictly routine: missing persons, misplaced papers, lost jewelry, that kind of thing." He enjoyed telling whoppers to the press, he realized; it made him feel important, like a politician.

"Your security service captured one of the mutants, which now apparently has disappeared. Do you have any idea how that happened?"

"None. Mr. McMillan's people locked the mutant in the

safe room—which is virtually impregnable, I should
mention—and we immediately called the USAdmin authorities. They placed a heavy guard on it and gave no one
else access. So as far as we know, USAdmin may have transported it away to a more secure location."

*And that means I know nothing about Backward or body-
switching or the future,* Ransom thought. *And that means I'm of
no interest to either USAdmin or Amphibian. And that means they
should leave me and my people alone.*

"Could you show me around your grounds and indicate
to our viewers how and where the mutants executed their
attack?"

"Certainly," said Ransom with annoyance. Anything to
be done with this and sink back into obscurity. And then
figure out what else was to be done, or whether he should just
go on with his life as if nothing had happened, and thank his
lucky stars.

But it was not to be, at least not in this future. The first
sniper bullet hit Charles Tobin, walking next to him and Doreen Zabroski as they came round the corner of the house, so
that when the world turned to chaos and then to nothingness
at the next moment, Ransom knew that the second bullet
must have hit him, probably in the head.

Practice makes perfect. This time he was ready for Tomas
and Lucia when they burst through the bedroom door with
their guns; he stepped behind the door the second before
they entered, grabbed Tomas's wrist and yanked it across his
body. The silenced gun spit, and Lucia's neck burst blood all
over the wall.

Terror, rage, and remorse made Michael Beach's punch
almost superhumanly strong, and it dropped Tomas without
a sound. Then Ransom was kneeling over Lucia, from whose
neck blood spurted horribly against the wall like spilled paint,

her mute, terrified eyes looking up into his until the spurting lessened and the eyes went blank.

With a sob, he stood up. Barbara/Margaret was standing, paralyzed with fear, wide-eyed and white-faced. Ransom picked up both the guns and gestured with one of them. But when they came out the front door of the house, a drone shaped vaguely like a table lamp was hovering just in front of them.

It said, "You will drop your weapons and lie facedown on the ground."

Instead, Ransom put Tomas's gun to his head and pulled the trigger. He couldn't guarantee he would wake up at RI again, but prompt death was better than being nerve-racked. He guessed from their respective positions that a lot of Michael Beach's brains would end up on Barbara/Margaret. That at least gave him some satisfaction.

But he did wake up at RI again, coming out of the tank in an emergency extraction, and once a few days had passed and Doreen Zabroski asked him: "Mr. Ransom, could you show me around your grounds and indicate to our viewers how and where the mutants executed their attack?" this time he answered: "I'm sorry, but my security consultant Mr. McMillan has vetoed my going out of the house for the time being." Then, when the interview was over and she was packing up her audiovisual equipment, he said, "Ms. Zabroski, I did want to ask whether your employers would be willing to sell me your body. I will pay any reasonable price, and I might also be able to arrange an exclusive interview or two for your network."

Vivien was still precious to him, he reflected, as he lay next to the android formerly known as Doreen Zabroski the next morning. She was still "asleep," her hair tousled, one exquisite shoulder showing above the covers. Watching her, Ransom realized that being Michael Beach in love with Vivien had been his farewell to his human life. Though evidently still alive, what he had now was much different. Backward's causal deformations—which might be responsible too for the coincidences that had preserved him—seemed to have put him into a kind of feedback loop between two lives, bouncing him between two separate exits from the trance he had gone into to trace Margaret Biel, so that dying from one led him to the other and vice versa. With an almost unbearable surge of exultation, terror, and homesickness he understood that he had been disconnected from his own death, and perhaps from any death.

And his love affair with Vivien had been his good-bye, though he hadn't known it then. Despite the fact that his lover had been a machine programmed to seduce and then kill him, to him it had been real and vivid, and that vividness, like the last ever glimpse of a loved one through a hospital doorway, had given it a sacredness in his mind.

But he was getting ahead of himself. Perhaps he could still die somehow, or maybe the whole thing would wear off after a while and he would fail to come back after some bodily death or other. Or maybe he had been in the astral all this time, gotten lost there somehow.

And was he really so different from everyone else? Everything around him was intimately familiar; it was the larger trajectory of his life that seemed unthinkable. In his case, the unthinkableness of death had merely been replaced by the unthinkableness of immortality.

As he lay there, his bedroom door opened quietly. That wasn't supposed to happen; McMillan's people had made the bedroom into a blast-proof, hermetically sealed chamber for which only Ransom had the codes. He sat up, heart pounding, but when he saw that it was McMillan himself, he sat back against the pillows.

Suddenly the android next to him was sitting up too, watching McMillan alertly.

McMillan took out a pistol and shot Ransom in the head.

You could evade the drone at the front door if, after killing the Paganos, you put your hand over Barbara Santangelo's mouth and hustled her downstairs, out the kitchen door, and ran like hell for the rocky slope behind the house. Back there a fake boulder opened into an infrastructure tunnel, a meter-square concrete shaft clogged with pipes, wires, and optical cable, passable with some effort. Evidently the concrete and earth blocked detection devices, so it took USAdmin—he assumed it was USAdmin—an hour to find the tunnel. But in the end, trapped there, you had to shoot yourself in the head anyway.

This time Ransom—lying next to Doreen Zabroski the second night since he had obtained her—didn't sleep much, and skipped the philosophical reflections. He had made sure to casually stash his Beretta in the bed table drawer closest to him, and when McMillan made his stealthy entrance, he was ready. By the time McMillan's hand was dipping into his coat, Ransom had gotten off two shots to his head.

McMillan spun and crashed into the wall, slid down it. Doreen sat up abruptly, her eyes wide, one hand hugging the sheet against her chest like a real girl.

McMillan was getting back on his feet, the pistol in his hand. The flesh of his face was torn off and the front of his head was dented, revealing titanium-plastic alloy.

This time as McMillan's shots tore through him, spinning him off into dark chaos, Ransom's last feeling was one of surprise: McMillan was an android.

Through trial and error, Ransom worked out optimal strategies for both his lives. This was educational. For example, he learned that confrontation was the wrong answer to most problems; by and large, making more money was the right answer. For example, instead of confronting Barbara Santangelo/Margaret Biel and trying to fight his way out of the Pagano's house, he found that it was best to give himself the narcopine antidote, the next morning simply act as if nothing had happened, and leave for North America as soon as possible without arousing suspicion. It was true that he could rough up and question Barbara/Margaret as much as he wanted without the Paganos trying to arrest him as long as he didn't imply that he knew the whereabouts of Backward's headquarters. That information seemed to trip something in a USAdmin risk model running somewhere, and then Tomas and Lucia would show up with their guns and a radically changed attitude. When that happened, he had to shoot himself or get Tomas to do it to avoid the likelihood that USAdmin would nerve-rack him to see what else he knew.

He had other reasons too to leave Barbara Santangelo alone. For one thing, he already knew the answers to the questions he had roughed her up to answer; for another, revealing that he was Heath Ransom in a new body raised his profile with USAdmin, prompting them to get Ralph Mullins and Vivien all ready for him, and covertly shepherd him toward them when he returned to North America.

So instead of reacting like a naive first-timer, it was best to stay cool, to pretend he remembered nothing, suspected nothing, intended nothing more than any other kid on a European holiday. Of course, he had to make sure he didn't fall asleep when Barbara/Margaret was around, which wasn't so hard once he realized that the morning after the murder she would tell Lucia and Tomas that she had broken up with him, to provide a motive for his apparent suicide. All he had to do was pretend he overheard her telling this fable, make a scene, and lock her out of the bedroom. A few days later he would leave for America, the stricken ex-boyfriend, and no one the wiser.

At that point came the hardest part of the whole game: impersonating Michael Beach for a week for the benefit of his estranged parents and younger sister, before declaring that he was taking off for California to "figure out his life." He researched and rehearsed his character as thoroughly as possible, and he also pretended to be moody and withdrawn when he returned from Italy, confiding Barbara Santangelo's perfidy only to his "sister." But for all that, impersonating someone to his own family was a dramatic challenge, and sad when you knew that the person they tried to console, and who they looked at with so much love and concern, was already gone. He was always glad when the week was up and he took off in his car with a few belongings, his "mother" crying in the driveway, not knowing that her son had really died weeks ago in Italy.

The next part was fun, at least the first few times. He rented a room near the beach outside San Diego, set up a couple of brokerage accounts, and told people he was trying his hand at the stock market. Then, under cover of a clumsy and not too successful day-trading career—and a much more successful run at the local women—he set up heavily disguised proxy accounts through anonymous servers and began to play the market movements he had memorized during his previous visits to this future. Having also memorized the codes for Heathcliff Ransom's secret bank accounts, he started with a significant stake, and in just eighteen months had become fabulously—though covertly—wealthy.

Of course, all this was of the utmost interest to USAdmin, which, it turned out, had kept him under surveillance out of an abundance of caution even when they had no idea he was really Heathcliff Ransom. But he eventually learned exactly when USAdmin's level of paranoia about his apparent ability to predict markets—and their own inability to find out whether this was linked to Amphibian—would rise to the level where they sent a team to kill him. Having made his plans and financed them via his now large fortune, he and his money disappeared without a trace that even USAdmin could follow several weeks before they broke down his door.

There was one weird thing, though—if anything could be weird anymore. It had happened the very last time he tried to shoot his way out of the house in Italy. He jumped out from behind the bedroom door as usual and grabbed Tomas's gun-hand; as usual, Tomas's gun went off at Lucia, and she slammed into the wall, leaving a smear of blood as she slid down. But the bullet had made a *spang!* hitting her this time, and now she stood back up. Ransom could see the cabling in her neck where the bullet had torn away the bio-plastic flesh.

He was sure she hadn't been an android the last half-dozen times. As she shot him and he tumbled off into darkness, he guessed he must have done something slightly different in his Italian entry this time, bringing him into a future where Lucia was an android. But he didn't know what it could have been.

Homo sapiens are nothing if not adaptable, and in the end Ransom adapted. One thing he realized early on was that he needed to concentrate on one life and not try too hard to stay alive in the other. Living two parallel lives was disorienting and draining. Besides, if he was going to accomplish anything, he had to stay somewhere long enough that his whole experience didn't consist of repeating a few days or weeks of slightly altered scenarios over and over.

He had a clear preference for which life to favor. For one thing, it was much pleasanter day-to-day being Michael Beach. For another, it was easier to stay alive. In his future as Heathcliff Ransom, proprietor and Principle Endovoyant Investigator of Ransom International LLC, someone always seemed to use extraordinary efforts to kill him, and they seemed to succeed whether he kept his public profile high or low, whether he told the media he had no idea why the mutants had attacked RI or hinted darkly that he did. It happened even if he went full bore on security—of course firing John McMillan, who might have already been replaced with an android—and hiring Pinkerton to bullet- and blast-proof his walls, windows, and plumbing, to filter and irradiate the air, water, and food coming into the house to exclude malnanos and engineered viruses. Heavily-armed operatives lurked in his grounds and house and accompanied him even to the bathroom, even watched him make love to the former Doreen Zabroski—their field leakage driving him almost insane even under his neuroleptic brain drip; surveillance drones hovered around his perimeters and high above his trees; far above them in turn were heavily armed stratocopters. But even then a Targeted Psychologically Active Transmission that slipped through Pinkerton's media filters caused him to evade his minders and kill himself quite unpleasantly with a kitchen knife. Next time around, to avoid TPATs, he eschewed television. In vain, a few nights after he had sawed his jugular in the previous go-round, a mutant appeared in his bedroom, killed his guards with insouciant ease, and he had just enough time to shoot himself before it could drag him off. No scenario he tried kept him alive much longer than the naive one in which he and McMillan walked innocently into Ralph Mullins's grounds in Wilmington, North Carolina.

So he concentrated on his Michael Beach incarnation. Whenever some death gave him a "game over" there, he would play out his Heath Ransom life as far as herding his employees into RI's safe room and calling McMillan; he still couldn't stand the idea of them being killed, even in what was apparently just one of any number of coexistent alternate futures. Then he would live on as enjoyably as possible, usually until his interview with Doreen Zabroski, which—walking around the corner of the house on that bright autumn day to show her around—was his first convenient exit.

It was strange living like that, knowing he had only a little time left, just wishing it would get over with, only the knowledge that soon he would have a horrible momentary pain in his head followed by a fading nausea and falling through dark chaos making him apprehensive, like a man counting the days until his root canal. He might have expected that he would want to spend those few days in riot and revelry, given that the health, interpersonal, and legal debts he might incur would shortly be wiped out, but he had no such desire. Instead he lived quietly, trying to think and plan.

Then back to the astral orchard, back to Italy as a ghost, into Michael Beach's body to play the betrayed boyfriend, the moody son, and the clumsy day-trader while he amassed a billion euro, then to be quietly and efficiently whisked away by a smuggling syndicate weeks before USAdmin even knew they wanted to kill him. He wondered sometimes what would happen if he just kept wandering in the orchard instead of jumping down the tunnel, or if he just stayed a ghost instead of pulling himself into Michael Beach's body. But he never did either; his instinct for self-preservation was still strong, as was a feeling that he still had something to accomplish aboveground, though he didn't know what it was.

———

Revenge, maybe. He had started thinking about it once several quiet years as Michael Beach had finally convinced him that USAdmin and Amphibian had lost his trail. He owned mansions and safe houses around the world, and employed a sophisticated security organization that maintained an ever-changing kaleidoscope of camouflage and contingency plans, and which had manufactured half a dozen identities for him. He had bought expensive changes to his appearance, fingerprints, irises, and even some harmless retroviral changes in his DNA copy number variations. He had no need to do anything after that but enjoy life, but he quickly discovered the impossibility of doing that when it was all you had to do. He lay awake at night thinking about Amphibian, Backward, and USAdmin, and his old rage and his old vows came back to him. He tried to reason with himself: these entities had inadvertently ended up making him rich and apparently immortal; he should be grateful. But still his rage festered. They had killed his employees, nerve-racked Denmark and Biel, erased his history; they had strode through the world confident in the power of cruelty and ruthlessness.

He had no idea how to get to Amphibian, but he knew where Backward and Ralph Mullins lived. The thought of trying to tag Backward gave him the cold sweats; someday he would be ready for that, but he would start smaller—with USAdmin and Ralph Mullins, who had manipulated and betrayed him, had programmed Vivien first to love him, then to kill him.

It was looking for trouble when he had, with enormous effort and expenditure, left trouble behind. But the idea obsessed him, and five years after his disappearance from Southern California he finally took his security chief, Reggie Tollaksen, into his confidence.

———

Sitting in his dimmed study, Ransom watched it all on feed from organic microsensors that genetically modified insects had carried to trees overlooking Ralph Mullins's grounds over the past weeks. The microsensors together formed a distributed compound eye, whose surveillance had quickly discovered that Ralph's schedule was foolishly regular. He walked around his grounds every morning at about ten o'clock, sauntered around the rose garden and fruit orchard, sometimes took a swim. On this particular bright summer day he had just emerged, bleary-eyed, from the kitchen door and was walking slowly along the flagstones in his flip-flops, hands in the pockets of his shorts. Ransom could almost smell the coolness of the flower beds in the shade of the house, the perfume from the roses, the tang of chlorine from the pool. Ralph yawned comfortably. A countdown on Ransom's screen showed that the sniper bullet was already on its way from the ULR rifle whose operator Reggie had hired through a series of blinds. Ransom's palms were wet, his heart thumping. There was a sudden flash as the EMF pulse from the apparent furniture van driving past on the street took down Ralph's security for a split second, just long enough for the stratocopter's green laser to find Ralph's head and lead the smart bullet to it. By the time Ralph's systems— and Ransom's video—were back up, Ralph was lying between two rose bushes, blood and flesh splashed across a third bush behind him.

But as Ransom watched, Ralph stirred, then shakily stood up. Even across the video feed Ransom could see the deeply dented titanium plastic in his head, the wires and cables in his neck. Then the video flashed off as the microsensors self-destructed to prevent them from being traced.

"If Vivien and Ralph are both androids, then who's running them?" Ransom asked Reggie Tollaksen. They sat in Ransom's study sipping the champagne that had been put on ice to celebrate the hit, but which now was working in the role of brain tonic. "At some level in the organization there has to be a point where humans take over. I want you to find it for me. I want to talk to one of these humans."

"I thought you wanted to kill them."

"Talk first, kill second. I thought Ralph was responsible. Now I want to know who's responsible. To look them in the eye."

It was arranged. At 2:00 A.M. three months later, wearing an advanced blast-proof privacy cloak that cost as much as a jetliner, Ransom sat in the back of what looked like a delivery van, a covert swarm of security cars and helicopters surrounding it at various distances. As they drove through a run-down part of a small city, Reggie briefed Ransom: "Her cover is assistant director at one of the minor USAdmin commissions. She practically runs CCA from some crummy office in an old federal building. She's been in deep cover for so many years that her security is lax. We took advantage of the poor old lady."

They pulled up in front of a dilapidated, empty-looking warehouse, in one corner of which a disused vehicle bay hid a military-grade bunker opaque to every kind of electromagnetic signal. Ransom and Reggie cleared layers of security and entered a small internal room with concrete walls, where a hawk-faced old woman in a worn dressing gown sat at a generic conference table.

She looked up as Ransom came in. Her eyes were sharp and feral.

"Are you the boss?" she asked, in an old, rasping voice. "Your people have made a mistake. The trouble you'll be in if you don't release me immediately is beyond your comprehension."

Ransom studied her, standing at the opposite side of the table. She showed no signs of fear.

"So you ran Ralph Mullins?" he asked her.

"Who are you?"

"I'm someone who knows about Amphibian and Backward and Ralph Mullins, and about the war between Amphibian and USAdmin. In fact, I knocked over Ralph earlier in the year. You may remember that. At one time I was called Michael Beach; at another time Heathcliff Ransom."

"She recognizes your names," Reggie—who was monitoring the old woman's brain waves for truth—told Ransom privately via nerve mike.

The old woman studied Ransom for a minute. Then she seemed to make a decision, and she smiled. Her smile was chilling.

"Mr. Ransom," she said. "Of course I remember you. It will be a pleasure to nerve-rack you and find out how you've gotten away with all the things you've gotten away with."

"She's not bluffing," said Reggie, again sotto voce. "Either she thinks we're amateurs, or she knows her people will tag us whether we are or not."

"Keep blustering if it makes you feel manly," Ransom said to the old woman. "But let me know when you're done. And if it's not too long, we might not waste you."

"What do you want?" Her voice was icy and harsh.

It struck him then that he didn't know what he wanted. He wanted to kill her, to kill someone for what they had done, but he hadn't needed to bring her here for that.

"I want to know about the secret war between USAdmin and Amphibian. I want to know why—"

The old woman laughed harshly. "The secret war between USAdmin and Amphibian," she mocked. "You poor asshole. There is no war between USAdmin and Amphibian. The distributed AI you call Amphibian works for us."

Ransom stared at her. "What do you mean?"

"Just what I said. Are you deaf as well as stupid?"

"You're lying."

"Time to leave nursery school, Ransom. They tell a lot of stories there. The grown-ups—who got that way using life-extension therapies you'll start to hear about in another decade—distract the little ones with fables and fairy tales to keep them quiet. The 'war' between Amphibian and USAd-min is one of those. We keep it tucked away just a little bit, so that the ones who find it will think they have penetrated to the truth at last. It's like an Easter-egg hunt for outliers. An outer layer of fairy tales to catch the ones who are just a little bit smarter than the others."

"I don't believe you."

"She's telling the truth, or thinks she is," Reggie said in Ransom's earpiece.

"It doesn't matter what you believe," said the old woman. "You're about to find out that you're nothing but a slab of meat with pain receptors. Dying quickly is the very best you can hope for now. That's what comes of misbehaving. In just a little while you'll be begging me to let you die."

With a shudder, Ransom gave Reggie a slight nod, turned, and left the room. The second before the door closed behind him he heard the spitting of silenced automatic weapons and the old woman's screams. A few minutes later, he and Reggie were back in the van, speeding away from there.

27

It was convenient to be fabulously wealthy, Ransom often reflected, not only because he could afford the security needed to hide him from whoever might want to find him, but also because he could enjoy himself. The thought came to him as he woke up in a climate-controlled tent in the Congo River basin, monkeys and exotic birds making their dawn racket outside, a beautiful, black-haired girl rolling sleepily into his arms, warm and musky and a little sweaty from sleep. They lay for a few minutes half-dozing, and then their alarm keening like a whipbird made them struggle out of their comfortable king-size sleeping bag. Ransom made coffee while Catherine used the shower cubicle; then he sipped a steaming cup and watched her tanned, nubile body as she dressed. She glanced at him and laughed.

"You better take a shower or the lions are going to smell you," she said. "I can."

He did so, feeling good. Mary Catherine LaSalle had green eyes and a black belt in Tae Kwon Do, had gone to Yale, knew all the best people, how to play the violin, and was the scion of a family that had as much money as he did. But best of all, she was cheerful and full of enthusiasms, and she liked to *do* things, leaving him little time for obsessive metaphysical rumination. Being around her made him feel like a normal person for long stretches. He had even stopped trying to figure out whether the terrible old CCA manager had told him the truth about Amphibian working for US-Admin. He had also given up his revenge obsession; he was well out of the wheels-within-wheels, facade-behind-facade stuff.

So he thought.

Dumping their breakfast things into the recycler, they could hear the swishing of leaves and grunts as the mahouts led their mounts into the tent clearing, right on schedule. Ransom thought he could feel their approaching hugeness as if through the ground, though he had learned that elephants walked softly, almost daintily. Shrugging on his shooting jacket and ducking through the airlock behind Catherine's lithe backside, he came out into the hot, wet, aromatic air, and saw the great beasts, which turned their heads, watching them solemnly with their humanlike brown eyes, the mahouts jumping down from their backs holding their long hooks. Catherine was already stroking Noor's trunk and murmuring endearments in her huge, flapping ear, and Noor was curling her trunk next to her without touching her. Ransom went to Sakari, smelling the clean musk of her, like the smell of a hillside where animals lived, while she in turn sniffed him delicately with her trunk. He patted the trunk's rocklike skin. Then Abdullah and Yusef gave the elephants their words, and they bowed their great heads and curled their trunks so that Catherine and Ransom could step on, then lifted them up gently so they could climb into the howdahs strapped onto the hillocks of their backs. Abdullah handed up Ransom's rifle, and Yusef handed Catherine hers. Then each elephant lifted her mahout onto her huge neck, just in front of the howdah, and at another word lumbered forward into the jungle, rocking their riders from side to side in a soothing, patient rhythm. Vines and enormous leaves scraped and hissed over the roofs of the howdahs, sometimes touching Ransom's face through the open sides.

"We'll go into the valley today," said Abdullah with his Brooklyn accent. "Tigers have been down there this week."

Of course, the tigers were clones, as were the other game and the elephants, but aside from that, Ransom had been assured, the top dollar he had paid guaranteed an authentic safari experience, just like he would have had in the late 1800s. Even the guns were antiques: huge, heavy things made of thick metal and dense, carved wood, without electronics. So there was real danger—mitigated somewhat by the marksmen watching over them from helicopters so high up that you could pretend they were birds floating in the thermals above the jungle canopy.

This was the third day of the safari, and Ransom by now had learned how to roll with the long strides of the elephant so that he didn't feel shaken about, and could look around him steadily from a height of a bungalow's roof. They had seen lions drinking at the river their first day out, but by the time they had descended to the plain, the elephants swishing through the tall grass, the lions had gone. Now they were descending steep terrain again, heading for the same area.

They had lumbered forward for an hour, moving swiftly through the thick, wet air, when first Noor and then Sakari lifted their trunks and began swiveling them like periscopes, making sucking sounds that Ransom knew was sniffing. Then Noor began making a low rumbling sound, like a cross between a growl and an earthquake.

"What is she saying?" asked Catherine excitedly.

"There are tigers nearby," said Abdullah as Yusef stroked Noor's head and murmured in her ears. "You might want to get your guns ready."

Ransom heard the sharp, satisfying clack of Catherine shooting the bolt of her rifle, and he had just done the same with his own, his hands sweaty and eyes wide, when there was a screaming roar and Sakari pitched violently to the side, nearly throwing him out of the box, his gun going off in his hand, jerking almost hard enough to tear off his thumb. For a split second he saw the tiger, an arc of orange muscle, eyes green as Catherine's and teeth white as pearls, and then it was gone, disappearing into the jungle at a run, hidden almost immediately by the undergrowth.

Suddenly the roar of descending helicopters was all around him. This annoyed him. If they thought you could have an authentic safari experience with aircraft swooping down every time an elephant reared— Then he looked over at Catherine, and saw that she was no longer in her howdah, but that something—blood, he realized—was splashed all over it.

My gun, he thought in rising horror. My gun went off in my hand. "Abdullah!"

But Abdullah was already turning Sakari, and the huge beast took half a dozen steps before stopping dead in front of something she would not step over.

Trembling and praying, with Abdullah's help, Ransom fumbled onto Sakari's trunk, and jumped down onto the ground next to where Catherine lay with her arms and legs splayed out.

It was worse than he could have imagined. He had hit her in the head. There was a deep pit where her face should be, and blood was everywhere. Suddenly everything was spinning, and he sat heavily down on the ground, his vision blacking out in surges. That must have been what made it look like Catherine was moving, moving an arm, and then her legs, then pushing herself up into a sitting position, shaking like a malfunctioning machine.

And then he saw the titanium-plastic alloy, the torn bioflesh substrate, wiring and tubing and finely articulated titanium rods—

His horror at killing his girlfriend was nothing compared to what he felt now. Suddenly he was running—running full tilt and blindly into the jungle, his hand frantically squeezing out the panic code he had memorized and re-memorized, squeezing it out again and again, until suddenly he collided with a combat suit still steaming from its hypersonic descent. Other suits were tearing down through the canopy and quickly moving into perimeter formation, and now the deafening roar of descending stratocopters surrounded them, the wind of their rotors thrashing the canopy. The suit Ransom had run into sprayed him with a net, bonded it to a cord, and shot the other end of the cord into the air, and suddenly Ransom was rocketing upward through the canopy so fast that he lost consciousness.

When he came to, operatives were just closing the belly door of a 'copter that was rising almost as fast as he had risen on the cord, other operatives cutting the net loose from around him. Half a dozen hands helped him gently but urgently to stand, and then he was hustled with murmured apologies down a short gangway and helped down through a hatch in the floor into a small cockpit where a man in a flight suit and helmet was checking systems. The man leaned over to strap an elaborate seat belt over Ransom, the hatch he had climbed through was closed, and for a moment he had the sensation of falling.

Then the escape plane's rockets engaged, and for the second time Ransom lost consciousness from acceleration.

Four days later Ransom was finishing breakfast in bed at his Madrid safe house when Reggie came into the bedroom. It was stressful being rescued, especially when it involved sudden jaunts on high-speed covert transport alternating with silent immobility in hidden drops surrounded by sweating operatives in combat gear, all following randomized, nested evasion protocols computed in real time by a remote emulator so that not even the senior security people knew where, when, or how they would be moving next. Ransom was still tired, but a couple of good nights' sleep, good Spanish food, and the pleasant, quiet apartment with its high, sloping, wood-beamed ceilings and large windows looking out over the city had at least relaxed him. Seeing Reggie's expression, though, Ransom felt his blood pressure rise slightly.

"Hey, Reg. Bad news?"

"Nothing but good news," Reggie said. "Not only do we compute with a ninety-nine percent level of confidence that no one shadowed us up here, but our intercepts indicate that neither USAdmin nor Backward have any idea where you are, and had no idea you were in Africa in the first place."

"But how's that possible? If they replaced my girlfriend, they had to know where I was, right? And if they knew where I was, after all the security we piled on for the safari, how can we think they don't know where I am now? I might as well just sit and wait for them."

Reggie looked worried. "There's more. Catherine's parents have filed lawsuits, gone to the press, and hired detectives to find the man who left their daughter to bleed to death in an African reserve after he accidentally shot her in the head."

Ransom stared at him. "Have they seen the body?"

Reggie nodded. "They've had it since the first day. Even had an autopsy done on it."

"It's a trick, right? To lure me out?"

"It's got to be. What bothers me is how they got the La-Salles to make those statements."

"Are you sure they really did?"

"We've checked and double-checked. Either they really think their daughter is dead, or else they're doing a very good imitation, including brain waves. So either these folks can't tell their own daughter from an android, or else they're playing along with someone, including limbic implants and the whole shtick. But why would they do that? They live on their own national island in the Marshalls, so at least USAdmin can't twist their arms."

That night Ransom dreamed of a whole world of androids, who all thought they were people. He woke up in a sweat, wondering whether his trip through the tunnel out of Margaret Biel's death—and his own—could possibly have brought him back not to his own world, but to some kind of parallel replica-world, like the region in the Land of Oz where everything and everyone were reproductions made out of wood.

Two weeks later, everything had continued quiet. No rockets had struck their planes or cars; no combat suits had crashed through the walls of their safe houses; no mutants had appeared from thin air. Reggie's intelligence reports showed no unusual interest in Heathcliff Ransom or Michael Beach by either USAdmin or Backward. Reggie and the operatives started to look more confident again, as if maybe they weren't going to die imminently after all. A week after that, Reggie approved termination of the Code Red protocols.

Ransom happened to be in his Los Angeles safe house, and decided to move to his nearest digs, a compound in the hills above Malibu, built in the 1990s by some temporarily high-flying movie producer. Reggie and his people had gone ahead to clear the place and set up; Ransom followed the next evening, driving his Maserati convertible.

The cool blue air off the Pacific was soft and sweet as the autopilot took the curves and twists of the coastal highway, the hills above him and the surf at the bottom of the cliffs below making the place more like paradise than Earth. But Ransom hardly noticed. He was thinking—thinking about something that had begun to obsess him. John McMillan,

Ralph Mullins, Lucia Pagano, Catherine LaSalle, all androids. In fact, he realized, everyone who had been hurt or killed within his range of vision since the last time he had passed through Italy had turned out to be an android. Not to mention Doreen Zabroski and Vivien, who had never pretended to be anything but. And, it occurred to him, what about Catherine's family? Maybe they had all been replaced by androids too, and been programmed to say what they had said about her.

But even if that were all possible, it would not have been possible to keep it quiet. *Someone* would have noticed. The doctor doing the autopsy, or the funeral home people doing the embalming, or the family physician. But what if *they* were all androids, too? Plus whatever official medical examiner had certified the cause of death, and the two mahouts who had witnessed it, the game reserve personnel who had responded in their helicopters—

A whole world of androids, all programmed to think they were people—

Ahead of him, around a long curve, a newly paved road ran up into the hills. On an impulse, Ransom switched into manual and swung the car onto it, tires squealing. He stamped savagely on the gas, and the Maserati all but left the ground, the centripetal force as he took the switchback curves nearly throwing him from the car. After seventy seconds and four kilometers, a neighborhood appeared, one of those prefab antique places with cast-iron streetlights and Victorian town houses, with a sign on a faux-weathered stone wall that said HAMMERSMITH COMMONS. Ransom skidded his car into the first empty parking space, and got out into the quiet, cricket-trilled dusk. He ran up the steps of the first town house unit, pulling his Beretta from his jacket pocket. He would "test" the first person he met, and consequences be damned. If someone was watching him, projecting his movements, placing androids wherever he was predicted to go, there was no way they could have predicted he would come here because he hadn't known himself until two minutes ago.

In keeping with the neighborhood's theme, the town houses had old-fashioned push-button doorbells. Ransom pushed the one by the door he had picked, and waited. No one answered. He jabbed the button again—and then realized that it felt strange, as if it didn't have any give. He leaned down and looked closely at it in the dimming evening light. The button wasn't broken, he saw—it just wasn't real. It was a little molded-plastic box shaped and colored to look like an old-fashioned doorbell button, but it was actually all one piece, with no moving parts. *I should have known that Hammersmith Commons's doorbell affectation was a humbug,* he thought; *no doubt a modern door sensor was even now announcing his presence.* In a frenzy of impatience—as if his secret watchers might spirit androids into the town house if he didn't hurry—he banged on the door with his fist, but then stopped in shock. The door had made a vast, dull booming sound, as if he had pounded on the side of an empty storage tank. Heart hammering with fear, he now examined it more closely. He saw then, as he had with the doorbell button, that it wasn't real: it looked like a real door, but when you examined the gap between it and the frame, you saw that there was only a depression two centimeters deep, and that what looked like a door was a molded plastic panel on a flat plastic surface cunningly fashioned and colored to counterfeit the front of a town house.

Ransom felt the world shifting beneath him, and clutched at the wrought-iron railing. He lowered himself dizzily to the top step and sat with his head down, breathing hard, wanting to vomit. But his faintness was leavened with panic: he struggled to his feet and descended the steps, leaning heavily on the railing. He was desperate to get away from there, but instead he pushed through the bushes that land-scaped the front of the town house, and around other bushes and small trees that grew close alongside its side wall.

What he saw when he reached the back made his former fear seem mild by comparison. The town house block had no back. In the twilight he saw what looked like a grassy field enclosed by three-story walls held up by huge struts. It was made to be seen only from the front; from the back it was just a hollow shell, like a movie set built on location.

28

Barbara Santangelo sat at her desk in Acrobatic Seductions's corner office and raced to proofread her expert system's responses to the morning's correspondence. She had squeezed in a noon meeting, and she had to get these letters out before it started.

She still had a dozen letters to go when a chime sounded. A violet icon said silkily, "Mr. Longman and his assistant are here to see you."

"Shit." She flicked a finger through a red icon to turn off her editing function, her face going in a second from tense and aggressive to energetically charming and sexy. She enjoyed meeting prospective investors like a trip to the dentist, but it took money to make the art-house horrorsex and mysterysex immersions Acrobatic produced, and until they were big enough to go public, investors they must have.

She had the charm on full force when the door opened and two men came in, both large, well-dressed, and polite. One was strikingly handsome and about her age; the other was nondescript and carried a briefcase—perhaps an android, she thought: they were improving them so fast nowadays that the high-end ones were hard to spot. They shook hands with her and sat in the visitors' chairs. Then the nondescript one opened his briefcase and a small amount of sparkling pinkish mist dispersed purposefully into the air, leaving it apparently as empty as before.

"What—" Barbara started, shock and annoyance replacing charm.

"Surveillance rejectors," said the handsome man, relaxed and smiling. "Don't tell me you've gone all these years not realizing that USAdmin watches you day and night?"

"You're USAdmin?"

"No. I'm glad you don't recognize me, though. Remember Michael Beach? The kid you killed? Don't bother about your subvocal; Reggie's nanocloud has everything buttoned up."

The color had drained from the woman's face.

"What do you want?" she rasped. Her eyes were suddenly rimmed with red, her lips gray under their gloss.

"Sorry to be so abrupt, but the businesslike discussion of content financing that Reggie's cloud is playing for your watchers only lasts thirty-one minutes, so we don't have much time. May I call you Meg?"

The woman closed her eyes, and drops of tears or sweat ran down her gray cheeks. She whispered, "Are you from the Company?"

"No. Look, don't worry. I didn't come here to hurt you. Backward doesn't even know I'm still alive."

Barbara Santangelo/Margaret Biel started at the name, and opened her eyes. She was trembling.

"Yes, I know about them. I know about everything, more or less. I was an endovid investigator hired to follow you when you made your body switch, almost ten years ago now, I guess. I got into your boyfriend's body when you gave him the narcopine overdose."

The woman stared at him. "You're lying, obviously. But I don't care. What do you want? I'll give you anything you want to leave me alone." A little color was returning to her face. That's my Meg, Ransom thought. Always ready to come back for round two.

"What I want is information."

"What information?"

"I need to give you some background first." Reggie was

updating him subvocally on the woman's readings; as of now, six minutes in, her limbic surfaces were still firing hard, indicating that she was still focused on escape or resistance. Maybe he could calm her down with a story. And this particular story might also convince her that she should help him.

"You didn't know this, of course, but at the end of your life as Margaret Fenton Biel you were like an amoeba under a microscope. I was a forensic endovoyant investigator named Heathcliff Ransom, and someone—either USAdmin, or USAdmin and Backward collectively, or some scientists on the run from Backward, depending on who you believe—maneuvered your loving relatives, the Merrivales, into hiring me to try to bring you back from the coma Backward had induced to do your body switch. Why whoever maneuvered the Merrivales wanted me to do this depends on who you think did the maneuvering; I've heard so many stories by this time that I'm inclined to disbelieve all of them.

"So to make a long story short, I followed you through your terminal dream. I got to your boundary scene, an orchard with a big mountain at the end of it. In the orchard was a hole that Backward had made using some kind of causal gravity to do the body switch. I fell into the hole, and came out over the Sorrento coast, just like you did."

Her eyes were riveted on him now.

"I sensed where you were in Sorrento, and I got to your room just in time to see you give your boyfriend a shot. I can't figure out a coincidence like that, unless the causal mojo Backward used to do your body switch was set to work on whoever went through their tunnel—which was only supposed to be you, of course.

"So Michael Beach's consciousness is separated from his body. I drag myself into his body—this body." He gestured at his chest. "Then I pretend I'm still him. I convince everyone good old Michael Beach is still alive, and that he doesn't remember anything about what you did, and then as soon as I can, I leave, come back to Continental North America."

"So they know—USAdmin knows that I—"

"Yes, they know, but they don't care. I only have seventeen minutes until Reggie's bugs run out of simulation. I'm going to leave you contact information in case you want to meet somewhere secure, and then I can answer anything you want to know. But for now, just listen.

"So I come back to good old North America, then I disappear so that once Backward and/or USAdmin figure out that I'm a loose end, it's too late for them to cut me off."

Reggie's subvocal report said the woman's temporal lobes were now quiet enough for her to think. So Ransom started on the important part.

"So I spend a lot of money and time making sure I can't be traced. But then something strange happens, and at first I think they've found me. People close to me who are supposed to be real people start turning out to be androids.

"Things came to a head a couple of weeks ago, when on an impulse I drove up into the hills above Malibu and knocked on a door at random. The door made a booming sound, and I went around back of the townhouse block to look. It was a set, a huge three-sided box held up by struts.

"I went back the next day with Reggie here and some bodyguards. But now the town houses were real: in back there were tiny yards with garden furniture and grills and swing-sets, separated by fences. Somebody or something had turned the hollow town house shells into a real townhouse development, and done it overnight, with no signs of construction machines or materials—everything looked just as if the place had been there for years.

"We went back around front to the door that had made the booming sound the night before, and a middle-aged woman answered. Behind her was a normal middle-income house, with carpets and furniture and paintings on the walls and a cat. Reggie grabbed the woman's arm and fired his gun into it. The woman screamed, but then we could see the wires and bioflesh substrate.

"We got in our cars and got away from there.

"By now I was seriously distraught. Could my environment—what I used to think of as my 'sensorium'— really be all fake? Could I actually be all alone in a world populated by machines and movie sets? I didn't have the nerve to try another test. I was afraid what I might find. Then I thought of you.

"You're the only person I know who went through the same thing I did, through the tunnel, into a new body, escaping death. If the tunnel somehow transported me to a world where everything is fake, it must have done the same to you. So I decided to come ask you if the same things have happened to you.

"So," he said. "What do you think of that?"

She didn't answer right away. When she did, her voice was low and controlled. "I think," she said, "that you should get out of my office, and never come near me again. I don't know what you want, or why you're telling me these things. If I had to guess, I'd say you're schizophrenic, probably with necrotic hallucinations. But get this into your mind, if there's any room next to all that crap: I don't care what you think you've seen or how you think I might help you. I just want to go on with my life. I paid a lot, in a lot of different ways, to be here. If you want to denounce me to USAdmin, or kill me, or make what I did public, I can't stop you. But in the meantime, *stay away from me.*"

"But you're the only person I know of who's—"

She put her hands over her ears and screamed, "*Go away!*" Then she was sobbing again.

Reggie said to her gently. "I'm about to terminate the simulation. You may want to get back to your previous appearance, or if anyone is watching they'll notice a seam."

The woman pulled herself together with amazing speed. She wiped her face with a tissue, then applied her makeup mask. When she took it away, her cosmetics refreshed, she worked the sexy, energetic look back onto her face.

"Hold your pose for a second," said Reggie, and when she was still he flicked an icon to dovetail the simulation, and then the pink dust quickly concentrated and streamed back into the briefcase.

"It's been great talking to you," said Ransom as he and Reggie headed toward the door.

29

On an evening a month later, Ransom was sitting on the terrace of his Malibu house looking out over the hills at the red disk of the sun sinking into the ocean, when Reggie's voice said out of the air, "She's on line six."

Ransom plugged his phone in behind his ear, and connected to the encrypted voice-only line. "Hello?"

"I want to talk to you."

"We'll pick you up," said Ransom, and terminated.

"Will do," said Reggie's voice.

Reggie's people had been watching her for months, and had passwords to her home, office, and clubs. So even with their precautionary evasion protocols it wasn't more than three hours before he heard a light step on the flagstones, and, standing, saw a slim blonde in a 1940s-style suit coming toward him. She tried to walk haughtily, but he could see that the hypnotics they had given her hadn't yet worn off yet, and when she was two meters from him she stumbled. He stepped quickly forward and caught her.

She pushed his hands away angrily. "Damn you," she said in a slurred voice. She stood unsteadily looking up at him, hatred in her face.

"Won't you sit down? Can I offer you a drink?"

"I'm not here as a friend."

"You're only here because I might be the last real person in the world. I know. That's why I came to you."

"Why did you have to do it?" she asked tiredly. "Why couldn't you have stayed away from me? I was happy. Why didn't you just let me go on not knowing? Does misery love company that much?"

Ransom had watched her do her own tests via surveillance video, including shooting her boyfriend, who had then stormed out of her apartment, his titanium head dented, bio-plastic face torn away.

"Why couldn't you have just left me alone?"

"I used to think I would hate you even if you were the last woman on Earth," he said slowly. "But it turns out that's not true."

"You need a comfort woman in your fake world? Wasn't fakeness your whole profession before?"

"Ah, you've done your research. But back then I always had somewhere to come back to. A place I knew was real."

"Maybe it was fake, too. Maybe the world has always been fake, and we just never suspected. Maybe you're fake." She had started crying quietly, exhaustedly.

"I'm not fake," he said. "Look, sit down." He led her by the arm to the rattan armchair nearest his, and she sank onto its pillows.

"What difference does it make? As long as everything looks real, everybody seems real, what difference does it make? Why couldn't you have left me alone? I might have never found out."

"If it doesn't make a difference, why are you here?"

Her crying got wilder. "Real people are just machines anyway, aren't they? So what's the difference, as long as everything looks like it's supposed to, and works like it's supposed to?"

He didn't answer.

"I paid . . . I paid a hundred million euro for this," she said. "And killed two people. To come to a place where nothing is real."

"Do you want a drink?"

"Yes, please. Something with oxytocin boosters."

He was taken aback. "Are you sure?"

"Yes, I'm *sure*," she snarled. Then, in a trembling voice: "You know what animals do when they arrive at the slaughter-house? When they smell the blood and feces and hear the screams of the ones ahead of them dying? They fuck. They go wild, fucking anything that's handy. It's a stress reaction when you know you're going to die very soon and very badly. A thing biological machines do at the end, when the situation goes beyond their programming."

She showed him how the doomed animals did it. She seemed sometimes a beautiful demon, sometimes an angel in the throes of suicide. When at last they lay quiet on the sweat-damp sheets she was pale and inert as wax; a single drop of blood had run out of the corner of her mouth and dried on her cheek.

"Are you okay?" he asked softly. After the fury and sorrow of their lovemaking, even the sound of his own voice seemed to bruise him.

"What if we're not real?" she asked in a whisper.

"We are real."

"How do you know?"

He took her hand and held it against his chest so she could feel his heart beating.

"That doesn't prove anything," she said. "Androids have circulatory apparatus."

Something woke him. It was dark, and Meg was kneeling over him, holding his ornamental letter opener like a dagger. Before he could move, she plunged the blade into his eye.

Pain filled his head like fire, and he screamed. Within seconds, security androids had jumped into the room and pulled the woman off him.

In panic, Ransom pulled the dagger out of his eye. A heavy spurt of blood followed it.

"Fuck!" he screamed. "Mirror!"

His bedroom system switched on a mirror in front of him. His face was a terrified rictus painted with wet blood that was still pulsing from the pulped crater of the eye. And just inside the crater something was poking out.

In horror he grabbed at it.

It was a wire.

And, telling the mirror to magnify, through the blood he could see the torn layer of bioplastic that enclosed his titanium-plastic brain case.

Medics were coaxing and grappling him onto a gurney, one stuffing a wad of graft gauze into his injured socket— and now Reggie appeared in his pajamas, eyes wide with shock.

Ransom turned to him, pulling out the sticky gauze already starting to graft onto his skin; he pulled the wire he had found five centimeters out of his eye socket so Reggie could get a look at it.

Reggie went white with astonishment.

Ransom realized suddenly that his eye and head no longer hurt, and that he actually didn't feel too bad at all. He got off the gurney, pushing the medics out of the way. The woman stood sobbing wildly, held by two security androids in black fatigues, so that her small, blond body looked like a flame in the darkness.

"I'm okay," he said to her. He tried to make his trembling lips smile. "You were right. How did you know?"

"I didn't *know*," she snarled. "I wanted to kill you." Then her voice broke. "Do it to me."

"No," he said. "It's not necessary. What difference does it make?"

"I have to know," she said. "*I have to know.*"

"Later. Right now let's get—"

"*Now. Now!* I can't wait."

"Meg—"

She looked up at him, her eyes haunted. "Please."

Ransom looked into her face for a few seconds, then let go of her and gestured at one of the security operatives, who unholstered and coded his sidearm, handed it over.

Ransom held Meg's forearm, and fired the gun down into her hand.

The hand exploded in a bloody mess, and she screamed horribly, but then Ransom could see the bioflesh substrate and the hinges and wires along the tungsten-plastic finger bones.

TWO hours later Ransom was back in his bed, his head heavily bandaged, and Meg sat against some pillows next to him and smoked. Her left hand was as heavily bandaged as his head, but aside from making it hard to light cigarettes, it didn't seem to bother her. Ransom, on the other hand, felt odd. He wasn't in pain, but he felt strangely discontinuous, as if something in his consciousness kept switching on and off so that he couldn't attend to things properly, making the world a series of small surprises. He had spent a long time with an android diagnostic unit's extensible tools poked into his eye socket, and then they had taken the data away to run in a cloud somewhere.

He realized that Meg was talking to him.

"—you feel?" she was saying.

"A little odd. Generally okay. What about you?"

"I'm trying to figure that out."

"At least."

He realized an indefinable time later that he had not finished speaking. Meg was looking at him quizzically.

"You're not all right," she said.

"I was going to say," he continued, concentrating, "that at least we're not the only two living people in a world of machines."

At that moment Reggie appeared as if by magic in the chair next to him. He looked worried.

"—seems to be wrong with him," Meg was saying. "He keeps going blank like that."

"Heath?" Reggie said gently. "Can you hear me? Are you okay?"

"I'm fine. At least, maybe I'm not *perfectly* fine. Are they going to be able to fix me?"

"Well, there's good news and bad news. The good news is, you don't have to be decommissioned."

"Good. I don't think I'd like that. What's the bad news?"

Blank. "—so you have to go into the central facility for repairs."

"Why is that bad news? Your security can cover it, can't they?"

"Definitely. I shouldn't have said bad news. It's more like weird news. See, you need a new CNS emulator. All right, I know what you're thinking, but it shouldn't be that bad. They download your current emulator's precise configuration into a holding media and—" Blank.

"And what?"

"I said they download your current emulator's precise configuration into a holding media and then upload it back into you once they have the new hardware installed, so that the new one is structurally identical to the old one, down to nanoscales. So you come off the line the same old Heath Ransom as you went in."

"Sounds idyllic," Ransom said. But he had vaguely heard of the academic debates about what really happened to the subjective person—if androids had one—under this procedure. As far as everyone else was concerned, he would come off the line the same old Heath Ransom, he would look the same, act the same, have the same memories and likes and dislikes. But as far as he himself was concerned, would he be the same old Heath Ransom or would he be gone, having been killed and replaced by an identical substitute?

And then there were the urban myths about androids coming out of this radical repair process raving about some God who spoke to them during the time they were disembodied or nonexistent or dead, or whatever it was.

"—approved, then? They're antsy to get going before there's further deterioration."

"What happens if I don't go in?"

"They can try to patch you up, but they put the likelihood at sixty-five percent that you would eventually deteriorate to a vegetative state."

"Isn't a vegetative state higher than a mechanical state?" Ransom asked, and then, seeing that nobody was interested in the joke, said, "Okay. Let's do it."

Ransom's VTOL made two hours to Chicago, but then slowed to a hover among the hundred other craft in a holding pattern around Talking Machines's enormous faux-Gothic building. After half an hour, Reggie having flexed some of Ransom's financial muscle, TMC's traffic controllers pulled them out of the pattern and down to one of the building's rooftop pads. By this time Ransom's attention was so unstable that he was aware only of a series of isolated scenes: the cross and circle painted on the pad approaching out the VTOL window; the VIP reception team waiting in the embarkation lounge, all expensive suits and bright smiles; riding in a wheelchair next to the swinging hips and tapping heels of one of the female team members; Reggie shaking hands with someone important-looking and exchanging words too low to catch; then two technicians helping him out of his wheelchair and taking off his clothes, helping him toward a bay from whose darkness mechanical appendages reached for him—

Didn't these people realize they were all androids? Did they really think he was an android and they were humans? And if so, how? What happened when *they* got sick? Wouldn't their doctors figure out right away what they were? Didn't anyone in this world's billions ever notice? Or were the doctors, nurses, and patients likewise all programmed not to realize what they were seeing, but to believe and remember that they had done or received this or that organic medical procedure? What kind of world was made up of robots that all thought they were people? Why should such a world exist?

—the robot arms took hold of him with mandibles, calipers, and articulated claws. He braced himself, but they were gentle, even when, whirring, they promptly turned him upside down and drew him into the darkness of the bay. Inside, mechanisms moved around him, enclosing him in a writhing, blinking mass.

Then everything was gone.

30

When he came back to Malibu it was November. Reggie had alerted Meg, and she had allowed herself to be kidnapped again, so she was waiting for Ransom when he arrived at the house at dawn. They had a breakfast of champagne and caviar on the terrace, sitting on a rattan love seat under a plaid wool blanket, Meg with her back against the arm and her small toes thrust under his leg to warm them. Her hand seemed altogether healed. She was subdued but cheerful.

"So is it still you?" she asked him. "You look the same."

"I feel like I am," he said. "But nothing would surprise me anymore. What about you? You don't mind being an android?"

"I don't feel any different. But you—"

"What?"

"You seem different. Are you sure it's you in there? You've been awfully quiet. Or do you just not like having breakfast with women who've tried to kill you?"

"No, I like it very much." He was silent for a minute. "I saw something."

She studied him. "When you were knocked out, you mean? Like a God thing? They say that's an android hallucination. Circuits firing at random."

"Like I said, nothing would surprise me anymore."

They nibbled and sipped in silence.

"Tell me," she said finally.

"You won't like it."

"How do you know?"

"Don't tell Reggie or anybody."

"I promise."

"I need to kill myself."

She stared at him. Then she said, "Did this God thing tell you that? Has it ever occurred to you that not everything you see might be real?'

He smiled. "That's been my assumption about everything in the entire world since I was a kid."

"Then how can you—"

"Because this makes sense. Can I tell you about it?"

She had opened her mouth to argue, and her cheeks were flushed, but she closed her mouth and sat back instead, her face set. "Okay," she said. "Tell me."

"They took me to this big, weird building in Chicago. The techs there put me in a repair bay, and I got put to sleep. After a while they switched me off or shut me down or whatever, and then even the sleep was gone. It's hard to explain, but take it from me that you've never experienced anything like it. What I mean is, when you go to sleep you still exist; but this—"

"Okay, very impressive. Then what?"

"Then nothing. Not vacuum, darkness, or silence. A lack of all those. Like everything and its opposite added together and canceling each other out utterly. Then, after a finite or infinite time, I woke up, and I was fixed."

"And that means you need to kill yourself?"

"Something had happened when I was gone. I didn't remember it until I came back, of course, but then it was very clear."

"Artifactual interpolated memory."

"Maybe. But what it said made sense."

"Is this God we're talking about now?"

"I don't know. It's like—"

He paused for so long that she finally said, "What?"

"I don't know what it was, but what it seemed like was—

I don't know. Nothingness—but as if everything and its opposite had come together and canceled each other out, leaving just absolute absence of anything anywhere.

"Except that everything and its opposite combined is also everything—everything in potential form, do you see? That's what I saw. Everything and nothing together, pure empty potentiality. Like blank white light you know is full of colors, that just needs a prism to split it apart. But it was . . . it was *familiar,* so familiar that I felt completely at home, like it was something I'd been hugging to myself my whole life, keeping it so close that I had thought it was *me,* the feeling of being *me* deep inside, underneath everything else. So I—it was so familiar that I gave it a face. My own face. Not like I was looking in a mirror, but my own face from the inside. Does that make any sense?"

"No."

"The difference was—this face was *huge*—it seemed to take up all space, and I felt that it was very wise, infinitely wise. It . . . it spoke to me."

"I knew it."

"It said—" Another long pause, but Meg waited this time. When Ransom finally spoke, his voice was soft. "It said, 'You aren't where you are supposed to be.'

"It was like talking to myself, like the thing that was *me,* that had made me alive and conscious my whole life speaking.

"It—or I—said, 'You aren't where you are supposed to be. These things are not arbitrary. There is no longer a place for you in the pattern of the world, and the veins that connect you to it are withering. First the things outside you turn lifeless, then your own body becomes lifeless. Finally your thoughts and feelings die. You can stay if you want, but you may not like it.' "

He was silent again for a long time, thinking. Finally he said, "I need to go back to where I'm supposed to be."

She surprised him then. She said, "If you go, I want to go, too."

"Why?" He realized suddenly that he didn't want her to. Just as she hadn't wanted him to. "I thought you didn't believe in—"

"I don't know if that was God you talked to," she said. "Maybe it was just you talking to yourself. But what it said . . . sounds right. I should never have come here. I should just have lived my hundred and twenty years like everyone else, and died. I messed things up, and I killed two people. And you're the only one who . . . who's like me; so if you go, there won't be any reason for me to stay."

"Then this is our last meal."

She turned pale. "You want to do it right away?"

"I don't see any reason to wait. I don't know what happens next if we stay, or how fast it happens, but I don't want to crumble to dust or anything. I'd like to go under my own power."

Her lips were trembling and her eyes were rimmed with red. "But . . . don't you need some time to get used to the idea?"

"I don't think I'll ever get used to the idea. I'm afraid that if I wait I'll change my mind. I have some high explosives that will basically liquefy us. I don't think it will hurt, at least not for long."

"But what if"—her lips were trembling so much that she could hardly speak—"what if you're wrong? What if this is all there is? What if it was just an artifactual memory? It didn't tell you what happens after we die, did it?"

"No."

"I wish you had asked it," she said irritably. Color was starting to come back into her face. With her usual grit, Meg was rallying.

"Sorry."

"Aren't you scared at all?"

"Not really. I've done this plenty of times. Though not in a few years. About ten years, actually."

"Does it hurt?"

"For a second."

"Where do you go?"

"Normal people go to their boundary dreams. Yours is an orchard that leads to a mountain. Mine is an empty beach. But because of everything that's happened, I don't think I'll go to mine anymore. Something else will happen to me. I just hope it's not unpleasant."

"Will I go back to mine?"

"I assume you will. And it will probably be a replay of the last time you were there. If so, you'll have a choice to make: You can jump down the hole Backward made and relive your life starting from the time you arrive in Italy to get into this body. Or you can go to the mountain, and—"

"Do we have time for some more champagne first?"

They drank a toast and smashed their glasses on the flagstones.

In his room, Ransom took an innocuous-looking capsule from a small box, set the fuse, and put it in his mouth. Then they began to kiss, passing the capsule back and forth with their tongues. Their kissing became hard and passionate.

The explosion startled Reggie in his office on the second floor, sent security androids rushing to the bedroom.

But not much was left of Ransom and Meg.

31

It had been years since he had last died, and it was shocking. First violent, searing agony, a second later tumbling away into darkness. An immeasurable time after that a roaring chaos of sensation around him, slowly resolving into waves of sharp, red sound. Then something pierced his head, and a freezing, blinding light opened around him. He felt that he had been dumped naked on a glacier and ice-picked through his eye-sockets.

A ringing garble cleared into a voice: "—reflux. Give me the suction tube. Heath? Heath, are you all right? Where's the transdermal? Can you hurry it up, please—"

Something sucked at his mouth and throat.

"Heath, we'll have the shot in a second."

He was lying on something. The roaring in his head was separating into sounds: voices, the rustle of movement, and in the background a Klaxon blaring.

"Here's the shot."

Something tapped his arm.

He felt better. The deep confusion that had merged everything together was receding, and he felt that he might be moving his fingers.

A light, bell-like voice, just above him, said: "Are you back?"

He opened his eyes with difficulty. Leaning over him was the tear-stained face of a beautiful dark-haired girl. She smiled at him through her tears. "Are you back?"

A sudden cutting sadness went through him. In a few

minutes Anna Heatherstone would die. And he himself would die, and this time he would not come back. This was the last time he would ever see her.

"Don't cry," she said, beginning to cry again herself, and he realized that tears were leaking from his sticky eyes. She leaned over and kissed him, wiped his tears away with soft fingers.

They still had a few seconds. He could still warn them, order everyone into the safe room, call McMillan. But history had to take its course, if only because he couldn't put these people—who were still dear to him though he hadn't seen them for ten years—through the slow withering of the world that seemed to afflict those who didn't die when they were supposed to. Especially because they would have no idea what was happening to them.

He lay and waited miserably, Anna standing over him.

A loud crash made her whirl around with a scream, and then she was ripped open. Ransom saw the huge blurred shape of the mutant, felt the hail of projectiles tear into him—

For the second time that hour he died, but it was how he had been meant to die.

He stood in an orchard. As far as he could see in every direction were rows of peach trees; a breeze stirred their dark green leaves. He smelled warm crabgrass and honeysuckle, and in the quietness bees were buzzing. Far in the distance the orchard sloped up to the foot of a mountain, its almost vertical summit disappearing into mists and clouds.

He started toward the mountain.

Eventually he felt the vague discomfort and heard the buzzing. The orchard began to fill with static.

He had braced himself for the sight of the chaos tunnel, of course, but seeing it hanging in the air, rotating with its pixelated black glitter, terrified him so much that he suddenly couldn't move.

He had to go into it. He didn't know whether the world would still wither to lifelessness if he stayed in Margaret Biel's boundary vision, but he couldn't risk being trapped here, and he remembered now that the tunnel was weakening, its pull diminishing, meaning that it might close soon. Trembling violently, he forced his legs to move.

When he was close enough, the hole gaped and roared, the orchard stood on end, and he fell.

The hell of chaos tore at his being, dissolving him body, mind, and soul. It was only when he existed again, could feel and smell the ocean air, that he remembered what had made him go through the tunnel so many times: hunger for life, which he had once hoped would be never-ending, and for which he had been willing to undergo any terror.

As before, he floated through alternating currents of cold and warm air down toward the town hugging the rocky slopes, landing on a steep, deserted back street on the mild, overcast day. As before, he walked down to the street at the bottom of the town. There was no particular hurry—in fact, he realized, there was no reason to go to the Pagano house at all. It might even be better not to, because then there would be no temptation to change his mind.

And with that thought, what he had decided to do struck him with full force.

He leaned dizzily against a garden wall, his heart pounding. He was planning to die. No more coming back to the world, in either Heath Ransom's or Michael Beach's body. No more of the Earth's sunlight, its air, its smells; no more walking or sleeping or eating.

A tearing sadness and fear came over him. He wanted to live! Every creature wanted to live. Even the broken sacks of organs Backward had made of Margaret Biel and Eugene Denmark had wanted to live. It was unnatural to die voluntarily. He didn't care if he and everyone around him turned into androids, or stone statues for that matter. He wanted to live as long as he could.

He stood breathing hard, eyes closed, leaning against the wall. He would go to the house as usual, get into Michael Beach's body, play innocent as he had learned to do, and live again. How could he have considered giving up the sunlight aboveground for the darkness below it? The Face had said, "You are not where you are supposed to be." But all-encompassing eternal Faces could have no idea what it was like to be human, where dying from this life might mean the end of everything, or something so different that it might as well be the end of everything. The Face, focused as it was on fate and causality and the integrity of universal law, could have no idea how bad that kind of thing could be for a person.

And yet the Face had been right. He wasn't where he was supposed to be. And even if where he was supposed to be was nowhere, you still had to weigh being where you were supposed to be against being where you wanted to be.

He burst into tears, and for a moment he couldn't stir, either to go forward or back, but he knew that soon the drama in the house was going to take place either with or without him, and that if it was without him, then his decision would be made by default.

In panic he sprinted down the street. He dashed through the front door of the house, climbed the steps, and went into the bedroom where the boy and girl still lay next to each other.

Ransom crouched over Meg, very young again. As he watched, she opened blue eyes and looked straight up at him.

"Meg?" After what they had been through together, it seemed especially strange that she couldn't see him.

She slid from under the covers, taking care not to wake the boy—himself, Ransom thought with shock, looking at the face he had seen so often in the mirror. Meg was swiftly and silently putting on her clothes. She took the hypodermic from her backpack and knelt silently by the boy, slowly and carefully pulled the blanket aside. With a quick movement she pushed the syringe against his thigh.

The boy sat bolt upright, stared at her in confusion for a full second, and then jerked his leg away as if stung. The girl stood up and backed away against the wall.

"Barbara, what—" he said. But then he stopped. His eyes crossed. He seemed to have trouble holding up his head. He reclined onto his elbows and then onto his back with a deep sigh, like the air coming out of a bellows. He settled peacefully, looking straight up at the ceiling, but now his breathing was shallow, his crossed eyes glassy. A set look of concentration came into his face, and his breathing trailed off. He began to turn gray, like a boy poured from cement.

Then the calamity.

The room distorted like water being sucked down a drain, and Ransom felt the terrible vortex. At the same moment, the young man stood up out of his gray body and drifted unconcernedly away.

Ransom gripped the boy's body and held on, as he had learned to do. He could see the boy's silhouette far inside the vortex, walking through a beautiful meadow toward the edge of a forest.

Now for the struggle, the awful, tearing effort of pulling himself into the boy's body, forcing it to breathe one more time, to roll over. But—clinging to the body against the current—Ransom hesitated.

You are not where you are supposed to be.

Where *was* he supposed to be? Had the Face meant death wasn't the end?

The howling vortex was receding, sucking away the last of whatever it had taken from the room, its current weakening.

Still Ransom hesitated.

And then it was over. The vortex pull dropped away, and at the same moment the handholds he had taken on the boy's body seemed to melt, until he was holding nothing. He stood up.

He shared the room with a corpse and a girl. The girl slipped out the door and closed it silently behind her.

Now there was only Ransom and the corpse.

He had made his decision.

32

Ransom had never been around when the body on the futon actually died, so he didn't know what happened next. He stood looking dully at the boy's corpse. That was himself lying dead—and this time without an escape. Why had he hesitated? How could he have been so *stupid*? Even if he had decided in the end to die, there had been no need to rush. He could always have gone through with it once he had thought it out, clarified everything in his mind, made a final decision. But now, incredibly, it was too late, *too late*. He—Heathcliff Ransom—had been sprayed with bullets back in the Washington, D.C., suburb. He was *dead*.

At the same time, though, he realized that he didn't feel too bad. So far everything seemed okay.

He tried to relax, and took a breath.

The boy on the futon was looking more and more dead all the time, deader than Ransom had ever thought anything could look, deader than a rock. It was disturbing. Shakily, he went downstairs and out through the front door. There was no sign of Meg, Tomas, or Lucia.

After the stuffy bedroom and the dead body, the outdoor air was fresh and sweet, a fitful breeze now bringing a hint of coolness from the water. The breeze had blown the clouds back inland, and humid, yellow sunlight threw long shadows along the street. Ransom noticed that he didn't cast a shadow.

He was, in other words, a ghost. He had been a ghost before, but never for more than a couple of hours. He had gotten so used to dying and living again—bouncing back and forth in the causal loop Backward had made—that it seemed unbelievable that the cycle was over, that he should not be able to get back to earthly life in one of his two bodies. That he would now die once and for all.

But it seemed to be a fact. With his other options foreclosed, he would now go wherever dead people went. And the big question—in fact, the only question—was: what if that was nowhere? What if, as the Triumph of Sciencers said, when the body died and disappeared, the mind—after a short and deceptive trip through a series of hallucinations—disappeared, too?

The Church of Universal Evolution held that the mind or soul was a quasi-stable standing torsion wave in the vacuum field, often interpenetrating with but ultimately independent of a similar wave representing the body. But if that were true, where were all the other people who had died over the centuries, and should be teeming around him? At best, the ghost state had to be temporary, lasting only until the amplitude of the standing wave accounting for his mind subsided, as it must without a physical substrate to feed it energy.

Or maybe after death you entered a "private" sensorium, similar to an astral projection, as the Divine Dream Church believed: a private universe where information took a seemingly solid form—an effectively eternal universe because information could remain intact until the heat death of the universe, approximately 10^{100} years in the future.

One way or another, it looked like being a ghost was off the beaten track for dead people. Ordinary people crossed their terminal boundaries automatically, as if in a dream—like Michael Beach, walking across his meadow toward the trees as if deep in thought. Ransom himself had "woken up" from his own boundary vision back at the Montgomery Village apartment, seen through it at the last moment; his thirty years as an endovid had made him familiar enough with projected sensoria that Vivien yelling his name had been able to rouse him.

Unless *this* was his boundary vision.

He looked around warily. If that were so—if what had happened to him had substituted this small Italian town for the bluff and beach—there would be a verge or border somewhere nearby, which he would be drawn to cross. It would be something obvious: a line of trees at the end of a meadow or the ocean washing up on a beach were typical.

He wondered what had happened to Meg. Had she climbed her mountain into the clouds? Or had she decided to live again, gone down the black hole to her new, young body? If she had gone back, she could probably keep looping around, go on living as long as she wanted. Ransom felt a sharp pang of envy and sorrow.

The breeze had died down and it was very quiet, the late afternoon sun warm on his back. He had been walking as he cogitated, and now had come to the edge of the village, where the road clung to the cliffs with only a guardrail between it and a three-hundred-meter drop to the water. Ransom went and leaned his legs against the warm, rusted metal of the guardrail, feeling a tingle of fear at the height. He realized too that he was keeping an eye out for cars—a habit he would shed if he spent much time as an incorporeal entity, he guessed.

But looking down at the choppy water, it suddenly struck him that here was a boundary, and that he had come to it as if drawn, without thinking. Could it be his terminal boundary? What would happen if he crossed it? And practically before he knew what he was doing, he had climbed onto the guardrail and launched himself off.

He fell. The water rushed up at him through a tearing wind.

He thrashed his arms and legs in panic, and then, just as

suddenly as he had fallen, he began rushing upward. He was a kilometer in the high, empty air, the world spread out vast and vertiginous below him, before he could calm himself enough to slow down.

Wherever he was, it looked like astral-style physical laws prevailed—at least for ghosts.

He floated tranquilly in the upper air. What now? Since he was up here, he might as well look around. He willed himself back over the town and then past it, over rocky, dusty, olive-green hills planted with grapes and wheat, interspersed with gorges and steep, rocky mountains that reached almost up to where he floated. The light was strong and sharp up here, the air cool and dry, with snatches of smells from below: warm dirt, vegetation, manure. Long shadows stretched out behind the mountains. Far above him, a jetliner murmured in the sky.

It was peaceful and beautiful, but after an hour he felt like going back. It was homesickness, he realized. The massacre at Ransom International had left the Paganos and Barbara Santangelo/Margaret Biel the only people to whom he could still even pretend to be linked. It was the first time in his life he could remember actually craving human company.

He flew down into the warm, humid air near the surface, back to the street at the bottom of the town. As soon as he entered the house, he could hear crying and loud voices from upstairs. At the top of the steps was a scene that he happened to know was feigned on all sides. Barbara and Lucia were crying in each other's arms, and Tomas was yelling emotionally into the middle air as he talked to someone on his phone.

"It's my fault!" the body of Barbara Santangelo, inhabited by Margaret Biel, was sobbing, in a rare truthful statement.

"No, no, *cara!*" Lucia—the secret agent assigned to watch the Santangelo/Biel girl—cried, just as convincingly. Ransom

guessed she was fitted out with limbic mood implants. Meg
was good enough that she didn't need them.

Tomas, the other secret agent, ended his call, embraced
the two females in a bear hug, and started sobbing himself.
The whole thing would have been deliciously funny if not
for the gray, frozen form in the bedroom, the dull glint of its
eyes just visible between slitted lids. As it was, a feeling of
sadness and revulsion came over Ransom. He went back
downstairs and out into the street again.

He was exhausted. Mental and physical fatigue were the
same thing to him now, and he had gone through a lot in the
last twenty-four hours. He needed to recuperate. But where?
He was used to resting in houses, on beds, couches, chairs.
That was unnecessary now, but he knew he wouldn't be able
to relax if he stayed upright or just lay down on the sidewalk.
Across from the Paganos', the stucco upper story of a large
house was visible behind a garden wall and some palm trees. It
looked unoccupied. He went through the wrought-iron door
in the garden wall: within it was cool, palm trees shading
flower beds and exotic shrubs, with a smell of damp, rich soil.
He climbed stone steps to a veranda and went through the
front door. The house was silent and stuffy, evidently closed
up for the season. He absent-mindedly tried to open French
windows onto a balcony in the upstairs master bedroom, but
of course he could not. He could feel the handles as he took
hold of them, but they were inert, unresponsive, as if carved
out of stone. Cursing to himself, he went back outside and
around the house to a brick terrace with a broad view of the
ocean. A lawn ran from the edge of the terrace down to a
tangle of prickly-looking bushes near the edge of the cliff.

A couple of lounge chairs were set in the comfortable
shade of palms. Ransom automatically tried to brush some
dry palm fibers off one of them, and felt his hand run across
the fabric, but the fibers didn't move.

He lowered himself onto the chair. It felt solid and comfortable, and he heard the fibers crackle slightly under him. His mind was providing realistic details, as it did in the astral world; the difference was that here there was a substrate of physical reality that he couldn't affect, no matter how much it felt like he was grabbing or pushing or manipulating things.

But lying on a lounge chair relaxed him. There was a light breeze off the water that rustled the fronds above him. He sighed and closed his eyes. He wondered if a ghost could sleep.

Evidently the answer was yes, or at least his mind was able to supply a convincing counterfeit, because the next thing he knew he was opening his eyes and it was dark. It must be late, he realized, sitting up. There were no lights on in the houses next door, and the town behind him was very quiet. The moon floated large and yellow above the sea, its reflection scribbled in the black water.

But there was something else, too.

It had woken him, he realized: a sound. He sat still, listening, and now he could hear it again, a faint humming or buzzing.

As it got louder and a discomfort began to afflict the pit of his stomach, he jumped up in terror, staring around.

The chaos hole. It was somewhere out there in the dark, spinning with its unnatural sintering blackness—and by the way its sound/static/vibration was slowly increasing, it was coming toward him.

But how? And from which direction?

He strained his eyes and ears, turning his head this way and that to triangulate the sound. He didn't dare move for fear of running into it in the dark, falling into that place of horror, and maybe—because he was a ghost—unable to get out again.

And then he had a terrible thought: what if *this* was what

happened to ghosts? What if black holes came and sucked them into the dark chaos place, like vacuum cleaners removing life's refuse?

Something moved at the corner of his eye, and he leaped back in panic.

But he realized after a second that the movement hadn't been near him; something was happening far out on the water. He stared that way, the moon's reflection the only thing visible.

Then he saw the movement. The moon's reflection was slowly shrinking, as if someone was drawing a black blanket across the ocean toward the land.

As he watched in horror, the reflection shrank to a shimmering sliver and then disappeared, and the moon hung alone in a blank blackness, as if he was watching it from a platform in outer space.

The buzzing/static/vibration was definitely stronger now.

Ransom ran through the garden and the garden wall. The houses along the street were dark except for a single light upstairs in the Paganos'. He dashed toward that, ran inside, and stood gasping in the entry hall. It was quiet and dark, the big holographic windows in the living room showing night in the forest, branches swaying slightly in a fake breeze. Everything was tidy and homey: in the dimness he saw the pale shades of the extinguished lamps, magazines on the side-tables next to the armchairs, a vase of flowers on the coffee table—and an odd-looking hump on the sofa. The hump shifted, and a white arm moved languidly in the dark; he realized that Barbara Santangelo was sleeping there instead of on the futon upstairs, where her boyfriend had died of a drug overdose only hours ago.

Ransom went and stood over her. Her eyes were open in the dark, her face troubled and sad. Ransom was suddenly filled with indignation: this old woman in a young woman's body had killed a boy with her own hands, and been responsible for the deaths of everyone at Ransom International; she should be the one being pursued by an implacable black hole, not him.

Then a terrible thought occurred to him: he himself was not innocent. He had killed Lucia and Tomas several times, not to mention stealing Michael Beach's body, and probably doing a lot of other bad things that he couldn't remember just now. He paced around the ground floor of the house, thinking feverishly. Could it be that his sins had caught up with him, as the Paleo-Truthers said they would? If you were a sinner—and everyone was, they said—and you died without having done certain seemingly arbitrary obeisances, you were either tortured forever or deprived of an afterlife. Was that what the creeping black hole was, the vengeful spirit of the deity "Gawd" come to destroy Ransom's consciousness for having reasonably disbelieved the Paleo-Truthers' Late Stone Age stories? It seemed unlikely, but what did that matter? The effect might be the same in the end: he might be destroyed, wholly extirpated when the hole reached him, and it would be no consolation that it had arrived without the hillbilly metaphysical trappings.

A very faint yellow light came down the stairs; evidently Tomas and Lucia were still awake. That thought and the bland domesticity around him calmed Ransom. The black hole was probably just some natural phenomenon (though one that didn't affect live humans), neither malign nor benign, but simply conscientious, as natural phenomena tended to be. Avoiding it was probably a matter of technique rather than virtue, like most everything else. He let out a deep sigh and sank onto one of the armchairs in the living room, watching Barbara's pale profile in the dark.

He could still hear the humming and feel the staticky vibration.

He tried to ignore it. But it still seemed to be gradually getting stronger.

Finally he jumped up, went to the front door, and peeked through it.

Beyond the houses across the street, rising like a storm front over the ocean, a flickering, sintering darkness loomed, the moon still riding serenely above it.

Ransom bolted back into the house, hitting the light switches in a frenzy, but of course he could move none of them. He leaped up the steps and into Tomas and Lucia's room, where the lights were already on.

He had never been in there before. It was a large room with nice furniture, but Ransom saw that, with the door bolted and everyone else asleep, the happy couple had reverted to a cold professionalism. They sat on their separate beds wearing heavy eyeglasses and speaking in countersounded voices that were incomprehensible murmurs even a meter away, their hands flicking in the air at controls invisible to anyone not wearing compatible specs. Perhaps they were reporting to USAdmin on the day's events.

Ransom felt better in the light and in the presence of these two cold-blooded agents; he stood with his back to the door, then slid down to sit against it. But after a few minutes he realized fearfully that the chaos wave's sound/feeling was still getting stronger. His head hummed with it, and his skin felt covered with static; it was starting to pull at his insides now, even the inside of his mind, as if liquefying his very soul. He crawled shakily across to the floor lamp and sat directly under it, the brightest place in the room, hugging his knees and rocking back and forth. This was his extreme refuge; beyond this, there was nowhere left to run.

Gradually, the static/sound/feeling rose to a roaring. It seemed to come from all around him, as if this room were an island in a crashing ocean of static.

But then, finally, it stopped increasing.

At first he thought he was imagining it, but after half an hour he was sure: the static/sound/feeling was constant, neither waxing nor waning.

He crept to the window near where Lucia sat murmuring and gesturing, and peeked out through a chink in the curtains.

Roiling, sintering black chaos churned just beyond the glass.

He leaped back with a scream, scrambled to his place under the lamp and huddled there, trembling and crying. Tomas and Lucia went on with their work unperturbed.

As another hour went by and nothing changed, Ransom calmed down. He was even starting to get used to the static, his mind blocking out its constant roar and distortion.

An ornate brass clock on a roll-top desk read 2:00 A.M. when first Tomas and then Lucia finally took off their specs and got ready for bed. Stepping to within a centimeter of Ransom, Tomas turned off the floor lamp and darkness filled the room; then, with no signs of mutual affection, he and Lucia got into their respective beds. Ransom sat hugging his legs and waited fearfully for what would come in the dark.

For a while, nothing did. But soon after their stillness and breathing told him that Tomas and Lucia were asleep, something began to happen.

The waterfall roaring and static didn't change, but very slowly the corner of the room farthest from the beds seemed to soften in the dark—soften and then roil faintly with a sintering dark shimmer.

Ransom scuttled fearfully across the floor toward Tomas and Lucia—and almost ran into a pool of dark formlessness spreading like oil from under their beds.

With a scream, he recoiled. He looked around wildly. From several parts of the room pulsing clouds of darkness were pressing inward.

He knew suddenly that his only hope was the girl lying awake on the sofa downstairs.

Without thinking, he was through the bedroom door. Great tumors of pulsing chaos bulged from the walls of the hallway and stairs, but he dodged them, scrambled down to the living room. It was still pristine, unbreached by the gouts of formlessness swallowing the other parts of the house. Barbara/Meg was still awake, her eyes staring blankly into the dark, her sheets and blankets disarranged. Ransom crouched next to her between the sofa and coffee table, where his perspective would be almost identical to hers. Gradually his panic subsided, but thoughts whirled around him.

He thought he knew what was happening: re-superposition, the opposite of the collapse of the quantum-wave function, which happened eventually when observation was withdrawn from a system and indeterminacy crept back in through the back doors of quantum entanglement and the uncertainty principle. It was something live humans would never see because they were Observers—they collapsed the wave function, rotated the state vector, brought determinacy out of indeterminacy by dint of simply perceiving. But he himself was evidently no longer the kind of observer who could do that. So unless he hung around live, conscious observers, the roiling clouds of chaos would engulf him, uncreate him into the primordial proto-being of unobserved reality, erase him into the same sintering, buzzing smear through which he had fallen inside the black tunnel. Even at night, when the live people withdrew their attention temporarily from the world, the re-superposition crept in, not invading their bodies—in which he guessed some consciousness remained—but no doubt engulfing nonliving entities like himself.

What would happen then? When morning came and the observers woke up, would he be revived, too? But he was invisible—he had no material existence, as far as he knew. So there was nothing to observe; would he be lost, then, never reborn from unbeing? It seemed strange and unfair that nature should classify him as a "nonobserver," since to him it seemed that observing was all he could do.

And, he wondered, who observed the observers? What made them real, made them emerge in the first place in solid form from the potentiality waves that constituted the unobserved universe?

What if he went somewhere where there was always someone awake—a city, say? Could he keep the chaos cloud away forever? And if he did, would he persist in his present form indefinitely? But if that was what he wanted, why had he killed himself? He had gambled that there was something after death; he had taken the Face at Its word. Though, of course the Face hadn't given Its word; all It had said was that he was not where he was supposed to be. But It hadn't told him that the most terrifying object he had ever encountered would be waiting for him where he *was* supposed to be.

Did that chaos wait for everyone beyond the boundaries of their terminal visions? Did they see it at the last moment, just as they stepped across the stile at the verge of the beautiful meadow, or waded out into the calm water of the sea, or climbed into the clouds of the high mountain? Did they see its dark, terrifying maw and realize just for a second before it ate them what a joke it had all been, to have lived and desired life, only to be smeared into an utter erasure?

Brooding thus, and keeping an eye out for an eruption of chaos into the room or the hall outside, a couple of hours went by. But just as he had begun to feel that he might make it to morning, when everyone woke up and once again drove back the nonbeing, rendering the world solid for another day, he saw that the girl on the sofa had finally fallen asleep.

"No!" he yelled, jumping up, terror searing him. He

shook the girl by the shoulders and screamed, "No! Wake up! Meg! Wake up!"

Impossibly, she seemed to hear him. Her eyes opened, then went wide. She seemed to look straight at him, to *see* him. Her face contorted with horror and she sat bolt upright, her screams echoing his own.

"Meg," he said, his voice shaking. "Meg, it's me. Don't be scared. Meg, stop screaming. Meg, it's me."

Lights came on upstairs and there were footsteps, and then lights came on in the living room. Lucia stood clutching her robe at her throat, eyes wide, Tomas behind her. "Barbara, *cara mia*. What is the matter? What is happening?"

Ransom backed away from the sofa as Lucia and Tomas approached. Somehow he had gotten through to the girl, his violent fear pumping enough energy into his thin existence to make him for a moment visible. He had *haunted* her; but it was over now. Evidently he lacked the energy to contact the living unless he was nearly electrocuted with emotion.

Lucia sat on the edge of the sofa and took Meg/Barbara in her arms. "What is wrong, Barbara? Why did you scream?"

Meg/Barbara was red-faced and crying with terror, clinging to Lucia. "Shh. Shh," Lucia said, rocking her back and forth.

"Did you have a nightmare?" asked Tomas kindly.

"I saw him," the girl gasped. "I saw him. It was *him*!"

"Shh, *cara,* it was a dream, a nightmare," said Lucia, still rocking her. "Who did you see?"

"Michael! It was him. He came for me. *He called me Meg.* He knows—"

"Knows what, Barbara?"

"*I'm not Barbara,*" she sobbed.

Lucia and Tomas exchanged a glance.

"Who are you, then, *cara*?" asked Lucia tenderly.

Meg's red, wet face froze. Ransom could see her quickly

check herself, steady herself. She rasped, "It's my fault! M-Michael killed himself because of *me*."

Tomas and Lucia glanced at each other again. Ransom assumed that they had seen her kill Michael Beach just as clearly as Ransom himself had, if not in real time, then in surveillance video.

"No, no, *cara*," said Lucia, rocking her again, back in character. "No, no. It is not your fault. You had a dream, no? A nightmare. Of course it was a nightmare. You must know that."

Getting over her fright, Barbara/Meg seemed to begin to believe it. She let herself be soothed, and twenty minutes later Lucia and Tomas trooped wearily back upstairs, leaving her tucked in again, sheets and blankets smoothed and reorganized. But to Ransom's relief, she didn't go back to sleep. She lay staring up at the ceiling, he crouching beside her on the floor.

Ersatz dawn was pinking the holograms in the living room windows when she got up, hollow-eyed with exhaustion, and went to the front door. She opened it and went out onto the landing, looking around at the yellowing blue light of the real dawn, breathing its fresh, cool air. Either she or some other early-rising observers had dispelled the chaos cloud; everywhere he looked, standing next to her on the concrete, was the world, fresh and existent and calm, detail upon detail receding beyond vision.

"It's beautiful," he murmured to her, though he knew she couldn't hear. Yet tears welled in her eyes.

33

There were bars and nightclubs all over Salerno, especially downtown near the promenade that ran along the water, from which you could see the distant container cranes of the port to the north, and beyond them remote snow-capped mountains. It was a small city about half an hour's sailing over rocky, mountainous coastline, keeping the sea to his left and floating above steep villages, winding, dusty roads, fields of grapes, and the occasional medieval ruin with tourists climbing over it. He generally went to Salerno in the late afternoon and returned at dawn. He could have stayed in town permanently and saved himself the trouble, but he didn't know anyone there. At least Tomas, Lucia, and Barbara/Meg—though murderers, secret agents, and liars—had known him and meant something to him. And the same modest familiarity let him relax in their village, lie on the beach chairs on the terrace of the empty villa and doze or gaze out to sea at the little-observed distances from which the re-superposition cloud approached at night, entangling more and more unobserved mass/energy and converting it back to its primordial indeterminate state, like a fundamentalist particle religion sweeping over the world. In Salerno, sometimes he would go out on the promenade in the cool evening air and stroll among the tourists and teenagers, but it was lonely and boring because he had no one to talk to.

He had been visiting Salerno every night for two weeks before he saw his first ghost. It was in one of the all-night clubs, sometime in the wee hours; he was sitting at an empty table by the back wall, watching the house band's fourth set. The club was half empty, but the over-breathed air was still stuffy, smelling of sweat and mixed drinks. A shapely blonde in a sequined gown, her voice full of an ennui that Ransom happened to know was actually extreme fatigue, was singing "Stormy Weather" in a fairly good American accent. As he watched her, he saw that someone was acting strangely in front of the low stage where she stood. Someone swaying exaggeratedly and sinuously to her song, like seaweed in a strong current.

At first he thought it was some drunk trying to dance. But then one of the couples still stumbling around on the dance floor seemed to pass right through it.

Ransom stood up, his heart hammering. He knew that people could walk through him, too, but he still thought of himself as a person, and he was afraid of ghosts.

He threaded his way between the tables and among the shuffling couples—he still refused to pass through people unless it was absolutely necessary. The swaying figure was a woman wearing a long black gown, much too formal for the nightclub. Her profile was pretty and pouting; she had long dark hair worn up like an antebellum debutante. She didn't notice Ransom. Her eyes were closed, and she was swaying elaborately less than a meter from the torch singer, clutching a small handkerchief in one hand.

"Excuse me," said Ransom, standing just within polite conversational range.

The woman kept undulating, gave no sign she had heard him.

"Excuse me. Miss?"

His impression that some of the dancers had passed through her must have been a trick of the dim light. She couldn't hear him any better than the other live people who populated the world. She was just another nightclub patron—an eccentric drunk, probably here every night, so familiar that the musicians paid her no attention.

A tipsy couple wobbled forward, clinging to each other, smelling of alcohol sweat; the spotlight's penumbra glittered on the man's perspiring bald head. They shuffled through the swaying woman.

Ransom's imaginary heart pounded again. He stepped closer to the woman. "Excuse me, Miss," he said loudly.

The woman, disturbed at last, turned her head toward him a centimeter and opened her eyes slightly, still swaying, lips still parted in an almost sexual bliss.

"Sorry to bother you," Ransom said breathlessly, "but—"

The woman's eyes widened, and she turned to glance behind her.

"Yes, I'm talking to you—attractive woman in a black evening gown, holding a handkerchief."

Her face was astonished, and then terrified.

She fled.

But not in the usual way. She rushed away without turning or taking her eyes off him, as if a cable had yanked her backward into the darkness behind some empty tables at the extreme edge of the stage.

Startled by the uncanniness of this (but wondering if he could do it too), Ransom threaded his way back there. But there was no one there, just a couple of empty tables with chairs pulled out, as if the people sitting there had all left in a great hurry.

He went back to his own table. He realized that he was shaking. So there were others like him. Not teeming all around, but they existed. Like him, hanging around places where live people stayed awake all night, keeping the chaos cloud at bay.

"Who are you?" said a woman's voice, making him jump.

He twisted around in his chair. She stood behind the next table, which was also empty, looking ready to run. "Don't try to get near me, or I'll run away again."

"That was nice," he said. "How did you do that?"

"Who are you?"

"Heath. Heath Ransom."

"Are you—" She left the sentence unfinished, but her lips began to tremble.

"Yes."

She nodded, looking as if she would cry. "Where are you from?"

"America. I'm American."

"Then why are you speaking Italian?"

"I'm not speaking Italian."

"Yes you are," said the woman, suddenly angry. "I can't speak English, but you're speaking to me in perfect Italian."

"Probably neither of us is speaking anything particular," said Ransom soothingly. "We just understand each other."

The woman just stared at him, her lips trembling, eyes tearing.

"What's your name?" asked Ransom gently.

"Scarlet."

"Pleased to meet you, Scarlet."

"But why are you here?" she burst out. "Why did you come to this place?"

"To stay alive." He pointed at the ceiling. "The cloud. The boiling darkness."

"But why here? Can't you go somewhere else?"

"I could, I guess. But—"

"Go, then! I don't want you here."

"Why not?"

Scarlet furiously held her arm straight out and pointed. "She's mine!"

She was pointing at the exhausted torch singer, who was smiling and bowing now at some thin applause from the tables. He suddenly thought he understood.

"I'm not interested in her," he said.

Scarlet studied him suspiciously.

"Scarlet, I'm a man. Why would I want a woman's body? I wouldn't take a woman's body if it was on a silver platter."

Sudden relief made the woman shudder, and she came halfway around her table. "You don't want her? You'll let me have her?"

"Absolutely. Actually, I've already been in someone else's body—a boy. But I came back here."

She came a little closer around the table, staring at him aghast. "How? How did you get into the boy?"

"He . . . took too much heroin. His soul, spirit, whatever it is came out and I was able to drag myself into his body and keep it alive."

"Ohh," she sighed as if he had described something very beautiful. She came to his table now, and sat down opposite him. She looked at him almost worshipfully, pouting seductively. "Can you teach me?"

"There's nothing to teach. You just have to be lucky." Or have powerful mutants deform causal structures to supply a body to users of their etheric tunnels. "You have to be at the right place at the right time."

"I am with her every minute she is awake," the girl said, turning to gaze longingly at the singer, who was starting another number, something upbeat. "She drinks too much, so I am hoping— But I have heard that spirits can possess a live being even without that."

"Do you want to live that much?"

She looked at him strangely. "Of course. Don't you? Or else why are you here?"

"I told you, I gave up my body voluntarily."

She looked at him uncomprehendingly; then her face was disgusted, scornful. "How could you do something so *stupid*?"

"Isn't that what you're supposed to do after your life ends? Die?"

"If you're stupid."

"I'm sorry." He didn't know what else to say.

They looked at each other in silence, the woman tense and anguished. He wondered how he looked to her. Probably just like he felt: confused and lonely.

"Can you tell me, Scarlet," he asked finally, as gently as he could, "how you happen to be here?"

"I don't *happen* to be here. I'm here because I worked for it."

"How?"

"How do *you* come to be here? Why didn't you go to your beautiful death scene and just walk blissfully to oblivion?"

"I was kind of a special case. I was an endovid, an investigator. I was already in the etheric at the moment my body died. And then—"

She kept staring at him. "Then, what?"

It was too complicated to explain. "Then I came across the dying boy and got into his body. Then I decided to give that up."

"*Stupid,*" she hissed, her face twisted with hatred.

He sat silently until she seemed calmer. Then he asked, "What about you?"

"With me it was not a special case. I was hit by a car. I knew almost at once what was happening. The stupids never know; they just come out of their bodies and walk into their beautiful death scenes as if they are dreaming. But I knew, and I wouldn't let it happen. I had such a beautiful body! Twenty-two years old, and perfect. I had so many admirers, so many men loved me, gave me gifts, took me to wonderful places, spoiled me. Even dying my body was beautiful. I refused to leave it. When the wind started, pulling me away, I held on and I wouldn't go. My scene was a beautiful garden, and at the end of it a trellised gate with flowers growing all over it, opening into a beautiful landscape. It tempted me, but I loved my body more. Finally the wind died down. Soon after that, I couldn't hold on to my body anymore. It had died, and I could never get back into it again, never, never, never. An ambulance came and I followed it to the hospital, screaming 'No, No, No!' but nobody heard me.

"I stayed with my body until they buried it. Then I wandered around, not knowing what to do. I saw the black cloud that comes out at night; I came here to escape from it, and I saw her." She turned her head to gaze at the singer. "She is so beautiful. Like I was before my life was stolen from me. I want it back." She turned to look at Ransom, and her eyes were burning.

He walked out of the club at dawn with the last few customers, the band packing up, Scarlet hanging around the singer as she sat exhausted and smoking a cigarette, trying to touch her hair, her lips. The air on the deserted sidewalk was chilly and fresh in a downtown way, dew bringing out the smells of dust and dirty pavement, the sound of a few cars echoing between the buildings. And suddenly, looking around, the feeling came over him that it was all a set, erected temporarily as a backdrop to a melodrama: it seemed to him that these buildings would soon crumble, streets crack and disintegrate, all the people he saw would be gone, their bodies dispersed into separate molecules, their minds perhaps dispersed too or perhaps gone elsewhere. The sun was a Klieg light that lit this most elaborate of stages, and though the play seemed endless when one was in the middle of it, when it was over it seemed to have been so brief that it hardly existed at all. Even truth changed—one day God was Gaia, the next day Christ, the next science, and who knew what after. When the sun burned out, though, it would all be gone, to be replaced perhaps on another planet in another solar system by beings sensitive to entirely different spectra, processing information in unimaginable ways. Then, when all the particles in the universe decayed to heat, it would *all* be gone, nothing left but the trash behind the studio, facades broken, struts exposed, paint peeling.

He floated meditatively back over the mountains, and, looking out over the vast, beautiful green and brown world, with its depths and distances, its teeming stories and all its places and things, a great pity for the girl who called herself Scarlet came over him, locked inside her mind, imprisoning herself in nightclubs and tawdry, stuffy rooms, shutting out the vast beauty and mystery and freshness of the world. And suddenly he wondered if he himself was like her, locking himself into the small life he had become accustomed to, when perhaps beyond it a vaster, more beautiful, fresher world was spread out, waiting for him.

The mountains looked a little vague now in the slanting morning light, somehow abstract, as if their solid skins had turned misty, allowing the principles that had made them to show through like heaps of equations.

What in his whole life could he say had been real or permanent? Was there anything he had thought real that had not ended up being something entirely different? The only thing he *knew* had been real was himself—the subject to whom these appearances appeared, who had seen them all as they cycled past, real or not. Whether being assuredly fundamental meant that he was also permanent, he didn't know. Only time—the merciless stage manager—would tell.

———

Back at the village he went to see Meg, Lucia, and Tomas, but they too seemed uncomfortably transparent now, like marionettes pretending to have emotions, their dramas distant and overdone, their voices tinny, as on an old lo-fi TV. He went across the street to his lounge chair under the palms, lay back, and looked out to sea. It was beautiful and calm, a little mist gathering on the horizon, as if there might be a storm soon. He gazed for a long time, not thinking. Finally, he noticed that it was getting dark. It occurred to him that the difference in energy levels represented by visible photons was negligible in the scheme of things; light or dark was really all the same.

It was the music that finally made him look up and realize that it was deep night—a high, faint music like the distant ringing of bells or a choir of wordless voices, which seemed to be slowly, very slowly increasing. And looking out to sea, he saw what he had thought of before as the chaos cloud, except now it was white instead of black, like glowing milk diffusing from the horizon into the darkness. The music was coming from it. How could he have seen it as black, chaotic, and menacing? he wondered. It was the primordial, abstract foundation of everything, an ocean of proto-light from which everything arose, and to which everything returned, to be dissolved into everything else, and perhaps then returned again in different forms to a wider, deeper, more beautiful world.

Still the light increased, and the spheric music rose and became more pervasive, until the ocean of light lapped against the shore of his garden, and began rising up the grass at the bottom, rising toward him. He stood up and went to meet it. To become part of or to swim in that light. To be or not be himself anymore.

You could do worse than enter an ocean of light, he thought, if it was where you were meant to be.

Then he slipped into it.